THE SLEEPWALKER

THE SLEEPWALKER

A Novel

CHRIS BOHJALIAN

Doubleday

New York   London   Toronto   Sydney   Auckland

Copyright © 2017 by Chris Bohjalian

All rights reserved. Published in the United States by Doubleday,
a division of Penguin Random House LLC, New York, and in Canada by
Random House of Canada, a division of
Penguin Random House Canada Limited, Toronto.

www.doubleday.com

DOUBLEDAY and the portrayal of an anchor with a dolphin are
registered trademarks of Penguin Random House LLC.

Book design by Maria Carella
Jacket design by John Fontana
Jacket illustration © Mohamad Itani/Arcangel

Library of Congress Cataloging-in-Publication Data
Names: Bohjalian, Chris, 1960– author.
Title: The sleepwalker / by Chris Bohjalian.
Description: First edition. New York : Doubleday, [2017]
Identifiers: LCCN 2016015531   ISBN 9780385538916 (hardcover)
ISBN 9780385538923 (ebook)
Subjects: LCSH: Sleepwalking—Fiction.   Missing persons—Investigation—
Fiction.   Man-woman relationships—Fiction.   GSAFD: Mystery fiction.
Classification: LCC PS3552.O495 S59 2017   DDC 813/.54—dc23
LC record available at https://lccn.loc.gov/2016015531

MANUFACTURED IN THE UNITED STATES OF AMERICA

1 3 5 7 9 10 8 6 4 2

First Edition

For Andrew Furtsch
For Eric Nazarian

I am terrified by this dark thing that sleeps in me.

—*SYLVIA PLATH*

PART ONE

IT MAKES ALL the sense in the world. You awaken and smell smoke and see that the cat at the foot of your bed is on fire. And so you scoop him up and race to the bathroom and douse him with water in the tub. You reassure him that he'll be fine—he is fine—telling him that everything's okay. You hold him firmly but gently under the faucet because you are worried about his burns.

The only thing is, you're not awake. But you're not precisely dreaming, either. After all, in the morning the sheets are wet where the cat slept when you both went back to bed, and there is fur in the tub. There are scratch marks on your arms and the back of your hands, because the cat was justifiably resistant to the idea of a shower in the middle of the night. And, of course, the animal was never on fire. Nothing in the house was on fire. And you're a reasonable person; you know that cats and dogs don't spontaneously combust. But in the middle of the night, in the fidelity of that instant, you were saving the cat's life and that was all that mattered.

Or, another time, you open your eyes in the charcoal dark and decide that you're hungry. So, you stroll to the kitchen and whip up an omelet, tossing atop the whisked eggs in the pan a little cheddar cheese and a handful of baby aspirin—a mortar and pestle, the ground orange a cure in the crock of a medieval apothecary—because in the murkiness of the moment, you are craving the sweet-and-sour tang of orange St. Joseph's.

Or you decide to go for a swim. In the river.

Or you are teased by a stirring between your legs, then a craving, and so you reach for the body beside you. And if no one's there? You push off the *sheets and climb from your bed. You will search out a stranger who will sat-isfy it. With any luck, you will wake before you find one. But not always.*

It is—you are—vampiric. And while it would be easy to use words like insatiable *or* unquenchable, *they would be imprecise. Because the libertine needs of your sleeping soul will be sated. They will.*

And that's the problem.

CHAPTER ONE

EVERYONE IN THE county presumed that my mother's body was decaying—becoming porridge—at the bottom of the Gale River. It was the year 2000, and we were but three seasons removed from the Y2K madness: the overwrought, feared end of the digital age. It was a moment in time when a pair of matching towers still stood near the tip of lower Manhattan. *Fracking* and *photobomb* and *selfie* were years from becoming words, but we were only months from adding to our vocabularies the expression *hanging chad*.

I was twenty-one that summer and fall, and my sister was twelve. Neither of us fully recovered.

☽

The experts were surprised that Annalee Ahlberg's body hadn't been found, since a drowned body usually turns up near its point of entry into the water. But *near* is a relative term. And so police divers had searched long stretches of the waterway and even dredged a section along the levee that was built to protect the road from the flash floods that seemed to mangle the great, sweeping curve there every other decade. But there was no trace of her. They had scoured as well the small, shallow beaver pond in the woods a quarter of a mile behind my family's red Victorian and found nothing there, too. Nevertheless, my younger sister and I thought it most likely that our mother was in that Vermont river somewhere.

We hadn't given up all hope that she would return alive—at least I hadn't—but every day it grew harder to feign optimism for our father or say the right things (the appropriate things) when people asked us how we were doing.

One day after school, a little more than two weeks after the police and the mobile crime lab and the Zodiac boats had moved on—when all the tips had proven apparitions—Paige took her swim fins, a snorkel, and a mask and had gotten as far as the edge of the river before I was able to convince her that she was wasting her time. My sister was sitting on a rock about fifteen feet above the water in her navy-blue tank suit with the profile of a seahorse on her hipbone, the suit she wore when she swam laps at the pool at the college where our father taught. Clearly she meant business. Paige was in the seventh grade then, already a daredevil ski racer to be reckoned with, and in the summer and fall, at her ski coach's urging, most days she swam laps for an hour or so. She was still young enough to believe that she was a force of nature. She still dreamt when she was awake.

"You know, the water is so low now, you really won't need your fins," I observed, hoping I sounded casual as I sat down beside her. I thought it was a little ridiculous that Paige thought her fins might be of use. It was the middle of September and it hadn't rained in Vermont in a month. It hadn't rained since our mother had disappeared (which we viewed as mere meteorological coincidence, not a sign of astrological or celestial relevance). The water was only shoulder high in that part of the river, and the channel was no more than ten or twelve yards wide. The fins would be an encumbrance, not an asset, to a swimmer as strong as Paige.

"Then I won't use them," she mumbled.

"Maybe at the basin," I suggested, throwing her a bone. The basin, a little downstream of where we were sitting, was at the bottom of a small waterfall. The water was perhaps a dozen feet deep there, and she could use her fins to push to the bottom.

"Maybe," she agreed.

The riverbank was steeply pitched, the slope awash with oak and maple saplings, the leaves already turning the colors of copper and claret. There were occasional clusters of raspberry bushes, the fruit by then long eaten by humans and deer. There were boulders and moss and mud—though that day, due to the drought, the earth was dry powder. Seven days earlier, Labor Day, the river was crowded with teenagers and children. Girls my age in bikinis sunned themselves on the unexpected rock promontories that jutted into the water. There were fewer swimmers than in summers past because, after all, it had been only a week and a half before then that the river had been filled with the search-and-rescue teams and the police. On some level, everyone who swam there or dozed on the boulders in the center of the Gale those waning days of summer feared they would stumble upon our mother's corpse. But still the swimmers and sunbathers came. Parents still brought their children.

The water was clear that late in the afternoon, and where it was shallow Paige and I could see the rocks along the bottom, some reminiscent of turtles and some shaped and colored a bit like the top of a human skull. Prior to our mother's disappearance, I doubt that either of us would have associated a rock with a skull; it was inevitable we did now. When we were quiet, we could hear the burble of the current as it rolled west, sluicing between boulders and splashing against the brush and a fallen maple on the shore.

I stretched my legs against a tree root. "And you know the water is a lot chillier these days than it was a couple weeks ago. It may be low in this section, but the temperature went down to forty degrees last night," I reminded my younger sister.

"It was sixty-five degrees at lunchtime today," Paige countered. "I checked at school."

"The sun's already behind the mountain. It's probably fifty-five now. Look, you have goose bumps on your arms. You'll last five minutes. Then you'll either get out or you'll get hypothermia. I'll have to dive in after you."

"I won't get hypothermia," she said, unable to hide her irritation with me. "And you wouldn't dive in after me, Lianna. You just don't want me to look."

"Not in the river, I don't."

"We both know—"

"If there were clues in there, the police would have found them. They didn't," I said—though the truth was, I did in fact believe there were clues in the river. I believed that probably there were more than clues. I couldn't help but imagine that our mother was in there. The body, in my mind, was lodged beneath the water somewhere between where the river passed through Bartlett and where it emptied miles to the west into Lake Champlain. The corpse was hooked to a jagged rock rising up from the bottom like a stalagmite. Or it was caught beneath a rusting car hood or trashed box spring or the barbed metal from a deteriorating wheelbarrow or boat or some other piece of detritus that had sunk to the bed of the river in those sections where it was deep. But if the divers hadn't found our mother—or any clues—there was no way in the world that Paige was going to.

"Well, we have to do something," Paige insisted, her voice morphing from vexation to pout. "I know doing something—doing anything except calling your friends at college or doing your magic or smoking pot—is against your religion. But I'm not you."

"I'm doing something right now. I'm trying to stop you from accidentally freezing to death. Or, at least, wasting your time."

Paige lay back against the bank and spread out her arms like she was about to be crucified. For a kid who made short work of Olympic-sized swimming pools, it seemed to me that my sister's biceps were sticklike. Paige had turned to the river that day only because she had given up her search of the beaver pond and the woods behind our house. I had seen her back there the other day, wading methodically in hip boots in invisible lanes from one end of the beaver pond to the other, scouring the water. In the end, she found nothing more interesting in there than a man's tennis sneaker. Another time she walked through the woods, hunched over like a witch from a children's picture book, studying the fallen leaves and humus for any trace of our mother. But this was land that had been searched and searched again by professionals and volunteers. Rows of women and men had walked side by side, almost shoulder to shoulder. They had found nothing. And neither had Paige. She had found nothing there and she had found nothing— other than empty beer bottles and candy wrappers and plastic coffee-cup lids—as she had walked for hours along the riverbank beside the road, kicking at the brush with her sneakers.

"What are you going to make for dinner?" she asked me after a moment, the question breaking the silence like a flying fish breaking the water.

"Can I take that to mean you're going to put your energies to better use than going for a dip in the river?"

"I guess."

"Thank you," I said. "I would have been really pissed off if I'd had to go in and drag you out by your bathing suit."

"You didn't answer my question."

It was a little before five. I had spotted Paige because I'd been walking to the general store for a bottle of Diet Coke and a brownie. I was only a little buzzed now, but I was still very, very hungry. I was also hoping that I might see something in the store's refrigerator case that I could put on our father's tab and call it dinner. Some potato salad, perhaps, and a couple of Mexican wraps. For a small store in a small village, the refrigerator case was impressive. When I was stoned—more stoned than I was that afternoon—the deli section made me think of a toy magic trick I'd had when I'd been younger than Paige was now, and I was first fantasizing that I might become a magician when I grew up. The trick was a red plastic vase no more than four or five inches tall, and it seemed never to run out of water. Or, to be precise, it seemed never to run out of water two times. Then it really did run dry. But twice you could seem to empty it before your—theoretically amazed—

audience. The refrigerator case and deli section at the Bartlett General Store were a little bit like that to me, especially when I had the dope giggles.

"Dinner. Let's see," I murmured. In the first days after our mother had disappeared, our father had been a cyclone of activity. He tried to make sense of the path the detectives and a K-9 dog named Max had outlined across our yard—the way the grass had been matted down in the night, the way you could see what they decided were her footprints in the dew, and (most compelling) the small piece from the sleeve of her nightshirt, ripped and found hanging on the leafless branch of a dead tree along the bank of the river. He had designed posters with her picture on them and had Paige and me plaster them on telephone poles and bakery and grocery store corkboards for miles. I had spent hours and hours alone in my mother's midnight-blue Pathfinder—an SUV my parents had gotten my junior year of high school because it was perfect for carting us all (but especially Paige) to and from the ski slopes, and because we would use it to haul my belongings to and from college—driving between Bartlett and Hinesburg and Middlebury, where my father taught at the college. He had placed ads with his wife's photo in the area newspapers to prolong the story's momentum and to prevent people from forgetting Annalee Ahlberg—because, he knew, quickly they would. People survive by being callous, not kind, he sometimes taught his students, not trying to be dismissive of the species, but realistic. How, he lectured, could we ever face the morning if we did not grow inured to the monstrosities that marked the world daily: tsunamis and plane crashes and terrorism and war? And even when the police followed up on a tip—an alleged sighting of a woman wandering aimlessly in her nightshirt, or a piece of clothing floating miles away in the river—and discounted it, he would investigate it on his own. His inquiries those first days often confused strangers and infuriated the police.

At the same time, he had shocked the dean of faculty and the president of the college by informing them the Sunday of Labor

Day weekend—barely more than a week after his wife had gone missing—that he still planned to teach that fall. It was, he said, the only way he could take his mind off the madness. Eight days later, Paige and I were sitting on the banks of the Gale. And while our father may have been himself in the classroom—inspiring one moment, glib the next—he had grown almost catatonic around Paige and me. He was utterly spent. He would drink till he slept in the evenings. In the days immediately after my mother's disappearance, he had depended upon my aunt—his sister-in-law—to make everyone dinner and do the laundry and, occasionally, brush Joe the Barn Cat. And then my aunt had left, returning to her own family on Manhattan's Upper East Side. My mother's parents, frail and inconsolable, tried to help, but my grandmother was descending fast into the murk of Alzheimer's. They understood they were making things harder, not easier, and soon had gone home to their colonial outside of Boston, where my grandfather could do his best to care for his wife in the surroundings she knew. The neighbors stopped bringing us lasagna and macaroni and cheese and bowls of cut fruit. And so the task of making dinner had now fallen to me. Though our father's classes met only three days a week, he had gone to the college every day since Labor Day. Faculty meetings, he said. Introducing himself to his new student advisees. His own writing. Talking to people himself who thought they might have seen Annalee Ahlberg. Each day he had left early in the morning and come home just before dinner. It seemed to me that he couldn't bear to be in the house. Did he believe that his wife was still alive somewhere? At first he said that he did, reassuring his daughters, but already he was more likely to speak of her in the past tense. I knew in my heart that, like me, he was convinced she had walked herself to her death in a moment of slow-wave, third-stage sleep.

For a couple more minutes I sat beside my sister on the bank of the river, and neither of us said a word. I was just about to rise and resume my walk to the general store when Paige surprised me and asked, "Did they fight a lot? I mean, in comparison to other married couples?" She was talking about our parents.

"Nah. Probably not."

"I hated it when the house would get all tense."

"It didn't very often—not, I believe, compared to other couples."

"They had that epic fight five years ago. I remember them yelling at each other. Screaming even."

"Just that once," I said. It really was the only time I could recall my parents raising their voices at one another, but it had been horrible. Paige had hidden in my room with me, my door shut, sniffing back tears as she buried her face in the quilt on my bed. For the only time in my life, I'd feared that my parents might actually strike each other. Usually when they fought, they fought rather quietly, their barbs sharpened on whetstones of condescension and sarcasm. My father's vocabulary seemed to expand, a black hole of erudite scorn. My mother was less articulate—less verbal—but she could be colder and her silences even more dismissive. What triggered the pyrotechnics that awful night, what led the skirmish to migrate from room to room and their voices to carry beyond the Victorian? It had something to do with my mother's sleepwalking and the way my mother's behavior was embarrassing my father. They both felt shame, but for different reasons: he because of what people saw and she because of what she could not control. "They were pretty stressed out that night."

"Why?"

"Sleepwalking, I think. I don't know for sure," I answered. "But they loved each other." I tried to sound more confident about this than I was. I presumed my father loved my mother—or, at least, thought he loved her, which even then I understood wasn't quite the same thing as actually loving someone. I was less convinced that my mother loved him back, but I was unwilling to admit such a thing aloud. I certainly wouldn't say that to Paige. But I sometimes wondered if my mother was in fact too smart and too creative and perhaps even too imaginative for her English professor husband: a man who had an endowed chair at an elite New England college. A man who had published widely and writ-

ten two acclaimed biographies of American poets. Annalee Ahlberg was probably too smart for most men. Moreover, she battled
depression: a shelf in the medicine cabinet in the master bathroom
was an honor guard of orange vials of antidepressants.

Still, I honestly believed that much of the tension between my
parents was born of the sort of fears and frustrations that would
cripple any relationship. Their marriage had almost certainly
changed between when I was born and when my sister was born.
I was nine years older than Paige, and separating the two of us
were five miscarriages. I had been old enough to recall vividly my
mother's despair and my father's disappointment after the last three.
I remembered well the months my mother had spent in bed, an
invalid, before Paige was born. The hours and hours I would have
to be quiet so Mom could rest. The sleepovers at friends so Mom
could rest. The week with my grandparents so Mom could rest.
And then Paige had arrived: not quite full term, but close. Thirty-
four weeks. A shade under five pounds. A week and a half in the
neonatal intensive care unit, that was all. In my opinion, my sister
had never resembled the aliens that are some premature babies. She
had raven-black hair from the moment she was born, a rarity in
my family: the Ahlbergs on my father's side and the Manholts on
my mother's all looked like extras in Scandinavian tourism com-
mercials. The women had long blond braids; the men, with their
high foreheads and wispy yellow hair, belonged in the background
of old Bergman movies.

And then, seven years later, there was my mother's sleepwalking. I was in high school. Paige was in second grade. I had read all
that I could about the phenomenon at the time, interested because
I had occasionally walked in the night as a child. I read about
other parasomnias. I read about dreams. (I also read almost every
word that my father had written: the published books and the
myriad articles in academic journals, as well as his notebooks of
unpublished—unpublishable, I sometimes feared—poetry. A lot of
it, I noted sadly, was about somnambulism.)

Our house was at the edge of the village in Bartlett, three-quarters of an acre across the street from the river and a five-minute walk to the center: a general store, a library, a firehouse for the volunteer firefighters, and a bed and breakfast. There was a brick church, ostensibly Congregational, but the worshippers—and there were seventy-five or so most Sundays—were largely American Baptist and Methodist, with a handful of Presbyterians. But it was the only church in the village, and so if you went to church, you probably went there. My family didn't, other than on Christmas Eve and Easter morning. And so I felt more guilty than grateful at the way the pastor, a woman with green eyes and short salt-and-pepper hair who looked more like a lawyer than a minister, had made warm overtures to take my family under her wing since our mother had disappeared. In the last week, the pastor had even gotten me a pair of gigs for later that autumn: magic shows at birthday parties for two kids in the Sunday school.

Our next-door neighbors, the McClellans, had heard what Paige referred to as that "epic fight" five years ago. I overheard Carol McClellan sharing her description of the shouting match with the police the day my mother vanished. And so my father was briefly a suspect, but I don't think anyone really believed that he had murdered his wife.

Besides, although it was Carol who told the police that she had heard the Ahlbergs screaming at one another that night, she was also the one who had told them about the time my mother had spray-painted the massive hydrangea silver by the lights from the bay window. The tree was in the front yard, twenty or twenty-five feet from the front door. I was the one who had heard my mother and brought her back inside, but the lights and our conversation had awakened the McClellans, too, and so Carol had witnessed Annalee Ahlberg's nocturnal eccentricities. (Somehow, the tree, though deformed, would survive. My father cut down the silver branches and tried to shape those that remained so that in time the hydrangea once more resembled a mushroom cloud.) And then there was the night when other neighbors, Fred and Rosemary Harmon, outside together to gaze at a spectacular full moon, saw me walking my mother back over the bridge across the Gale River by the general store a little past midnight. I knew it was an old wives' tale that you shouldn't wake a sleepwalker, and so I had woken my mother. By then she had climbed atop the concrete balustrade and was poised like one of the marble angels that stand watch on the bridges across the Tiber and the Seine. The bridge was high enough that had she jumped she would have been crippled or killed: she would have broken her back or crushed her skull or (merely) drowned. She was naked and I, seventeen at the time, was struck by how very beautiful she was. When she was back on the ground, I covered her up in the cardigan sweatshirt I was wearing and led her home.

When my mother was sleepwalking, it seemed she was oblivious even to the cold. One March night, after a late spring blizzard had turned Bartlett into a Currier and Ives print, she took her Nordic skis and went on a cross-country journey throughout the woods behind our house. She had no recollection at breakfast the next morning, but her clothes were drying beside the woodstove—which she had also started in the night—and I followed her tracks the next day when I came home from school.

What all of this somnambulism had in common was that it occurred only when my father was out of town—including the night when she vanished once and for all. It was why the police almost instantly discarded him as a suspect. He had been at a poetry conference in Iowa City.

Of course, that also meant that my mother's disappearance would be a source of guilt and self-loathing for my sister and me. After all, neither of us woke up that night. Why did neither of us hear something, climb from our beds, and stop her? And as the older sibling, the one who once before had pulled our mother back from the precipice—the one who understood as well as anyone her noctivagant tendencies—I felt the remorse especially deeply. It was why I had chosen not to return to college for my senior year. I couldn't bear to leave my father and my sister alone. I couldn't bear to resume a normal life. Amherst had understood. The plan, as much as I had one, was that I would return after Christmas, in time for the spring semester.

Some people speculated that I was waiting for my mother to return—that I wasn't giving up hope until a body was found and all hope was lost. I wished that were the case, but I knew deep inside that it wasn't; it was heartbreak, not hope, that was keeping me here.

"Do you know what time Dad will be home tonight?" Paige asked me.

"I don't."

"Have you talked to him today?"

"I haven't."

Paige sat up and shook her head dismissively. "Mom would have talked to him. She would have known what's up."

"I'm not your mother. I'm your sister." When Paige said nothing, I rattled off a litany of questions as sarcastically as I could: "How was school, Paige? How are you doing with your polynomials? Did you bring home your *Lord of the Flies*? What are you going to be for Halloween? Or is that too far away? Are you and your little friends too old now to dress up?"

Paige looked at me and her dark eyes grew small. I knew that the girl was going to be a knockout, especially when she was pissed off. When some people are annoyed, their mouths collapse and their face falls into neutral. Not Paige. Even at twelve, she smoldered well. "Why do you make fun of everything?" she asked me finally. "Everything's just patter for you. Why are you always so . . . so cynical?"

I sighed. Most seventh graders didn't use words like *patter* and *cynical,* either. But most seventh graders didn't have an English professor and wannabe poet for a father. They didn't have an older sister whose summer job was magician: Lianna the Enchantress. (Before our mother had vanished, I had been thinking it was time to tweak my stage name. Come up with something that sounded less like a personal ad for an escort.) I knew that when I had been Paige's age, I had also taken great pride in my vocabulary. "I work hard at it. People think it's easy to be like this. It's not," I said simply.

"You smell like weed."

I probably did and it made me feel guilty. I guessed it was my clothes. Dope stuck like Gorilla Glue to L.L. Bean flannel shirts. Of all my good friends from high school, only Heather Prescott had not chosen a college in Maine or Massachusetts or New York, so I'd been hanging around mostly with her lately. She was a senior at the University of Vermont, and still a very serious partier. I had spent the afternoon with her and a couple of nice but not especially bright frat boys. Now I inhaled my sleeve and, sure enough, it was a tad pungent. Skunky. It was a testimony to how much slack people wanted to give me—Warren Ahlberg's daughter, the girl whose mother had disappeared and who hadn't gone back to college— that not a single person those days ever asked me why sometimes I reeked like the backroom of a head shop.

"So, I'll call Dad at the college and see what time he's coming home for dinner," I said, not wanting to escalate the fight. I really did feel like a bad role model; on some level, I wanted to do better for Paige. "I was just going to get us wraps and potato salad at the store. But maybe I'll make a meat loaf. Do you want me to make a meat loaf? You love Mom's meat loaf."

"You know how to make meat loaf?"

"How hard can it be? It's, like, hamburger meat and ketchup and onions. Maybe an egg. But I'll check a cookbook. Trust me, Mom isn't the French Chef. I think that's about all she does."

Paige nodded. "Okay." And then she repeated the word and started to reach for her swim fins so she could carry them home. But then she stopped and gazed down at the water in the river as it meandered past us. When she looked up again she was crying. Soundlessly. I started to hug her, but she swatted at my arm with one of the fins. "Don't," she said. "I'm fine."

But, of course, she wasn't. Neither of us was.

YOU CAN'T ARGUE *with a dream.*

Because you don't know it's a dream.

It may be nonsensical, but in the insinuating, slow-motion faithfulness of this nocturnal world—its grave commitment to its madness, the confidence it has in the rightness of its unreason—you respect this new normal. The world is a fog, especially when you are in the solarium-like heat that lives under the sheets.

They tell you there is no connection between sleepwalking and dreams. Perhaps. After all, you can remember your dreams.

You have heard of people who can wake themselves up from a bad dream. Or control the environment. The experience. You are not among them. You can neither turn away nor turn back. You make the best decisions you can.

CHAPTER TWO

I DECONSTRUCTED MY mother's last night countless times as summer segued into fall that year. I described everything I could recall
for my father. For the police. For myself. I talked it through with
Heather Prescott when we were sitting around her dingy apartment in Burlington just off the UVM campus, and with another of
my high school friends, Ellen Cooper—who hadn't gone to college, but was making what seemed to me at the time to be scary
amounts of money designing jewelry and candlesticks at a pewter
smith in Middlebury—when she would stop by my house on her
way home to Bartlett. The thing I kept coming back to was how
pedestrian my mother's last night really was. There were no warn-
ings, no ominous asides, nothing that could be construed by even
the most rabid conspiracy theorists as foreshadowing.

My father was a time zone to the west at his academic conference. Scholars and professors dissecting poetry. Because he was
going to be gone for two nights, it had crossed my mind that my
mother might sleepwalk. It had crossed all of our minds. After all,
it was only when her husband was gone that she would arise at
some point in the night and embark upon one of her journeys. But
she hadn't left her bed in the night in nearly four years—at least
that we knew of, and wouldn't my father have known?—which
was why my father was even willing to leave for the conference.
(There had been some discussion that my mother might accom-

pany him since I was home and could look after Paige, but it had never struck me as very serious: my mother had her own work here in Vermont.)

And so this was the first time that my father was leaving Annalee alone in their bed since her work at the sleep clinic had, my family believed, given us a course of treatment for her somnambulism. Proper sleep hygiene. No alcohol. Hypnosis (which, in the end, my mother felt had not been a factor). And, most importantly, a small tab of clonazepam before bed. The clonazepam, perhaps in concert with her antidepressants, knocked her right out. She slept, it seemed, without waking. The polysomnographs of her brain when she was on the drug were fascinating to the physicians and technicians at the sleep center; they actually showed montages of Annalee Ahlberg's EEGs to students at the adjacent medical school.

Nevertheless, my father reminded me to be alert. He said, his eyebrows raised, to refrain from any recreational activities that might diminish my attentiveness. But I had just turned twenty-one and my father knew that I would approach this responsibility with the appropriate gravity. I was a grown-up.

And I had indeed taken my father's words seriously. I hadn't partied that night at all, even though it was the end of August. I had stayed home and watched TV with Paige, petting Joe the Barn Cat—we were as likely to call the eighteen-pound bruiser Joe the Barn Cat as we were Joe, even though he had lived inside our house for five years now—when he would jump into my lap. I had slept with my door open. I reassured myself that I had brought my naked mother in from the bridge when I was seventeen; I reminded myself that I had awoken in time to save half our hydrangea from being asphyxiated by silver spray paint. I would awaken if my mother left her bedroom; I would let no one down.

And I took comfort in the reality that I myself hadn't gone sleepwalking in fifteen years. I had experienced a relatively brief, not uncommon pediatric arousal disorder, and I had outgrown it quickly. No one believed it was worrisome; no one considered it a sympathetic reaction to my mother's sleepwalking, because it had preceded her nocturnal forays by nearly a decade. By nearly ten full years.

☽

My mother picked up Paige at the college swimming pool late that August afternoon, and the two of them returned home to Bartlett about twenty minutes after I did from Heather Prescott's—who was still in Bartlett in August, though she and her UVM friends were about to move into their apartment in Burlington. Already I had pulled carrots and cherry tomatoes and a green pepper from the garden in the back of our house, and made a tossed salad to accompany the curried chicken salad our mother was serving for dinner.

After supper, the three of us were a little on edge, but no one said anything about it. We were acutely aware that Professor Ahlberg was in Iowa, and Annalee would be alone in the master bedroom. It had crossed my mind that perhaps for this big experiment I should sleep in the room on my father's side of the queen bed with the massive mahogany headboard. But I didn't want my mother to feel like an invalid, and so I never even made the suggestion.

Paige and I watched a cassette of *You've Got Mail,* one of our favorite movies those days. It wasn't merely a love story with bookstores as the backdrop. It was set in Manhattan, about as far from Bartlett, Vermont, as one could get in glamour and spirit. Our aunt and uncle and cousins lived there, and Paige and I always loved visiting them. And, of course, the movie ends with Harry Nilsson's affecting cover of "Over the Rainbow."

I went to bed last. I peeked into my sister's bedroom and then my mother's, and I took comfort in the fact they were both sound asleep. I e-mailed my friends, including an Amherst boy I had some interest in named David, who lived in Los Angeles. I remembered to keep my door open to increase the likelihood that I would wake up if my mother had an incident. A little before one in the morning, I put down the novel I was reading, checked my e-mails a final time, and turned out the light. The fact it was almost one in the morning was reassuring, because my mother had gone to sleep around ten p.m. The witching hour when sleepwalkers arose like the undead—those first three hours, that first third of the sleep cycle—was past.

$$\mathbb{D}$$

In the morning, Paige shook me awake. I opened my eyes and instantly understood this was bad. My sister had both of her hands on my shoulders and was practically pummeling me. For a fleeting second, in the murk between sleeping and waking, I thought we were on a train hurtling down a wooded mountain pass—the remnant of a dream. But then, even before I comprehended what Paige was saying, I realized this was about our mother.

"Mom's gone!" Paige was telling me, not screaming precisely, but her panic evident. "She's gone!"

I was sleeping only beneath a sheet, but I kicked it off without saying a word and stumbled toward our parents' bedroom. My sister followed me, continuing to babble. "I went into their room to check on her the second I woke up, and she wasn't there! She must have left sometime in the night!" Outside, the sun was just over the mountain and so it was still early. I wished I had glanced at the clock to see what the hell time it was. I understood on some level that it made no sense at all to go to our parents' bedroom first, since Paige was pretty clear on this one fact: our mother wasn't there. But I went anyway; I had to see for myself.

For a moment I stood in the doorway and stared at the empty bed. Then I went and touched my mother's side. The sheets and the pillowcase were cold. I glanced around the room to see if her summer nightshirt was there. My mother liked to get dressed before breakfast, and over the years I had noticed that she usually tossed her nightgown onto the foot of the bed. Sometime after breakfast—after she had gotten Paige and me off to school, after her husband had left for work—she would go upstairs and make the bed, and put whatever nightshirt or pajamas she had slept in under the pillow. Invariably, I remembered from the days before I left for college, the bed looked as perfect as an image from a Bloomingdale's catalog by the time I returned home from school, because my mother was an architect—and an architect who cared deeply that her own spaces should be as finely articulated and comfortable as the homes she designed for others. But there was no sign of the nightshirt. Not on the foot of the bed, not draped over the chair by the window, not on her nightstand. Not on the floor.

"You've checked downstairs?" I asked Paige. "You've checked the kitchen?"

"Of course I've checked downstairs."

"The garden? Outside?"

"Yes, I went outside." Then, to make her point, Paige shrieked at the top of her lungs, "Mom!" extending the single syllable for at least three or four seconds.

When there was no response, I asked simply, "The basement?"

Paige put her hands on her hips. We both knew that Paige was a little scared of the basement. I was, too. It was a terrifying, windowless world with a dirt floor except for the cement pads for the hot and cold water tanks and the washer and dryer. The walls were stone. The ceiling, mostly decaying insulation, was low. It was lit by two swaying lightbulbs at opposite ends. It was like a dungeon and we rarely went there—and never after dark when we were alone.

"Yes. I checked the basement. I checked everywhere."

"Is her car here?"

My sister sighed but said nothing. I went to the window and looked out at the carriage barn. In the summer, our family never bothered to close the garage doors. The bay where our father parked his car was empty, because he had driven to the airport yesterday. Our mother's SUV, however, was in its usual spot.

"Okay, I'll call Dad," I told Paige. I was pretty sure that Iowa was an hour behind Vermont. "What time is it?"

Paige pointed at the clock. It was a little before seven.

"Oh. Right," I said. "Thank you."

When I lifted the handset from the cradle, I was struck by its weight and shape. My parents had each owned what we called a car phone for nearly four years by then, though the phones were no longer tethered to their vehicles and my mother always had hers in her purse when she wasn't behind the wheel. But it was only that summer that they had gotten me my first cell phone. Earlier that year a tower had been built not far from Bartlett, and suddenly we had cell service in the village. Of course, coverage across most of Vermont was still spotty at best—my parents used their car phones mostly on the interstate or while they were in Burlington—and so I had used my stubby new phone no more than a dozen times in the six weeks I'd owned it. Already, however, the transition from landlines to cell phones was beginning, and I couldn't help but notice how different the bedroom phone felt in my fingers.

"Call him!" Paige was demanding.

Slowly my father's number came to me and I rang him. I got only his recorded voice at the other end, suggesting that I leave a message.

"Hi, Dad," I said, trying to sound calm. "I hope you have your phone with you. I'm sorry to call you, but we maybe—kind of—have an emergency. Paige just got me. It's, like, seven in the morning here and Mom's gone. Call me the second you wake up."

Then I hung up.

"You didn't say who you were," Paige said.

"I think he probably figured it out."

"Call the hotel. Wake him up."

"I don't know what hotel he's at," I said. And then, without consulting Paige or telling her what I was doing, I dialed 911.

☽

The emergency call did not follow the script I expected, at least as much as I had a script in mind. But I had anticipated that instantly there would be police officers—state troopers, sheriffs, detectives—on their way to our house. There would be grown-ups wanting to help us.

"How long has she been missing?" the dispatcher—a woman with a very calm voice—asked me.

"I don't know. But she was in bed last night. And she's not in bed now."

"Is her car still there?"

"Uh-huh."

"Is there a note?"

I glanced around the bedroom and didn't see one. "Hold on," I said to the dispatcher. I put my hand over the phone's mouthpiece and asked Paige, "Did you see a note?"

"No, but I wasn't looking for one," she answered defensively. "Mom doesn't leave notes when she does this."

"I don't think so," I told the woman on the phone. "But I'm not positive."

"Is there anyone in the house other than you and your sister?"

"No. Our dad is away at a conference."

"What kind of conference?"

"Poetry," I answered, unsure why this mattered. I envisioned the officer scoffing.

"Have you let him know?" she asked.

"We just left him a message."

"Was your front door locked?"

"I don't know."

"Okay. Is there any reason why your mom might have left the house for a bit? An errand, maybe?"

"In the middle of the night?"

The dispatcher sighed audibly. "Is there some sick neighbor she might be helping? Could she have gone to a friend's house?"

"She sleepwalks."

There was silence on the other end of the line. Then: "Thank you."

"So, you'll send people over to help us? You'll send out a search party or something?"

"How common is her sleepwalking?"

"Not common. She hasn't done it in years. But—"

"We're just about to have a shift change. The night shift is almost done and the day shift is checking in. Your mother really hasn't been gone all that long and you say she hasn't been sleepwalking in a while. If she isn't home in half an hour or you can't find where she is, call us back then, okay?"

"Is that it?"

"That's it."

I thanked the dispatcher, and in my haste to get off the phone I failed to summon the proper sarcastic tone. I imagine I sounded only curt, rather than frustrated or annoyed. The moment I hung up, however, the phone rang, startling me. I knew it was my father even before I had answered it.

"Your mother's gone?" he asked me. "Tell me the specifics. How long?"

"I don't know. I just got up."

"Have you called the police?"

"Yes. They weren't seriously helpful."

"I don't understand."

"They said to call back in half an hour if she isn't home."

"That's not right. That makes no sense."

"I guess."

"God. Okay, call Elliot Sheldon. Call Donnie Hempstead. They're both first responders. Start with Elliot. I'm sure he hasn't left for work yet—but he will soon. Call them the moment we get off the phone. I'll call the state police myself. I'm so sorry I was in the shower when you were trying to reach me."

"She's probably fine, right?"

"Right," he said. "But let's leave nothing to chance."

"Should I try and find her? Should I see if she's in the woods or the village or someplace? Maybe the bridge?"

"No," my father said. "Just get our neighbors out looking for her."

When I hung up, I saw that Paige was about to cry. All it took was the word *bridge,* and what memories that word exhumed. Paige hadn't witnessed our mother standing on the balustrade above the Gale, but she had seen her when I had brought her home. It was one of those haunting third-grade memories that only grew worse over time.

☽

Annalee Ahlberg was strikingly beautiful. My mother had Swedish blue eyes that made her look a little possessed when she smiled. Lapis lazuli. A Kodachrome photo would not have done them justice. Think CGI. Only a computer could create eyes like that. She wore contact lenses during the day, but eyeglasses— stylish turquoise ovals—at night and those days when she worked from home. Her hair was a blond so yellow that it almost looked bleached, but it was natural. And she was tall, almost as tall as my father, and he was six feet. Her legs went on forever. If she had had a better nose—less upturned, perhaps—and more patience when standing still (she had none, her soul craving movement even when she was asleep), she might have been a model instead of an architect.

And so when the state police from the New Haven barracks were interviewing Paige and me later that morning while they waited for my father to fly home from Iowa City, they probed the possibility that our mother had run off or was having an affair. Obviously less attractive women than Annalee Ahlberg had extra-marital dalliances, too, but one of the troopers, a squat, heavyset detective sergeant in his late thirties with a state police sort of buzz cut and a birdy little nose, tried—clumsily—to see whether Paige or I had suspicions that our mother had a lover. Or, perhaps, lovers. It was infuriating and I felt my family was being violated. I understood why they had to ask, but that did not make this line of investigation seem any less absurd or, on some level I could not quite parse at the time, degrading.

It was a little past nine o'clock in the morning now and we

were in the living room. I was seated on the couch, and the sergeant was facing me in a ladder-back chair he had brought in from the dining room. I was convinced that the only reason the two officers finally came to our house was because my father had gone ballistic when he'd called the state police. It irritated me that they hadn't taken me seriously. A shift change? Yeah, right. The search parties had been wandering in the woods around Bartlett and following the river for at least ninety minutes now, and no one had found my mother yet.

"So," the sergeant was asking me, "did your mom have any . . . friends . . . she might have met?" The badge on his uniform said C. Hardy. Paige was showing a second trooper the upstairs of the house and the bedroom where our parents slept.

"I told you. She was sleepwalking."

"You said you're twenty-one, right, Lianna?"

"Yes."

"College, right?"

"I'm about to start my senior year."

"Okay, then, I am going to ask you some very adult questions. May I?"

I stopped myself from rolling my eyes. "It's fine."

He smiled approvingly at me. I hated him already. "Did your mom and dad ever squabble?"

"Sometimes, sure. But she's a sleepwalker. That's what this is about. Ask the people at the sleep clinic in Burlington."

"What did they fight about? I can see all these pictures of her around the house. She's a pretty lady. Do other men, you know, hit on her?"

"She's my mother," I snapped at him, disgusted by the way his tone managed to be both cloying and condescending. "I have no clue if men are hitting on her. But she wouldn't care if they did."

"Uh-huh. So what did they argue about? Your parents, that is."

"I don't know, what do all parents argue about? What do all people fight about? I guess they fought about money. They fought about my mom's sleepwalking—what to do about it. They fought about the stuff that disappointed them. The stuff that's hard."

"What do you mean, 'the stuff that's hard'? Give me some specifics."

The sergeant had a notebook, but as far as I could tell he had written almost nothing down. For the first time, however, he seemed really to be listening. Cop schadenfreude.

"Depression. My mom can get depressed. But she's been treated for it. It's under control. I promise you, she didn't kill herself."

"Are her drugs upstairs?"

"Yes." He wrote that down, I noticed. "What I guess I meant by stuff that's hard," I went on, trying to explain and get the conversation back on track, "is that she had miscarriages. But this isn't about that either."

"Your mom had a miscarriage? When?"

"Look, you want to write something down?" I said. "Write down *sleepwalker.*"

He leaned as far back as he could in the chair, tipping back on the two spindly rear legs, visibly irritated with me. Instead of heeding my suggestion, he dropped his notebook into his lap and folded his arms across his chest. "And you're absolutely sure there wasn't a note?"

"There was no note."

"Because you wouldn't want to hide evidence. That's not just a crime, young lady. It makes our job harder. It makes it way more difficult for us to find your mother."

"I told you: there wasn't a note."

"And so you want me to believe that she just went sleepwalking in the middle of the night and still hasn't woken up?"

"No, I want you to believe that she just went sleepwalking in the middle of the night and is somewhere in the woods or near the river or something," I said, and the combination of the awful truth of what I was saying and my escalating frustration with the officer caused me, suddenly, to break down. My face fell into my hands, my elbows on the thighs of my blue jeans, and I was sobbing, sobbing in a way that I hadn't in years.

Somewhere far away I heard the other trooper and Paige on the stairs, my kid sister coming to my aid, but the sergeant didn't move from the ladder-back chair.

YOU WISH YOU could remember their faces when you're awake. But they dissolve. They become indistinguishable, the faces on the deck of a great ship as it pushes away from the port. You are aware mostly of their arms waving.

You wish when you were down the rabbit hole that the laws of physics applied. That you couldn't have sex on a cloud. That your college roommate wasn't judging you. That the cars on the roller coaster weren't airplanes—actual Airbuses. That your bed wasn't a chaise lounge beside a hotel swimming pool, and there on a towel beside the recliner was your lover—naked, ravenous, wanton—reaching up to you from the coralline deck.

No one ever thinks of dreams as playful. But they are. At least they can be. Think of an amusement park that is utterly oblivious to the conventions of nature. It's only when the dreams lead you from your bed—from sleep—that the amusements become dangerous.

CHAPTER THREE

IT WAS JUST after noon when one of the first responders, a volunteer firefighter from Bartlett named Elliot Sheldon, noticed the small piece of fabric dangling from the dead finger of a dead branch on the steep pitch of the riverbank. It was beside the road, the Gale aligning there with the asphalt. The scrap was navy blue and it seemed to be cotton. It was perhaps the size of a playing card. There was a toothpick-wide bit of red piping. He thought it was part of a cuff, but it might just as easily have been part of the hem. He knew not to touch it.

I was sitting on one of the black leather barstools around the kitchen island my mother had designed, fretting and staring out the window when the kitchen phone rang. It was from Elliot's niece, a girl a year younger than I was and not a kid that I considered a part of my posse, and she was looking for me. I liked Sally Sheldon just fine, but Sally was the sort of girl who had played lacrosse and softball in high school, and she was now a lacrosse star at Syracuse. She was, God help her, kind of like Paige: athletic and enthusiastic and social. She wasn't the brightest bulb in the tanning bed, but I thought she was sweet and well-intentioned.

Sally was inadvertently terrifying in her directness. "My uncle found a piece of clothing on a tree by the Gale," she said. "I heard it on one of the scanners. The police are about to ask you about your mom's clothes—what she was sleeping in."

I felt sick: I got dizzy and thought I might actually black out, and so I put my forehead down on the counter. I took a few deep breaths and after a moment forced myself to sit up. "How big?" I asked. "Do you mean a whole piece of clothing, like a shirt? Or a piece of clothing, like part of a sleeve? And what kind of clothes? Did you hear?"

But before Sally could tell me, a female trooper who couldn't have been more than thirty was sitting down on the barstool beside me. I told Sally I'd have to call her back in a couple of minutes.

The trooper had creosote-colored hair cut short and insisted that Paige and I call her Rosanne. She rubbed my back and asked, "How are you doing?"

"I'm doing bad. I'm kind of freaking out."

"Yeah. I get it. Your father's plane lands in about an hour. He should be home soon."

I nodded. My father had caught a plane from Iowa City to Chicago, and then another from Chicago to Burlington. It was twelve fifteen now. I was about to bring up Sally Sheldon's phone call, but Rosanne beat me to it.

"We may have a lead," she began. "A volunteer found something a few minutes ago and they're bringing it to the mobile crime lab right now. Can you tell me what your mother was wearing when you last saw her? You know, before bed?"

"A summer nightshirt. Navy. Victoria's Secret. Buttons down the front."

The trooper wrote down the description.

"Is that what they found?" I asked. "They found her nightshirt?" If they had, I wondered if that meant my mother's sleeping self had stripped off the nightshirt to go skinny-dipping. I knew waking Vermonters who did—whole families in the privacy of their backyard ponds or in secluded corners of the Gale—but most still had a bit of hippie in them. My mother? As far as I knew, it would only cross her mind in her sleep to peel off her nightshirt and go for a swim. And even then, skinny-dipping wasn't really her style. That time when I pulled her naked from the bridge? That wasn't somnambulant skinny-dipping. That was something else entirely. Somnambulant soaring, maybe. Somnambulant base-jumping. Believing in her sleep she could fly.

"They found a piece of fabric—not a piece of clothing. They found a little piece hanging from a dead branch beside the road. By the banks of the river. It's near here. Between here and the store."

I glanced down at the kitchen phone and thought of what I had just asked Sally. I took a breath and repeated that short, critical, two-word question: "How big?"

"It's little. It's small. Maybe a couple of inches by a couple of inches. It got caught on the branch."

"What color is it?"

"Navy."

"So it is from my mom's nightshirt."

"We don't know that."

But, I understood, they did. They did know that.

$$\mathbb{D}$$

My father had told me that he had long ceased trying to understand the meaning of the code: he left and his wife would rise like the undead from the sheets. No one, he insisted, had been able to explain to him or to my mother why she only walked in her sleep when she was alone. One time, I had watched my parents and two of their friends joking that she was trying to find him, though the attempt at humor seemed to make both my mother and father uncomfortable. Did my mother fret that she would find her husband in bed with another woman? Did my father fear the same thing?

Now I tried to push my memory of that conversation from my mind. I tried to push the fragment of nightgown from my mind. I tried to reassure myself that my mother had walked to the nearby elementary school and broken an ankle, and the only reason it was taking so long to find her was that the school was empty in August. Or she had walked to her friends the Bryces and broken her leg on a fallen tree in the woods. She was closer to Marilyn

Bryce than she was to her husband, Justin, but I knew she enjoyed his company, too. Marilyn was a painter her age, and Justin was a restaurateur, older than his wife, who owned bistros in Burlington and Middlebury that specialized in what he considered comfort food: the menus were rich with variations on macaroni and cheese and French fries.

But the fact that my mother hadn't been found yet was obviously a very bad sign—especially since at least once before she had walked to the river. To the bridge.

I wished I were more comfortable with prayer. I wished I were that little girl again who actually went to Sunday school for a couple of years when I was in preschool and kindergarten.

Jesus loves me! This I know,
For the Bible tells me so.

We sang that in the little classroom in the wing off the sanctuary every Sunday morning. We drew pictures of angels and sheep and pinned them to one of the walls. In the end, my parents had preferred sleeping late to walking me to and from the church, and so I had stopped going. Eventually, the awkwardness brought on by the fact that neither of my parents was sufficiently inspired to attend more than twice a year meant that I, too, had slipped from the fold. I sighed. I regretted that in a paper in college I had grouped the origin stories of the Christian church with—and I felt guilty remembering this, a vestigial shadow from those days in Sunday school—the lunacy that grounded Scientology.

I wondered why my parents had grown further from God (any god) as they had aged. One of my professors had lectured that faith was an upside-down bell curve: a U. It grew weaker through adolescence and adulthood, and then—as mortality started to rear its ugly, cadaverous head—started to rise. Faith made it a hell of a lot easier to put one foot in front of the other when your feet were old and swollen and riddled with arthritis; when your hair was thinning and gray; when your neck was showing its first signs of caruncle droop. My parents weren't precisely atheists; they did go to church on those two important occasions each year, and at least my mother defined herself as a Christian whenever she was asked (though clearly she was uncomfortable with the question). But neither of them leaned upon the church in times of need, either because they felt it was beneath them or because they had never—even after five miscarriages—felt the church would offer much comfort. I guessed I was like them in that regard.

I shook my head. This wasn't about my parents growing old or infirm in ten or twenty years. This was about the here and now and the reality that my mother was missing, and how my life might be about to change in ways for which I was neither prepared nor trained. I was, I realized, scared. Very scared. I would take comfort wherever I had any chance of finding it. Any chance at all. And so I went upstairs to my bedroom. I looked out the window, actually up at the cloudless blue sky, and there I did something I hadn't done in years. I prayed.

☽

Our red Victorian had three porches, one with glass windows that faced south, one with screens that faced west, and one that was open and faced east. The southern porch doubled as a greenhouse in April and early May, incubating the tomato seedlings and pepper plants until it was likely the last spring frost was past and we—my mother and I, and then my mother and Paige—could transplant them into the garden outside. The open porch was at the front of the house, and near the entrance: a pair of heavy, cinnamon-colored doors with slender stained-glass windows in the top halves. Half a dozen feet to the right of the doors was a white wooden glider swing, long enough for two people to sit comfortably. Before my mother had spray-painted the hydrangea silver and my father had been forced to trim and cut away at least half its branches, it had shielded the glider from the street. Less so, now. Sometimes in the summer my mother would have her coffee on the swing and read the newspaper there in the morning; my father would occasionally grade final papers there in mid-May and read books in June and July. By August, the sun had moved, and the swing would remain empty until my father took it down in October and carried it up to the attic.

But not now. It was August, and my sister and I had gone to the swing to sit and wait for our father to return from the airport. I had brought a deck of playing cards and was absentmindedly shuffling it with one hand. Some people bit their nails; I cut cards, equally adept those days with either hand.

Our father had called home the moment he had landed in Burlington, asking for news—which I had, a story in a scrap of a nightshirt—and telling me that he would be here in an hour. I guessed he would be home any minute now, well under an hour, because most likely he was speeding. In my mind, I saw him passing the slow-moving tractors and manure spreaders that congested the two-lane roads between the dairy farms in Starksboro and Hinesburg, and roaring past the pickups and sedans that were flirting with the speed limit. No doubt he was racing near seventy-five in the fifty-mile zones, and topping fifty where he was supposed to be traveling along at thirty-five. Inside our house, detectives were combing my parents' bedroom and had set up a command center of sorts in the kitchen. I imagined them writing down my mother's prescriptions from the bottles in the medicine chest in the master bathroom; perhaps they were even confiscating the bottles for analysis.

I saw Donnie Hempstead trudging from the woods across the street. He was among the first responders my father had asked me to call. He was wearing jeans and a white T-shirt that was filthy from the woods and his sweat. He had a radio on his belt. He saw my sister and me and paused before us. "We'll find her, girls," he said, running one of his hands through the trim brown beard that followed the line of his jaw. "Any minute now. Hang in there, okay?" We nodded; we hadn't a choice. Then he continued on into our house.

A moment later, Paige and I heard a dog barking somewhere near the river. We looked at each other and my sister spoke first. "That sounds like one of those dogs the police brought," she said.

"Maybe," I said. I wasn't convinced. About an hour earlier, the K-9 team had arrived, a pair of German shepherds and two handlers. They had gotten there moments after the piece of my mother's nightshirt had been discovered. I had overheard the troopers discussing the animals' deployment, and the plan was to bring one dog to that spot. The other had set off from our house's front yard. The dogs were named Tucker and Max. The names of the handlers hadn't registered with either Paige or me. Before the dogs had started off, I had had to give their handlers a piece of clothing my mother had worn. Originally I had brought down a pair of her summer shirts to choose from, but they were clean. The handlers had asked for dirty clothes, items that would be rich with the scent of Annalee Ahlberg. And so I had gone to the clothes hamper in my parents' bathroom and retrieved the black sweatpants and maroon sports bra she had worn to the gym the day before. It had felt like a violation, but I did it. "Of course, it could be Dandelion," I added, referring to our neighbor's yellow lab. Dandelion barked at almost anything that moved: Squirrels. Cats. Extra-large butterflies.

Paige shook her head. "I don't think so. I think it's Max." Max had sniffed at our mother's sports bra from the front steps and then yanked his handler across the yard and off toward the woods by the Gale.

I tried to imagine what would cause the animal to bark now. Would another scrap of clothing do that? Or would it demand a body? My mind had just begun down that especially menacing track when Paige and I saw our father's car approaching. We hopped off the swing simultaneously and ran to the spot on the driveway where we knew he would glide to stop.

☽

I could see that my father was being emotionally drawn and quartered, pulled in more directions than any one body could handle. He was having a conversation with the state police, and though I could tell that while they believed they were asking him questions, my father—ever the professor—had the upper hand and mostly was interrogating them. But he was also trying to field phone calls from my aunt—my mother's sister in Manhattan—and from his father-in-law in Massachusetts. Paige was on the couch beside him, half in his lap, her head against his chest. I feared that my kid sister, disarmingly mature most of the time, was now such a wreck that she was a snippet of bad news away from sucking her thumb. Already she was chewing on her lower lip.

And then there was the guilt our father seemed to be shouldering. I, too, was feeling its weight. He had gone away; I hadn't awoken. He should have stayed; I should have slept on his side of the bed. We both had let Annalee Ahlberg down. Our guilt coated the house like pollen. I told myself it was my imagination, but the more the state police learned, the more I felt judged.

I listened to the conversations until I couldn't bear it and then went back outside. I heard a helicopter nearing and was surprised for only a second: of course there was a helicopter. I was confident that soon there would be a second and a third. I watched it hover over the village on the far side of the river and then continue on its way in the direction of the elementary school and, eventually, the forest. I noticed the sun on the maples at the edge of our driveway—the light almost like honey—and saw that a few of the leaves were already starting to turn. A state police truck rumbled by the house with a pair of Zodiac rubber boats on a trailer behind it. There were two state police cruisers in our driveway now, as well as the mobile crime lab—a long green-and-white van with logos and shields for the State of Vermont—parked on the street.

I turned and saw a fellow in a gray tweed blazer and a silver-and-black-striped necktie emerging from the barn where we parked our cars. I hadn't spotted him earlier, and wondered if he was a reporter nosing around our property. I guessed he was in his early to midthirties, trim, thin yellow hair just starting to roll back. He had a leather attaché slung over his shoulder. When he reached me, I saw that his eyes were hazel, a kaleidoscopic (and rare) spatter of brown and green. I thought he was cute, and then felt guilty for noticing.

"A sleepwalker, eh?" he said to me.

"Yes," I told him firmly, unsure whether he was asking because he doubted the story. Most people, I had learned, were skeptical of sleepwalkers. They couldn't believe the things a person could do in that state. "My mom walks in her sleep. You can check her medical records. It's all there."

He nodded. "I wasn't doubting. I'm Detective Rikert, ma'am."

"Ma'am? I'm twenty-one."

"Would you prefer I called you Lianna?"

"I would," I said. I wasn't surprised he knew my name. It was clear I was the missing woman's older daughter. "And you're not a reporter? You're really a detective?"

"Yes. Let's start again. I'm Detective Rikert. I'm with the Bureau of Criminal Investigation in Waterbury—a part of the state police." He reached into his jacket pocket and pulled out a leather wallet with a badge and ID card. "The G stands for Gavin."

I waited. When I said nothing, he continued, "You're the magician. And you're home from college for the summer."

"I'm not a magician. I do kids' birthday parties to make money and clubs sometimes in Massachusetts. Small clubs. It's not exactly a career path."

"What is your career path?"

"I'm an English major. I have no idea."

"Teaching, maybe? Like your father?"

"I doubt it."

"Writing?"

"Maybe."

"Can I ask you a few questions about your mother?"

"Why not? Everyone else has been," I answered, exasperated.

"I've looked through a lot of the team's notes about her and thought about what we know. What I know." He shook his head. "She wasn't having an affair. She hasn't run off with some other man. The fallacy with that theory is you and your sister. My sense is she wouldn't just up and leave the two of you because there was some man she loved more than your father. And for that same reason—you and your sister—I don't think she killed herself."

"I agree. Thank you."

"Nah, don't thank me. At least not yet. All that means is . . ." His voice trailed off.

"Is what?"

"It means nothing," he said, trying to sound definitive. But it was clear he was backpedaling.

"Tell me."

He sighed. He looked away. "All that means is that she's probably had an accident. It means that we need to find her soon or this doesn't end well."

I was shocked by his candor. But I also sensed a subterranean ripple of pain as he spoke. Of empathy. And, of course, I knew he was right; I'd known it for hours. He was simply the first person to verbalize the obvious around me. I understood it had taken some courage to speak so frankly, and, in truth, a part of me was grateful. I swallowed hard and asked, "If that's true, what happens next?"

"Tell me if I'm being too honest—Just stop me, okay, Lianna?— but if we don't find her in the next day or so, all of this activity will turn from a search-and-rescue mission to one of body retrieval."

"And then you'll find her?"

"I expect so. We'll find her in a ravine somewhere. Some corner of the woods. Maybe even in the water. There's actually a lot of research into—forgive me—how far a body will drift."

Once again, I felt a little sick. "So, you think she might already have drowned?"

He took a deep breath. He looked a little forlorn. "It's my fear, yes. Think of where we found that scrap of nightgown: it was by the river. Think of the time you pulled her down from the side of the bridge. So, yes, we have to consider that possibility." He motioned ever so slightly with his head in the direction of the village. "So, let's hope she's in the woods and the accident is a broken leg. Worst case, a concussion. But let's pray she's not in the water."

"I can't handle this," I said slowly, carefully, staring at my legs and trying to lose myself in the blue of my jeans. I was angry with myself for pressing him and wished that I hadn't goaded him into elaborating. I had to remind myself that he was only saying what I already knew. If my mother were alive and unhurt, she would have woken up by now and come home; if she were alive but injured, someone would have found her and the radios would be crackling with the news. After all, how far could she have walked?

"I said too much," he said. It felt like an apology.

"No. You were just being straight with me."

"But I am sorry. Like you, I want to find her."

"What can I do?"

"I want you to tell me everything you know about her sleepwalking the last few years. Anything that's happened this summer. Anything she might have said about it."

"Why?"

"Because it might be useful," he said, and then he paused. "And because I can probably relate."

"Your mom was a sleepwalker?"

"No. I was."

"You?"

He tapped his pen against his pad, once more unwilling to meet my eyes. "I actually met your mom some years back," he said. "We were going to the sleep center at the same time. We met in the waiting room. It's why I'm here now."

$$\mathbb{D}$$

The detective wouldn't say why he didn't want to speak with me in front of my father. When I suggested I go get him, he said only that he wanted to chat with me first. We could get him in a few minutes, he added. My sister, too, because he was going to want to chat with her as well. Besides, it was madness right now in the house, he observed. *Madness.* That was the word he used. He walked me toward one of the cruisers and opened the passenger's-side door for me.

"Are you taking me somewhere?" I asked. I wasn't precisely afraid of Rikert, but I was wary.

"Nope. Get in," he urged. "You'll be more comfortable sitting down."

And so I did, but I kept my right leg dangling outside on the pavement so he couldn't shut the door. He didn't seem to care and went around the front of the vehicle, rapping the hood with his knuckles as he passed it. I stared for a moment at the radio micro-phone and then at the radar gun; I'd never seen one up close.

"A magician," Rikert said when he got in. He removed a yellow pad from his leather attaché and then tossed the bag into the backseat. "I think that's really interesting."

"It's not," I corrected him, my voice cool. "I told you, it's a summer job, mostly."

"Times like this I wish there was a little real magic in the world," he said. "Make disappeared people reappear. Make the kids in the Subaru I once found wrapped around a tree breathe again. Just get up and walk away from the wreck."

"So you know my mom?" I asked. I had no idea where this was going, but I wasn't happy with the digression.

"Yup. Sleep may not be as intimate as sex, but it's a weirdly personal experience."

The word *sex* stopped me. "Does that mean you two slept together? Not had sex, but . . . slept?"

"No. We were in separate rooms for the sleeping. But we had the same doctor. The same technician. And there's no such thing around here as a sleepwalking support group, so we sort of created our own one."

"God."

"And when I saw your mother was missing, I asked my captain

if I could help. I told him I knew her—and how I knew her—and he agreed it was in the best interests of the investigation for me to get involved. So, here I am."

"What did you talk about?"

"Your mom and me?"

"Uh-huh."

"We talked about why we were at the sleep center. Our sleep-walking. You assume everyone else is there for something like sleep apnea. But that wasn't her deal, obviously. Or mine."

"Did you ever meet outside of the sleep center?" I asked. It was a hunch and I thought—I feared—I knew the answer.

He hesitated. Then: "Yeah, we did. In fact, after we met that first time in the waiting room, we *only* met outside the sleep center. But we were just friends. And we were just friends in the context of our sleepwalking. We had something in common that neither of us had with anyone else."

I thought of how Rikert didn't want to speak with me in front of my father. I felt unsettled in the claustrophobic air of the cruiser, as if something was ever so slightly wrong and I was learning things my mother would never have wanted me to know. I watched the search teams, the state troopers, and the local police coming and going from our house. A second TV news van had rolled to a stop behind one of the state police pickups. Had there ever been this many people at one time in the Victorian? I doubted it. "How often?"

"How often did we see each other?"

I looked straight ahead. I nodded.

"I'm the one who usually asks the questions. It's why I brought you over here," he said, his voice light. When I remained silent, he continued, "We got together maybe eight or nine times."

"Does my dad know you two are friends?" I thought of how I was referring to my mother in the present tense. I was afraid it would be disloyal and jinx any chance of her safe return by transitioning now to the past.

"We were friends. I hadn't seen her in almost three years."

"Did my dad know?" I asked again.

"There would be no reason why he wouldn't. There was nothing illicit about our relationship."

"Why did you two stop seeing each other?"

"No reason, really. I was promoted and transferred to Waterbury: the Criminal Investigations Unit. Your mother didn't have clients in my neck of the woods. Plus I was traveling more. But the big reason, I guess, was that our sleepwalking was under control, so we no longer had that in common."

"Was under control," I repeated.

"I hear ya," he said, and when I turned to look at him he was shaking his head. "Anyway, we talked about family, which is relevant because I know how much she loves you and Paige. And we talked about dreams, which are irrelevant when it comes to sleepwalking, but still pretty damn fascinating if you have a parasomnia—and you're on really interesting drugs like clonazepam or imipramine."

"I wouldn't know."

"Which is good!" he told me. "Your mom have any new friends?"

"You should ask my dad."

"I will."

"Because she probably told him more than she was likely to tell me."

"Why?"

"Well, they're married." I watched him scribble a note on his pad. "And, remember, I've been away at school the last three years," I said.

"You'd be amazed at what married people don't tell each other."

"I don't remember her mentioning any new friends."

"Ornery client, maybe?"

"Not one she told me about."

"What dreams did she share with you when you were home?" he asked.

"She actually used to share more—when she was sleepwalking.

But since she stopped—or while she stopped, since it's pretty clear she started again—we don't talk about them all that often."

"What was the last dream you recall her telling you? Any you can think of her bringing up over breakfast this summer?"

"It's weird."

"All dreams are weird. Their secrets are encrypted. Was it a good dream or a bad dream?"

"Bad dream."

"Sometimes I'm not sure which hits us harder," he said, his voice growing wistful, "that relief when we wake up from a nightmare and realize it was just a dream, or the sadness when we wake up from a good dream—a really good dream—and realize that nothing was real."

"And then there are moments like this: you're wide awake and wish you weren't. You wish it was just a dream."

"That is the worst, I agree. So: that dream. Your mother's bad dream."

"She and the minister here were pulling dead bodies out of some weird underground bunker."

"Who's the minister?"

"Katherine Edwards."

"Your mom isn't a big churchgoer. Is your dad?"

"None of us are."

"Where was this bunker?"

"I don't know."

"Did she recognize any of the bodies?"

"She didn't say if she did. And she didn't sleepwalk that night. Obviously."

"Tell me another."

I put my head in my hands and closed my eyes, trying to concentrate. It was hot inside the cruiser, even with the passenger door open. "This was a while ago, when I was home in the spring. We had a swimming pool in the dream. It was in-ground. It had screens over it. A plane crashed into the hill just beside it."

"Little plane?"

"Big plane. Airbus kind of big."

"More bodies?"

"Yes. And a lot of the locals were there, trying to help. The volunteer firefighters. Our neighbors. The guys out looking for her right now. Elliot. Justin Bryce. Donnie Hempstead. But, again, Mom didn't get out of bed. She hasn't gone sleepwalking in years."

"Others?"

"There was a chimney fire, but it wasn't this house," I said, and I motioned with the back of my hand at our home. "It was, like, a house from her childhood."

"In Stamford, Connecticut."

I looked at him. "She told you a lot."

"She liked that house. She loved the bookcases her mom and dad had someone build in the family room. She loved the brook in the backyard at the edge of the woods. What happened during the fire?"

I honestly couldn't recall any more of that dream—or any other dreams. But the unease I had been feeling grew more pronounced; it disturbed me that my mother had shared so much with this stranger. They had discussed, it seemed, even their childhood homes. "I don't remember," I said.

"As far as you know, she's been taking her meds?"

"As far as I know."

"We'll check, of course. And—just confirming—this is the first episode she's had since she was treated, correct?"

"That's right. It was the first time my dad went away since then. She only does this when he's away. This was kind of a test." *And she failed it,* I thought, but I kept the short sentence to myself. *We failed it. I failed it.*

"She have any problems sleeping?"

"Not that I know of. But, again, you should ask my dad."

"How about you?"

"No."

"Your sister?"

"Again, no," I told him. "I want to go check on her—and my dad. Is that okay?"

"I'll come with you," he said. "I want to talk to them, too." Then he handed me his card and we both climbed from the cruiser. "I'll stay in touch, but you stay in touch with me, too. And Lianna?" I waited as he leaned over the roof of the car. "I'm going to say this one more time because I want to be sure you believe me: your mother and I were not having an affair. We were friends who shared one very uncommon personality trait. That's all."

I nodded. I wanted to believe him. But the idea that he was so adamant only made me more dubious.

THEY TELL YOU *the term is "arousal disorder." An arousal disorder occurs during NREM sleep. Non–rapid eye movement. Non-REM. The patient seems to be simultaneously awake and asleep. There are subsets: Sleep terrors. Confusional arousals. Sleepwalking. The patient is oblivious to the environment. The patient is, more or less, inaccessible.*

In the morning, the patient is amnestic. The patient remembers nothing or next to nothing, or presumes that whatever occurred was merely a dream.

Merely a dream. Only a dream. Parents say that to comfort their children a dozen times when they're young, right? "Shhhhhh. It was only a dream." They go to their room (if the children have not already come to theirs) and hold them tight, murmuring those magic words. Only. A. Dream. How many times did my own mother say that to me?

Arousal disorders are, most of the time, benign.

Only rarely is the term an inadvertent and wholly unintended pun.

CHAPTER FOUR

NOT QUITE THREE weeks after my mother had disappeared, I was folding laundry and practicing patter in my bedroom. It was a little before nine at night and my father had come home for dinner, spent a little time helping Paige with her analysis of the novel her class was reading, and then fallen asleep in front of the television downstairs. A glass, still a finger width of amber at the bottom, was on the table beside him. The scotch seemed to help him sleep.

I took real pleasure in folding laundry then, especially sheets and towels. I savored their warmth when I pulled them from the dryer, and I derived a strangely deep satisfaction from the rectangles and squares I would create. The stacks of ivory (sheets) and blue (towels). It was work that was orderly and utterly mindless. My thoughts could roam or I could rein them in and focus. That night I was thinking about a magic trick called the Square Circle, and how little kids absolutely loved it. I would show them an exotically decorated, bright yellow cylinder and a square cage that looked vaguely Ottoman: it had wire screens in frames shaped liked minarets. I would take great pains to show my audience that both the circle and the square were hollow—sometimes I would whisk my wand through the circle and run my arm through the square—before placing the tube inside the square. Then I would pull a dozen scarves from the cylinder, the scarlet and purple and canary-colored silks tied together so the rope would seem endless. And just when the kids would think that was it—the circle was empty—I would pull a Beanie Baby squirrel from inside it. I was tweaking my patter that evening because I was considering replacing the squirrel with a Beanie Baby kitten. The story would have something to do with a runaway kitten that was frightened. A scaredy cat. That would be the pun. The key would be to find a way to integrate the scarves into the tale. I wondered if Hello Kitty made kerchiefs or bandanas. They would have to be thin or I would have to use fewer of them, because the secret sleeve was only so big. But I thought the kids—especially the girls—would appreciate the kitten more than the squirrel.

I was bringing a stack of sheets to the linen closet when the phone rang. I put the laundry down on the hallway floor outside my parents' bedroom and reached for the phone on the nightstand beside their bed.

"Hello?"

"Lianna, it's Detective Rikert. How are you?"

I sat down—collapsed really—onto the mattress, suddenly scared. They had found my mother's body. I tried to convince myself that he was just checking in again with nothing to report: he'd done that a week earlier, calling only to ask how Paige and I were holding up. But why would he do that at nine at night? This was different. This was not what my parents referred to as "normal business hours."

"You there, Lianna?"

I swallowed. "Yeah. I'm here."

"You okay? You don't sound good."

"You found my mother's body, didn't you?" My voice sounded very small and childlike in my head.

"No. God, no. I'm so sorry I scared you. I'm not calling about the investigation at all."

"Okay."

"This is about business, however; but it's about your business."

"What do you mean?"

"This is kind of last minute, forgive me. But I just got off the phone with my sister in Middlebury. Her daughter—my niece—is having a birthday party this Saturday. Feel like performing? Are you up to working?"

"How old is she?" I was fragile and didn't want the hassle of working with middle-schoolers.

"She's going to turn eight."

"In that case, sure. What time?"

"It's in the afternoon."

"Okay."

"Okay, you'll do it?"

"Uh-huh."

"Excellent."

"How many kids will be there?"

"No idea. I'll have my sister call you with the details."

"Will you be there?" The question was a reflex.

"Of course. My niece is a sweetheart. Her name is Julie."

When I got off the phone, I saw that Paige was watching me. "Who was that?" she asked. She was wearing her reading glasses atop her head like a hair band. She was in her pajamas.

"A person with a job for me."

"A magic show?"

I nodded.

"Then how come you look like you're going to throw up?" she asked.

"I just . . . um . . . stood up too fast."

"Can that really happen?"

"Yes."

"How old is the kid? Four? Five?"

"Turning eight."

Paige shook her head. "Wow. She's in third grade and still wants a magician at her party. Can you spell loser?"

"Some people like my shows. Even older kids. Even people my age."

"They don't have to listen to you practice. Hello, Kitty? Seriously?"

"You were listening?"

"Not by choice."

I grabbed a small throw pillow off the mattress and heaved it at her good-naturedly. I had no idea why I hadn't told Paige that the person who called was one of the detectives; I just knew that I wanted—that I needed—to keep the information to myself.

☽

Later that night, I watched my father dozing in the chair with the mesa-red Aztec upholstery. He had fallen asleep in front of a Red Sox baseball game. Our cat was sitting like a sphinx on the arm of the couch. The TV—the only television in our house—sat in a mahogany cabinet our mother had had specially built, and was surrounded by matching floor-to-ceiling bookcases. One of the shelves, which had a pair of glass doors, held the two biographies my father had written, including the British and French editions. I sat on the nearby footstool and looked at the not-quite-empty scotch glass on the table beside the chair. The alcohol was a beautiful color. I didn't drink much at college, but I understood from a Valentine's formal how good the warmth felt on your throat and chest when you took that first sip.

My father was part of a long line of New England writers who romanticized the Red Sox. When I was in high school, he had explained to me that the love was born of the team's quixotic dream of derailing the Yankees and someday winning the World Series; the fact they often were tantalizingly close only deepened the allure. Since then, of course, the Red Sox have won multiple world championships. But in the autumn of 2000? Rooting for the Red Sox was an exercise in poetic heartbreak.

Finally I put my hand on the knee of my father's khakis and gave it a gentle shake. He opened his eyes abruptly, startled, and for a split second seemed scared. Then he saw it was me and smiled. He had a strong jaw and a dimpled chin. His eyes were a moonstone, Ahlberg blue. His teeth were nearly perfect. And yet he looked now as if he were on the downward slope of middle age. He had aged in the past weeks. We all had. I recalled a sociology course I had taken the previous fall and a book with the term "sandwich generation." I thought I was too young to be caring for my father on the one hand and raising Paige on the other. But I wondered if this was my destiny.

"Lianna," he murmured simply.

"I thought you might be more comfortable if you went to bed."

"Thank you." He gazed over my shoulder at the television and saw the score. "When I dozed off, they were winning. No longer, it seems."

"Sorry."

"I was having the most lovely dream." Briefly he studied his wedding band. Then he rubbed his eyes.

"What was it?" I asked.

"I was reading aloud to you from one of Roald Dahl's books. *The BFG,* I believe. We were on a plane to Disney World. I was doing my terrible Scottish accent, and a fellow in one of the seats ahead of us turned around. He was British and disabused me of the notion that my brogue had the slightest basis in reality."

"That really happened, Daddy. I was, like, seven."

He shook his head. "In my dream, the other passenger was the BFG himself. The Giant."

"Oh."

"But what was beautiful was that your mother was asleep against the window. Remember how she always loved the window seats on planes?"

"I do," I said. Sometimes I wanted to correct him when he spoke of his wife—my mother—in the past tense. But I never did. Who was I to condemn what I knew in my heart was realism? I was not at that place yet, but I understood that eventually I would get there.

"That was the best part of the dream," he went on. "The presumption of normalcy. Your mom with her head against the window."

"She does sleep great on planes."

He grinned a little mischievously: "She was always well medicated: Xanax. And the wine helped. And the white noise."

"Maybe the sleep doctors should have explored white noise or wine."

"Maybe white noise. Not wine. Alcohol can trigger a parasomnia."

"That's right, I forgot," I said. Then: "I got a gig for Saturday. A little girl's birthday party."

"Oh, really? Wonderful. Where?"

"Middlebury."

He raised an eyebrow. "Anyone I know?" I could tell he was hoping that he was somehow the conduit. Maybe the party was for a faculty brat.

"I don't think so. I don't know the details yet."

"What's the family's name?"

I shrugged. "The mom is going to call me. A . . . friend recommended me."

"Well, I'm thrilled. Whoever it is, they are very lucky to have you."

"We'll see."

He took a deep breath and stood, stretching his long, rangy body. He lifted the glass with the last of his scotch and went to turn off the television. He stroked the cat's fur and smiled down at the animal. As he was leaving the room, I considered calling after him, telling him that the friend who had recommended me was the sleepwalking detective who had once known his wife. But, once more, I kept the source to myself.

☽

Despite the fact there was no body, my father was far from alone when it came to referring to my mother in the past tense. I had friends at Amherst and at home in Vermont who would make the leap that she was dead (because who were we kidding? of course she was), and then tell me how they had never had a person close to them die or the only funerals they had ever attended were for their grandparents. One evening when my friend Ellen Cooper and I were sitting around her bedroom, both of us buzzed, she confessed that she had never been to a funeral. Her grandparents were still alive. Then she added, "I mean, I've had dogs die. And a cat. But they don't really count, do they?"

"They count," I said, partly to be kind but also because I loved Joe the Barn Cat and I had loved his feline predecessors in our home. But I knew what she meant. It spoke volumes about the cocoon in which my friends and I lived and how lucky we really had been. Yes, some of us had lost grandparents we loved. I had lost both of my father's parents, and based on how devastated— and frail—my mother's parents had been when they had come to Vermont in August, I expected soon I would lose them, too. But my friends and I had been spared our peers' violent deaths in automobile accidents and we had been spared our parents' deaths from cancer and ALS and the sudden, tectonic change that accompanies a fatal heart attack or ruptured aneurysm. My mother's disappearance was a sad, strange wake-up call for so many of my friends. It scared them. My presence scared them. I reminded them of the one thing in the world we want most to forget.

☽

It may have been the sound of Gavin Rikert's voice and his connection to my mother—my living, breathing, sleepwalking mother, not the ever-fading specter whose disappearance the detective was investigating—but the next day I drove to the hospital sleep center in the beige brick building in the midst of the University of Vermont campus in Burlington. I'd been considering a visit for a week now, ever since the shock of my mother's disappearance—the mourning, the listlessness, the exhaustion— had begun to morph into something else. Real life. Regular life. Gavin's voice had rallied me.

I didn't phone ahead because I had a feeling that calling would accomplish nothing. The minute I said who I was, the receptionist would take a message and the doctor would be appropriately guarded when she called me back. I understood the basics of HIPAA and patient privacy. And with a criminal investigation surrounding one of her patients? The woman would be especially circumspect.

But perhaps in person I could get something out of her, though what that something was I couldn't say. Still, I would play the gamin. I would look pathetic and lost—which really wasn't all that difficult those days.

When I arrived, a little before lunch, I took a seat in the waiting room on the third floor of the building and gazed out at the Adirondacks and Lake Champlain in the distance. The room was across the corridor from the reception desk, but I didn't introduce myself. My plan, as much as I had one, was to catch the doctor as she strolled toward the elevator bank for lunch and walk with her wherever she was going, even if that meant only the parking lot. I had met the woman once but had researched her on my laptop—brand-new that summer, my first—before leaving Bartlett to refresh my memory. Cindy Yager had been running the sleep center at the hospital for eight and a half years now. She was fifty-six ("and holding," the woman joked in a recent newspaper interview I had found about her and the center), and planned to stay at the hospital another few years before retiring. She had brown eyes and curly, auburn hair that was starting to gray.

I had been in the waiting room over an hour, alone for most of the time, browsing through the magazines on the small side table. Just after one I saw the doctor. She was walking a young man in blue jeans and a windbreaker who might have been a college student like me to the elevator. I got up and followed the pair, and was relieved when Yager didn't get into the elevator with him. The moment the doors slid shut, I said to the physician, "I am really sorry to bother you. My name is Lianna Ahlberg. We met one time when I was in high school and my mom first came here."

The woman was holding a clipboard and lowered it against her skirt. "Yes, I remember meeting. Of course. How are you?" She emphasized the verb, lengthening the single syllable. She tilted her head ever so slightly and smiled at me.

"Not great. But not awful. I mean, I haven't given up all hope," I told her, craving a professional's reassurance. "I've got this fantasy that maybe my mom has some head injury or something and got amnesia. You know, she fell while sleepwalking and hit her head just right. People get amnesia all the time and then, suddenly, get their memories back. Right?"

"Oh, maybe they do all the time in movies. But not in real life." Her eyes were gentle, her tone definitive.

"Or maybe she was abducted. Maybe she's locked in a bedroom or building somewhere, and any second now the police will find her and rescue her." After I had verbalized the idea, I felt guilty for wishing such a thing on my mother, and naïve to suggest it was likely. But wasn't imprisonment better than being dead? Wasn't it?

"Yes," the doctor agreed, "I guess that's possible." But I could tell that she didn't believe it, and I felt patronized—and I knew I deserved to feel that way.

"But it's not very likely, is it?"

"No." Then: "What can I do for you, Lianna? How can I help?"

"I want to talk about my mom's sleepwalking. I want to know—"

"I'm not allowed to discuss any of that," she said firmly, but not unkindly. "Your mother was a patient and there are very strict laws that protect patient confidentiality. I am so sorry, but that's just how it is."

"I get it. And I know the police have probably asked you a thousand questions already. But can I ask you a few things that wouldn't be confidential?"

"Like what?"

"About sleepwalking generally, I guess. I mean, I learned a lot from those days when Mom started to sleepwalk when I was in high school. And I've researched it a ton the last couple of weeks. But there is still so much I just don't get."

Yager looked at her watch. "I have a patient in a few minutes and I was going to try and squeeze in a moment with a banana and a granola bar I brought from home. But if you don't mind watching me eat, join me in my office."

"Absolutely. I'm crazy grateful," I said, and I followed the doctor back down the corridor and through the reception area, past a narrow room with a bed and a wall of sleep apnea masks and tubes that looked like props from a horror movie. It was unfair, but I imagined a serial killer wearing one and wielding the hose like a noose. The physician's office was small, but it faced the grassy quadrangle in the center of the UVM campus. Yager motioned for me to take the chair in front of the desk, and she sat in the larger, leather one behind it. She reached behind her for a knapsack and extracted the banana and granola bar. She broke the granola bar in half and handed me a piece.

"My very glamorous life," the doctor said. Then: "So: sleep-walking."

"I miss my mom," I said, surprising myself with this first short sentence. It wasn't at all what I had planned. I had thought I was fine, but apparently the presence of this older woman—a physician who knew the demons who came to my mother in the night—was going to dismantle the wall of grown-up resolve I had built. The words began gushing like the prattle from an overwrought child, and none of them were the reasonable, adult things I had imagined I'd say. "It feels like she got sick and I went away to college. I had a couple of summers. And now she's gone. I want to know where she is. I'm doing my best for my family, but it's just not enough. It's just not very good. And I didn't hear her that last night when I should have. And—"

"And this isn't about sleepwalking at all, is it? No one should have to shoulder what you are right now, Lianna. It must be horrible. But I'm not a therapist. I'm so sorry. Even if I knew how

to help you, I couldn't. Tell me: do you have general sleepwalking questions for me?" The doctor was leaning forward across her
desk, her hands folded between piles of papers on the blotter. I saw
in her eyes how sad she was, either because she was mourning my
mother, too, or because so far there was nothing in the world she
could do for me.

"Okay," I began again, gathering myself. "I'm sorry."

"Don't apologize. You've done nothing wrong."

I started again. "No one's found her body. Someone did find
part of her nightshirt beside the Gale River. At least once before
she walked to the bridge. So, let's say that the worst thing that
could have happened did happen—what a lot of people believe.
She walked into the river that night near where they found the
scrap of nightshirt. Why didn't she wake up when her feet hit the
water? Can you be in that deep a sleep when you're sleepwalking?"

"Maybe she did."

"Wake up."

"Yes."

"And it was too late? She was already drowning?"

"Could be."

"Have you ever had a patient die while sleepwalking before
now?"

"No. Thank God."

"So why then is everyone so sure my mom did? Why are you?"

"It's rare what your mother may have done in her sleep. But far
from unprecedented. A few years ago, a woman walked into a lake
in North Carolina and drowned."

"I saw that online. I found that news story."

"There are lots of stories similar to that in their degree of sadness . . . of strangeness. There are lots of accounts of sleepwalking
excursions that could only be called . . . extreme. People cook in
their sleep. They have sex in their sleep. They commit crimes in
their sleep. I had a patient a few years ago who was driving in her
sleep. One night, she backed her car out of the garage and into the
mailbox. That's when she woke up—and that's when she came in

for treatment. But there had been at least one other time when she didn't wake up. She drove around. How do we know? She drove to the parking garage down by the waterfront, parked on the top floor, and then walked a mile or so back home."

"I read that sleepwalking runs in families. Is that true?"

"It is. It certainly can. Are you sleepwalking, Lianna? Have you had an incident? Is that why you're here now?" She sounded concerned.

I thought about the word *now*. I guessed my mother must have told the physician that I had walked in my sleep as a little girl. Maybe my mother had filled out that detail on some form. A patient questionnaire. A family history. "No."

"Good. But please come in if you do—if something happens. Deal?"

"Sure. I'll call if something happens."

"Is that it?"

I shook my head and asked, "I know sleepwalking is a non-REM phenomenon. Why is that when people sleepwalk?"

"We only have theories. If you look at the delta waves on an electroencephalograph—an EEG—most of the time you really won't see a big difference. There isn't a huge physiologic marker."

"Is it as simple as the part of the brain that controls judgment is asleep, while the part that controls motor activity is awake?"

"You might say that. But it may also come down to one little chemical messenger in the brain: gamma-aminobutyric acid. GABA. It's an inhibitor that calms the brain's motor system. In little kids, the neurons are still developing, which might explain why childhood arousal disorders are so common. And for some people, the inhibitor may always remain a little undeveloped, even into adulthood. Or it may be easily affected by all those environmental factors that we know can trigger a parasomnia. A lack of sleep. Exhaustion. Stress. Certain medications."

"Had my mom changed her meds?"

"I can't discuss that."

"I mean, maybe because my father was going to be gone, she

did something different to be sure she'd stay in bed. But whatever she did, maybe it had the opposite effect. Is that possible?"

Yager looked at me, but said absolutely nothing.

"You really can't tell me," I murmured.

"I can't. I just can't."

"Can you tell me why she only walked in her sleep when my dad was gone?"

"No."

"Because you don't know or because of patient confidentiality?"

"I have my suspicions," she said, and waved her hand vaguely.

"Have you had other cases like hers?"

"It has certainly happened before: people sleepwalking only when they're alone in bed. Again, it's not common. Nothing about sleepwalking is. But there are plenty of documented cases."

"May I ask one more thing?"

"Of course. I just worry I won't be much help."

"Is there any chance my mom killed herself?"

"You mean on purpose?"

"Yes."

The doctor gazed at the UVM commons for a long moment. Then she turned back to me and said, "No. I can't say that definitively or categorically. Like I said, I'm not a therapist. We'll probably never know for sure. But speaking as a mother myself and speaking from my conversations with your mother while we were treating her parasomnia, I would say no. I understand she was taking antidepressants. But there is a chasm between taking antidepressants and taking your life. Okay?"

"Okay," I said, but it really wasn't. Over my shoulder I saw the receptionist in Yager's doorway. I didn't have to ask if my time was up. I knew it was. The doctor and I stood almost at the same time. She rounded her desk to hug me, and then I thanked her and left.

☽

Annalee Ahlberg was gone, but my mother remained as present and real as a shadow in the red Victorian. She was, at once, never there and always there, as undeniable yet untouchable as the sky. Though my father spoke of my mother in the past tense, in many ways he remained as incapable of moving on as my sister and me. It was still early autumn: Didn't missing people reappear all the time many months later? And so there lived a hollowness in the heart of the house. The three of us were missing the semaphore that was wife and mother. We needed a new language and new rituals, but it was going to take time for them to evolve.

My mother's clothing sat folded in her dresser and hanging in her closet in the master bedroom. The book she was reading, a beautiful black-and-silver doorstop of a novel about Marilyn Monroe, was on her nightstand, the bookmark still between pages 218 and 219. Her jewelry sat where she had left it on her dresser, the different pairs of earrings she wore most often (the hoops, the love knots, the teardrops) on a small silver tree denuded of leaves, perhaps six inches tall. Her charm bracelet was half in and half out of her jewelry box, and I took the cat and the barn and the butterfly and the heart and folded them back into one of the box's small drawers. I picked up a heavy bangle she slid over her wrist often when my parents went out in the evening, a silver cable with blue topaz at the tips, and held it in my hand a long moment, comforted by its totemic heft. My mother clearly had loved it. I put it back atop her necklaces, coils of moonstones and gold and one string of pearls that had once belonged to my grandmother.

The police had taken her computer, hoping there might be a clue somewhere among the e-mails and web history or in a document (there wasn't), but when they returned it, my father had placed it back in the guest room, where she worked those days when she was designing and drafting from home. (It was an unspoken rule that computers, along with television, did not belong in the sanctum sanctorum of the bedroom.) Her briefcase with the sketches for the vacation house she was designing in the White

Mountains hung over the back of the wrought-iron barstool on the far side of the kitchen island. Until Paige had been born, our mother had worked for a large architectural firm in Burlington and commuted to and from the city daily; she had also traveled with some frequency for work. But she had left the firm when Paige was born, because she wanted to choose her own hours and be available for her children. Her two children. She had worked exclusively from home until Paige had begun first grade, and then gotten a small office on the second floor of a building near the bookstore in Middlebury. I dropped by there one afternoon weeks after she had disappeared and saw that once the police had finished scouring it, my father had made sure that it looked exactly as it had before they had arrived. He had even placed his wife's favorite coffee mug beside her drafting table, and it waited for her there like a faithful dog. I wondered how much longer he would pay rent for the space.

One night, Paige and I spent hours with some of our family's photo albums on our laps, flipping the thick pages with the images in clear plastic sleeves. We weren't looking for clues (at least I wasn't). We simply wanted to see our mother once more. See her with the two of us and with our father. See her in a bathing suit on a friend's deck on Lake Champlain, or having a hot chocolate with other friends after skiing. See her with our father at a restaurant in Burlington. See her with clients as a house she had designed was being built, its shape starting to grow in the timber framing above the foundation. It was disturbing to see her with people far away who probably had no idea that she had disappeared. An acquaintance from college who now lived in Greece. A childhood friend who had moved to London. And then there were the photos of our neighbors in local Fourth of July parades or in the background of images of Paige and me—at the base lodge of the Snow Bowl, watching me perform, eating cupcakes at the volunteer fire company's annual fund-raising barbecue—some of whom, I knew, had driven my father a little crazy those last days in August with their public prayers and cloying remarks about courage and hope.

Mostly, however, it was just . . . us. The Ahlbergs. Here was our story: Me in a purple flapper wig when I was ten, and Paige making a snow angel at the base of a ski slope when she was seven, her skis planted like trees in the snow behind her. My sister still has her race bib on. There are my mother and father, not much older than I was then, young lovers leaning into each other on a bench in Washington Square Park; there they are again, years later, parents now, one time when we were all visiting my aunt and uncle and our cousins who lived in Manhattan. There are the three Ahlberg females on a half dozen Christmas mornings, always in the dining room, our stockings on the table around the coffee cake that my mother baked every Christmas Eve. There is my mother mugging with a chocolate bunny on an Easter Sunday four or five years ago. There she is at the drafting table at her office in Middlebury, playfully feigning exasperation—those turquoise eyeglasses a pointer in one hand—because she is trying to work. There are all four of us on Captiva Island six years ago, Paige in a pink bathing suit with the Little Mermaid on the front, our mother in a modest two piece—but a bikini of sorts, nonetheless. There is my mother kissing my sister on the forehead when Paige can't be more than six months old, and there is my mother swinging my sister in the air when Paige is perhaps a year and a half. (The two of them are, I speculated, dancing to a song by 10,000 Maniacs my mother adored. There was a period when both my mother and father would dance with Paige before dinner to 10,000 Maniacs. I was in middle school then, and far too self-conscious to join the fun.) There I am, a toddler, sitting on a blanket outside by the vegetable garden, a board book in my lap, while my mother seems to be weeding the channel between the first lettuce and the first peas. There I am again, sixteen years older, about to leave for the prom with my high school boyfriend, Stewart Godwin, my dress a white strapless sheath that I still rather liked, but I recalled was difficult to dance in. Stewart looks a little awkward in his tux, but he is a good-looking guy roughly my height, and I had only fond memories of him. And there I am as a girl magician on the stage in a New Year's Eve talent show in Burlington, a silver sequin skirt, a black leotard, and a dark purple cape as my costume. I have just made three large, seemingly solid metal rings link together. There were dozens of pictures of me performing my magic, just as there were dozens of my sister skiing. There were dozens of our father lounging with a notebook in his lap on the shore of Lake Champlain or in one of the Adirondack chairs in our backyard or at the Bread Loaf campus in Ripton. There he was laughing with colleagues (and visiting luminaries) at Middlebury.

But the ones that were hardest for us both to look at were those of our mother. We each picked out three photographs—a number we chose because it was finite, not because it was spiritual or symbolic—and brought them back to our separate bedrooms, where their sentimental importance to us grew daily that autumn.

☽

Sometimes when I was alone in the house—when Paige was at school and our father was at the college—I would hear the sound of my mother's voice. This wasn't a ghostly apparition. This was only in my head and it was almost always a recollection of the prosaic, not the profound.

Fettuccine Alfredo okay for dinner?

I saw the most beautiful field of sunflowers.

Bring your phone: I want to know I can reach you.

Other times when I was alone, I would catch Joe the Barn Cat looking a little anxious as he sniffed among my mother's shoes in the mudroom just off the front door. And so I would sit on the floor beside him and pet him. I would take him into my lap. These were the moments when I was most likely to stare up at the ceiling and either blink back the tears or, as I did equally often, embrace the solitude and cry.

☽

When my mother started to sleepwalk, my family joked that she had gotten it from me—some sort of bizarre reverse inheritance. I had always been told that I was the first Ahlberg to have an arousal disorder, though they hadn't used that term when I was a child. They hadn't even taken me to the doctor when it first happened. My mother had only mentioned it, almost in passing, to the pediatrician some months later when I had my annual physical. The physician had asked a few questions, and when he'd understood that only three or four times had I actually gotten out of bed in my sleep (and not once in the last month), he'd smiled and said there was nothing to worry about. It was not an uncommon occurrence among small children. Even the way I would seem to be awake—wide awake—and not recognize my father or mother. The physician had reassured my mother that I would outgrow it. And I did. The disorder may (or may not) have had something to do with starting kindergarten, the brain wanting to process all these new experiences and stimulations, or it may have been part of a growth spurt. Or maybe I was responding to stress in the house. But it didn't matter. I would sleepwalk a couple more times over the next two years, but by the summer between first and second grade, I was sleeping through the night. When I saw my mother and father, I always knew exactly who they were.

☽

"So, we have a box—an antique box I brought back from Egypt," Lianna the Enchantress was saying to the dozen girls and boys at the party on Saturday afternoon. I was wearing my purple harem pants, a white dress shirt I had tied into a midriff, and a paisley vest I had found at a vintage clothing store in Burlington. My feet were bare, and I had painted my toenails a shade of lavender to match my pants. The costume was neither inappropriate nor revealing, but never before had I tied my shirt up to expose a part of my abdomen. As I worked, I was aware that some of the moms and dads were watching me as avidly as the children. But mostly I was aware of Gavin Rikert. The detective was leaning against the fireplace mantel of his sister and brother-in-law's house, wearing blue jeans and a black turtleneck. I tried not to think about him, but it was difficult. His gaze was lionesque and he was standing perfectly still. I felt a bit like a gazelle.

"Did you bring it back on a flying carpet, Jasmine?" The question was shouted by a boy on his knees, a chubby kid in camo pants and a John Deere sweatshirt. In addition to interrupting my patter, he was leaning in a lot closer than I liked. But I guessed I had earned the Jasmine joke. I had spotted the boy right away as the child in the audience most likely to drive me crazy, and so I had brought out the Clatter Box earlier in the show than usual so I could involve him right away and win him over early on. Usually I wasn't a fan of rewarding bad behavior, but the rules were different when I was performing: I did whatever it took to bring the skeptics and hecklers into the fold.

"As a matter of fact, I did," I said. "What's your name?"

"Foster."

"Well, Foster, I need your help," I told him, and with the speed of a lemur he bolted to his feet and was standing beside me. The box was about five inches square and decorated with neon-red camels against a banana-yellow desert on three sides and a cocoa-colored pyramid on the fourth. It was made of tin and had a gold tassel at the top. I gave him the box and asked him to hold it by the tassel with his right hand. Then, so he couldn't use his free hand to examine the box, I gave him a silk to hold in his left.

"As you all can see—as you can see, Foster—the box is empty," I said, opening the box's front door, the side with the pyramid. The children and the parents all peered into the blackness. Meanwhile, I babbled about the mysteries of the pyramids and the way treasure hunters disappeared inside them. "The treasure chests were booby-trapped by the ancients to shoot daggers if someone ever opened them," I added ominously.

I reached onto the card table beside me for a cobalt-blue scarf. I closed the pyramid door. Then I made a tube with my left hand

and pressed the scarf into it with my right, reminding everyone
how very different Egypt was from Vermont. I encouraged them
to imagine how spooky it must be to wander through the dusky
corridors and tombs inside a pyramid. When I opened my left
hand, spreading my fingers into a starfish and exposing my palm,
the scarf was long gone.

"But is it really gone?" I asked the kids, raising an eyebrow.
"Does anything really disappear forever?" I glimpsed the detective
against the fireplace and briefly our eyes connected.

"No!" the kids shrieked at once, aware that this was most certainly the correct answer, and I regained my focus.

"Indeed," I said. "Now, my hope is that the scarf is inside this
box. I would hate to think I needed a new one. Foster, would you
please open the door for me?"

The boy did. And the trick worked like a charm. Foster pulled
on the tiny front door handle, the very same one I had used, but this
time all four sides and the base of the box exploded out, falling to
the floor with a clatter. Only the roof and the tassel remained in the
boy's fingers. And there, dangling from a hook in the ceiling, was
the cobalt-blue scarf. The kids squealed and their parents clapped,
and Foster would be putty in my hands for the rest of the show.
I could now turn my attention to the birthday girl, a child with
blond hair and a blue bow and a white party dress—which I did.

But always as I worked, I was aware of Detective Rikert.

〗

"That costume is quite the bold fashion statement for Vermont," the detective said to me. He had a bottle of soda in his hand
and was leaning against the counter beside the dishwasher in the
kitchen. His niece was opening her presents with the other kids in
the living room, and the two of us were the only adults not watching. His sister had offered me a glass of wine, but I had declined.
I hadn't been twenty-one all that long, and I didn't believe that
Lianna the Enchantress should be drinking in front of children:

it would be like the clown removing his makeup. Besides, I usually left the party as soon as I finished. The mom or dad would discreetly slip me a check and I'd be gone. Finally I had accepted a Barbie-pink paper cup of lemonade, but it was only so I would have something to do with my hands.

"It . . . evolved," I began. I wasn't nervous, but I was wary. He was a detective, and I knew I still had much to learn about his relationship with my mother. And yet I was drawn to him: he was handsome and glib, and I felt a little unsteady around him. "There were iterations. When I was a kid—"

"Spoken like someone who is facing midlife with real courage," he said.

"You know what I mean. When I was in middle school, I actually wore a cape and black pants. I had a top hat. But the whole outfit was, I don't know, too manly. So I started trying to be more feminine."

"Always play to your strengths."

I tried not to be self-conscious. I would have untied my shirt and covered my stomach, but I feared that would only draw more attention to what I was wearing. "At first, I went with a sort of Merlin the wizard vibe. This was before Harry Potter, so he was the gold standard for me. I got a church choir robe and dyed it black. But I looked like I really was wiccan. And I couldn't move the way I wanted. I need very free arms and very free hands."

"Which do you practice more? Your sleight of hand or your stories?"

"Sleight of hand. I could ad-lib the patter if necessary—especially when my audience is second and third graders."

"I liked the stories and I am way older than the kids on the floor. Some of your stories reminded me of Indiana Jones."

I smiled. "When I was a junior in high school, I actually toyed with an Indiana Jones persona. But the safari jacket I tried on looked kind of ridiculous on me."

"So you went with something less ridiculous: harem pants."

"Thanks."

"I'm kidding you! I'm teasing. They're perfect—especially for Lianna the Enchantress."

I took a sip of my lemonade.

"What do you wear on your feet when it's too cold to be barefoot?" he asked.

"I have a pair of beaded slippers. They're supposed to be Persian."

"Supposed to be?"

"I'm pretty sure they were made in China."

"How many shows a year do you do?"

"Eleven or twelve during the summer when I'm home. Maybe three or four during the semester when I'm at college."

"And you told me you do a couple of clubs," he said.

"Wow. You have a good memory."

"It's okay. It helps, given what I do. What about when you're home in Vermont? Any clubs here?"

"Nope—though I did do a country club on the Fourth of July. It was just outside of Burlington. I entertained the kids on a patio near the barbecue."

"In your harem pants."

"You really are fixated on them."

He shook his head. "Nah. You just don't see them much around here."

"What was your favorite trick?"

"I think when you made the ball levitate behind the scarf."

"Why?"

"I liked the story you told. 'Believe in ghosts,' you said. That was it, right? You said you found the ball at a haunted minor league baseball stadium."

"Yup."

"And I never could see the wire."

"Not a wire."

"Oh, you really are magic?"

"A magician never reveals the secret behind a trick."

From the other room we heard a crash—a table overturning—

and then the detective's sister saying it was okay, not a big deal. In seconds, Gavin's brother-in-law was in the kitchen with us, grabbing a dishtowel off the handle of the stove and the entire roll of paper towels on the counter. "Fruit punch spill," he said. "Nothing to worry about, unless you care about the beige upholstery on the couch."

"Need help?" the detective asked.

"No. We can't fit another person in the living room. Would be a fire code violation."

When he was gone, I said, "You just can't have a kid's birthday party without a spill. Trust me, I know."

"You're good with kids."

"I like them. You couldn't do what I do, if you didn't."

"I got the sense the day I came to your house that you're good with your sister, too."

I shrugged. "I guess."

"How's she doing?"

"Oh, sometimes she's still her own search party. She's still out there looking for clues."

"Find any?"

"Nope."

"What else?"

"She tries to get on with her life, I guess. She goes to school and does homework. She sees her friends. She swims."

"And you?"

My answer was brutally honest. "Me? I just wait."

"For your mom to walk in the front door . . ."

"Maybe. I don't know. But I wait for something."

"You wish you were back at college?"

"Yes and no. I miss my friends. I miss classes and studying. I miss my life. But I want to be here for my dad and Paige. I *need* to be here for them. I mean, it hasn't even been a month yet since Mom disappeared. And, I have to admit, I don't think I'd be able to focus away from home right now."

For a moment we were quiet. We had both felt the air in the

room grow heavy. Then I took a breath and asked, "Is there any news about her? Any new leads?"

"We get fewer new leads now than the first couple of days. A lot fewer. But someone will spot a homeless woman who looks even a teeny bit like your mom in Rutland or Albany, and we follow up. Someone will see something in the river or the lake that they think might be your mom, and we follow up."

"But it's never her."

"No. It's never even a clue."

"At first, it was the biggest story in Vermont. Now, it hasn't been in the papers in days. I don't think there's been a mention on the TV news in over a week."

"The news cycles move on. The media interest wanes."

"And the police interest?"

"Sadly, that wanes, too. Human nature. Detectives lose interest when we're getting nowhere. When we've exhausted every possibility. And, for better or worse, we don't have any reason to believe this is a homicide investigation."

"No."

"At one point, there must have been a dozen of us working on the case. But once we'd talked to your mother's friends and her clients, once forensics had analyzed her computer and phone, once we'd followed up on every crazy sighting"—he put his soda down on the counter and extended his hands, palms up, a universal sign for capitulation—"what's left? So we wait for a break. We work on other things."

"Do you still think her body is in the river?"

"If it is, the drought helps. Maybe eventually the water will get so low that we find it. We dragged part of the river, but maybe it was wedged perfectly under a rock."

I bit my lip and looked away, hoping Gavin wouldn't notice how the image had unnerved me. As painful as it was for me to hear the conjecture, I didn't want him to stop.

"I said too much," he murmured. "I'm sorry."

"No. I need to know. Go on."

He took a sip of his soda. "Maybe the divers stirred up just enough sediment in the water that they missed her," he said. "It happens. Think of that poor kid from Dartmouth."

I nodded. I recalled the story. When I'd been in elementary school, a junior there had disappeared the first Friday in February. He'd left a friend's dorm room late at night and vanished. But no one seriously suspected foul play, because there were footprints his boot size that led to the crew team's boathouse near the Connecticut River. He'd been a member of the team his first two years at the college, a rower in the shell's engine room. He was no longer on the team, and apparently he grieved that loss immensely. His friend said he had been drunk when he had left that last night.

"The kid's body wasn't found until June," the detective said. "But it had been in the water the whole time, in that very spot no more than a half mile from the boathouse. So tragic. So sad."

He finished his soda and rinsed out the bottle in the sink. "But your mom? We just don't know. We assume she's there because of a scrap of nightshirt and because one night years ago she walked to the river—to the bridge. But there are no footprints in the snow this time."

"Then she might be alive?"

"I didn't say that. I wouldn't want to get your hopes up. But, yes, without a body, we can't rule out that possibility."

"But she wouldn't just leave my dad and Paige and me. You said that yourself."

"I did, yes. I believe that."

"So you're thinking . . . what? This might not have been a sleepwalking thing? She might have been murdered?"

"At the moment, I'd say that was unlikely. But, yes, it's a possibility. Maybe she was killed while she was sleepwalking. Maybe she was killed after she woke up—on her way home."

"But there would still be a body."

He nodded. "One would think so. And we certainly found no one who would seem to have any reason to want her dead. She didn't have enemies. No one in her address book, none of her clients. None of your neighbors. You didn't want her dead. Paige didn't want her dead. Your dad didn't want her dead. I mean . . . people loved her. All of you loved her."

I opened the cabinet under the sink where I suspected there would be a kitchen garbage can. There was. I tossed my lemonade cup into it. Then I stood up and asked another of the hard, horrible questions that had been gnawing at me as a woman. "Okay, here's another gruesome question: Are you investigating if she was raped? A random thing? She was outside alone at night and someone attacked her?"

"So she was raped and murdered? Yes. But so far that track hasn't gone anywhere."

"Have you ever had a case like this?"

"I haven't. And I've been doing this twelve years."

Instantly I did the math in my head. I supposed he was thirty-three, a dozen years my senior. My mom was forty-seven. That meant she was fourteen years older than he was. My mom had been forty-two when they met, and he had been twenty-eight.

"It's baffling," he was saying. "But you do this long enough, you get a case like this. Every cop does. Sometimes you solve them. And sometimes you don't. They just grow cold."

"God," I murmured. "If only I'd slept on my dad's side of the bed that night."

"Yeah, but that still assumes you might have woken up. This isn't your fault, Lianna. Your mom worried if something ever happened to her you'd feel this way. But she never wanted you to feel even a twinge of guilt."

"She talked about something happening to her?"

"Of course she did. You pulled her off a bridge, for God's sake."

"Did she think she'd go back there?"

"She was more afraid she'd set the house on fire. She was more afraid she'd accidentally hurt you or your sister."

"Is that why you asked me about her dreams the day she disappeared?"

"Not really. There's only the most mundane association

between sleepwalking and dreams. They occur in different parts of the sleep cycle. It's not like a sleepwalker is acting out a dream."

"Then why?"

"They tell us a bit about a person's inner life, don't you think? And in your mom's case? Plane crashes. Dead bodies."

"She was scared of leaving people behind?"

"Possibly."

"Lucky guess."

"But her dreams may not mean that at all. A lot of shrinks will tell you a plane crash dream is about failure. Nothing more. You're not achieving your goals."

"Or maybe you're out of control?"

"Maybe. And your mom did remember more than a lot of sleepwalkers. She sure as hell remembered more than I ever did. Most of us have amnesia. But not your mom. At least not precisely. She would remember a detail here and there, and sometimes she'd think it was a dream. She'd actually hope it was a dream."

"Where did you two used to go to talk?"

"You should be the detective."

It was getting late in the afternoon now, and I felt a chill on my stomach. I went ahead and untied my shirt and then buttoned the three lower buttons. "That's not an answer."

"No, it's not. Sometimes we went to the coffee shop near the hospital and the hotel they use for their sleep studies. Sometimes we'd head downtown. We'd go to that bakery across the street from the library on College Street."

"My mom did love their cupcakes."

"And their coffee. Decaf, of course."

"Of course."

"Did you inherit her love of cupcakes?"

"I did."

"Ever have the time to come to Burlington?"

I chuckled. "These days I have nothing but time."

"The bakery has more than cupcakes. They have pretty good

sandwiches. Want to come to lunch on Monday? It's one of my days off this week."

His voice was casual, but once more the room shifted. I wanted to see him again, but I needed reassurance that he and my mother had never been romantically involved. I met his eyes: "You swear that you and my mom were not having an affair?"

He raised his right hand. "I swear. It was never, ever like that. She loved your dad. And I was dating someone else back then, too."

"What happened?"

"She moved to Boston. We grew apart."

"And you're not, I don't know, crossing some ethical line as a detective?"

"By taking you to lunch?" He smiled. "Arguably."

"So I shouldn't," I said. It was a statement, not a question. I felt a pang of disappointment.

"Oh, I'm sure some people would frown. But like I said, we have no reason to believe this is a murder investigation. And I promise you: it won't cloud my ability to explore what happened. So you should."

"Okay," I said. There was a tremor of doubt in my voice, and he heard it, too. I told myself that by seeing him, I was in fact the one playing detective. I might learn something more about my mother and her disappearance. But there was more to it than that: I understood the way I was attracted to him.

"Okay, we're on?"

"Uh-huh. We're on. What time?"

"Twelve thirty?"

"I can squeeze you in," I said.

"Excellent."

When I left the party a few minutes later, driving home in my mother's Pathfinder, I considered whether I would tell my father and Paige that I was seeing the detective for lunch. But I knew in my heart that I wouldn't. That I shouldn't. I had the sense that

Gavin wouldn't want them to know. I convinced myself—and it really took very little work—that they didn't need to know. No one did. There was absolutely nothing wrong with my meeting the detective at the bakery; there was absolutely nothing wrong with my meeting him anywhere.

Nevertheless, a part of me wondered what the hell I was doing.

THE DREAM HOLDS *you tight. The voices inside you drone on, but you ignore them because this is but a dream.*

So you give in. Lovers don't enter your life out of the blue. You summon them in your sleep.

A lucid dream? A technical term. A term coined by a Dutch psychiatrist just before the First World War. In a lucid dream, people wield some control over their sleeping world. They choose to fly. Or they choose not to. But they are aware that they're dreaming. There is activity in the parietal lobes.

A lucid dream is particularly vivid. The physical sensations can be . . . remarkable.

You have all the cerebral activity but none of the control. None. Your dreams are lucid, but you are not technically a lucid dreamer.

And so when you see a new lover, you start to unbutton your shirt.

Or not.

You have no recourse but release, and so sometimes you don't even bother to undress.

CHAPTER FIVE

THAT NIGHT, WHEN the *Saturday Night Live* rerun was over and I
was confident that my sister was asleep and our father had passed
out—that was how I was starting to view the sleep that followed
his drinking—I went to the guest bedroom. My mother had usually worked at her office in Middlebury the last six years, but she
kept a computer and an old drafting table in the guest room so she
could still get something done those days when Paige was home
with a cold or strep throat, or the roads were too snowy to drive
to Middlebury (which usually meant some combination of all of us
were home anyway, because there was a snow day and the schools
were closed). I swung open the door and, as I expected, saw my
mother's handbag and cell phone on the credenza beside her drafting table. On a separate desk was the computer. I paused: I had
never appreciated the warm molasses of the wood and how meticulously my mother must have selected each piece.

I switched on the cell phone, wondering if Gavin Rikert's
name would be among the contacts. I imagined my mother phoning him to coordinate their calendars and schedule their little support group—their discussions of their sleepwalking over coffee.
There were perhaps twenty-five or thirty phone numbers stored,
and his wasn't among them. But this meant nothing, I decided,
because my mother's phone was only two years old.

So I booted up her computer. I was struck by how much bigger
the screen was than my laptop as I searched it for Gavin Rikert's

name, too. I typed his first name, then his last name, and finally both names together in the search bar on her e-mail program. It never appeared. There was no trace of the detective in any of her documents either. He wasn't in her lengthy address book full of contacts.

Still, before shutting the machine down, I scanned some of the e-mails between my mother and my mother's clients and some of the e-mails between my parents. I read some random e-mails between my mother and my grandfather about my grandmother's Alzheimer's diagnosis, and it was heartbreaking to see the two of them outline the options for care as, in the coming months and years, she deteriorated. I guessed this was an invasion of privacy, but certainly the police had done this. And clearly they hadn't found anything of importance as far as the investigation was concerned, because they wouldn't have returned the computer if they had. They wouldn't have returned her cell phone. That was just common sense. I was moved by how many of the e-mails were about Paige and me. Our mother seemed to brag a lot about the two of us. I was touched by how often our parents e-mailed, and how domestic it all was. A lot of their e-mails would have been texts a half decade later, they were so brief: grocery store reminders ("We're out of half-and-half") and references to newspaper articles ("They found the plane's black box!"), or the times of the movies they wanted to see. Sometimes my father was pleading with her to join him at a college function or thanking her profusely when she did. Sometimes she was referencing one of their inside jokes about their friends, like Marilyn Bryce's husband, Justin, a self-proclaimed foodie restaurateur, who mostly just added truffle oil to starch. Other times she was asking him to endure Bill and Emily Caldwell for a dinner in Burlington, even though they both agreed that Bill was a world-class bore. It made me a little sad that—as I had always assumed—my father seemed to love my mother more than she loved him. He often signed his e-mails "Love, W." She never signed hers at all. He told her how beautiful he thought she was. She never responded. I never found a single e-mail where my mother complimented my father at all. Her e-mails weren't cold; some were even playful. But the romance, such as it was, felt almost unrequited.

It was in the e-mails about my sister and me that I was able to glimpse the mother I recognized: passionate and funny and loving. So warm. So creative. So clever.

And I saw that my father was her equal when it came to his girls. Among the e-mails that left me wiping my eyes was one from my scholarly and (yes) bookish dad, observing how much he loved chatting with me about fiction and poetry and whatever I was reading. He had recently driven me back to college, and he had written how the car ride had left him wistful because I was so grown up. Discussing with me a Kent Haruf novel that was a finalist for the National Book Award that year had left him "proud and moved because she has become so astute. She is a much better reader than I am." It wasn't true, but it made me happy he thought so. And I remembered that afternoon ride well. I remembered most of our journeys well.

And, of course, some of the oldest e-mails on the machine between my parents were about the sleep study. But these were, again, all very businesslike. The schedule. When she would be gone. He'd express his concern. She'd tell him not to worry. There was no mention of a support group or a detective. There was no mention of any other sleepwalkers.

But then there was this: an e-mail my mother had sent my father that very June. It was the subject line that caused me to pause: "MCA and Miscarriages." My mother had written:

> This is all ancient history. The study might be new, but it should mean nothing to you and me anymore. Nothing. Okay?

She was responding to an e-mail from my father. I followed the chain and understood quickly that MCA stood for "male chromosomal abnormalities." My father had found a study published in the *New England Journal of Medicine* that suggested chromosomal defects in male sperm were occasionally the cause of recurrent or multiple miscarriages. Based on the e-mail he had sent her, he had come across the article that day and was bringing it home to show her— even years later, it seemed, trying to take the bullet for my mother's miscarriages. Clearly, he had made this argument before—taken the blame. My mother, meanwhile, had her two girls and wasn't especially interested in the study. Even if this research suggested that all of the miscarriages she'd endured had had more to do with his biology than hers, she didn't care. Clearly two of his swimmers had been athletic and healthy. Paige and I were the proof.

I shut the machine down, heavy-hearted and stoop-shouldered with grief. I went downstairs and woke my father and walked him up to his bedroom. Then I climbed into the gym shorts and T-shirt that I was sleeping in those days and went to bed. For a long time I tossed and turned in the dark, tortured as much by what I knew as what I didn't, before finally getting up and pulling up the shade and opening the window. In the chill air I watched the night sky and stars from my window seat and I listened to the river, and over and over I asked my mother where she had gone.

☽

Once, when our family was starting to understand the connection between my father's absences and my mother's nocturnal journeys, my father had asked one of the clinicians at the sleep center whether I should lock my mother in the bedroom from the hallway when he was gone. Of course we would have had to add such a lock to the outside of the door. Or, he had suggested, we could add an electric light beam with an alarm to the frame. The alarm would sound if his wife walked through the doorway, at the very least awakening me. I had not been present for the discussion, but my father had shared it with me. Unfortunately, there were problems with both solutions. What if there were a fire and my mother couldn't escape the bedroom? What would we do when I left for college in a year? Paige was still so young. No, the best

solution was that my father simply wouldn't travel until the medi-
cation took hold and it seemed likely that his wife's sleepwalking
was cured—or at least in remission.

⟩

The next day, Sunday night, my father and Paige and I were
fighting another losing battle against awkward silences over dinner.
I had improvised a Chinese stir-fry using the very last of the carrots and green peppers from the garden and the last chicken breasts
they had at the general store. I promised myself that someday I
would actually drive to the supermarket and buy a week's worth
of groceries. Wasn't that what grown-ups did? Homemakers? My
own mother? I watched Paige push the vegetables around her plate
as if they were elements of a board game. Finally I asked my sister,
"You have a lot of homework?"

"Nope."

"Any?"

"Nope."

Our father looked up from his plate and smiled. I studied him
and waited, but he said nothing and then rather delicately cut a
piece of the chicken into a pair of even smaller cubes.

⟩

After dinner, I cleaned up the dining room and loaded the
dishwasher. My father offered to help, but both of us knew I would
decline. By the time I was done, he was sitting in the den with
a book in his lap, already dozing. I went upstairs and peeked in
on Paige and saw that she was lying on her back in bed and playing with her Game Boy. She had gotten into her pajamas but was
wearing a sweatshirt with the logo for her ski team above the kangaroo pocket.

"What do you want?" Paige asked, not looking up from the
device.

"Nothing. But . . ."

"But what?"

"You know you're not supposed to be playing video games on a school night."

"It's Mario Brothers. It's for kids."

"That's not the point. I wasn't judging its suitability. I was just reminding you that Mom and Dad don't want you playing video games on nights when you have school the next day."

"Well, Dad is half in the bag—"

"Where did you hear an expression like that?"

"Ally McBeal."

"Since when do you watch *Ally McBeal*? Since when do you even understand *Ally McBeal*?"

She raised her eyebrows and looked at me as if the questions evidenced previously uncharted realms of utter cluelessness.

"Dad's not half in the bag," I said.

Paige dropped the Game Boy on the mattress beside her and pulled herself up against the headboard. "Okay. He's not half in the bag. He's all the way in the bag. And Mom's dead."

For a moment we stared at each other, the last word—a single syllable—as tangible in the air between us as smoke. Without thinking, Paige had verbalized the unthinkable. And then, aware of what she had done and how now she could never go back, she repeated the adjective. "She's dead. She's dead and we both know it."

Still I said nothing. I wanted to reassure my sister that we didn't know this, there wasn't a body. But those words would have been unbearably hollow. Paige was smart. It would have been insulting to try and dissuade her of the truth. So instead I went to the bed and sat down beside her. I felt my own eyes welling up, but Paige didn't seem close to tears. It wasn't at all like that moment by the edge of the Gale, when Paige had started to cry and swatted away my arm with one of her swim fins. Instead she seemed resigned, maybe a little numbed by what she had said.

"Wow," I murmured simply, gently rubbing her back.

"Why? Is it because I finally said what you've wanted me to say for weeks?"

"I didn't want you to say it."

"But it's what you believe."

I bit my upper lip so I wouldn't break down. "I don't know what I believe," I said carefully.

"Of course you do. We both know she's gone." She put her hands in the sweatshirt pocket.

"I guess."

"You guess," Paige said, her voice dismissive and curt.

"Can I ask you something?"

"Sure."

"When you would wander across the beaver pond those afternoons . . . when you would walk along the road beside the Gale . . ."

"Maybe I was looking for clues. But I was also looking for the body."

"Oh."

"She's never coming back. I'm twelve. Not retarded."

"Why would you use a word like that?"

"Twelve?"

I waited.

"Fine. I'm twelve. Not mentally challenged. Whatever."

I looked at the Game Boy. "Can two people play Mario Brothers?"

"No, they invented and designed the whole thing without a multiplayer mode."

"You're being sarcastic, aren't you?"

Paige nodded. "Uh-huh." Then: "You're going to suck at first, but I can teach you."

"Thanks."

She shrugged and moved over, giving me more room on the bed. That night we would play the game for close to an hour, and although I thought Mario looked ridiculous—blue overalls barely restraining a throw pillow of a paunch, a tennis ball for a nose, and a pair of great hairy wings for a mustache—he would come to me in my dreams.

☽

The next morning, I made Paige her lunch for school and then phoned one of the girls I would have been living with had I returned to college. Erica was a double major in chemistry and political science who was going to change the world by irrigating Central Asia. I had been friends with her since we had had rooms next to each other our freshman year.

We discussed how little news there was about my mother and then segued somehow to the guy Erica was thinking of dating. Erica talked about our mutual friends, telling me what they were doing and whom they were seeing. What they were planning or hoping to do in eight or nine months when school (at least their undergraduate years) was behind them. She asked me if I had heard from David, another senior in whom I had admitted some interest as classes had been winding down the previous May, and I said I hadn't since those very first days after my mother had disappeared. But, then, I hadn't reached out to him either, and the reason had something to do with Gavin: the detective interested me a bit like a thunderstorm. Erica did not bring up any mutual professors, because we had none. Finally she asked me whether I was returning for January term and the spring semester. I supposed Erica was dressed by now, and in my mind I saw her in her crewneck sweater the colors of corn silk and red maple leaves. I presumed that her hair was brushed. Me? I was still in the gym shorts and T-shirt I had slept in. My hair was, I feared, a rat's nest.

"I don't know," I said. "That's still the plan. Coming back."

"J-term?" she asked, using the shorthand for the brief burst of classes that some of us took in January.

"Maybe. Maybe February. In time for the spring semester."

The college had filled what would have been my bedroom in the suite. The dormitory flat had four bedrooms, a living room, and a bathroom. Erica said the new girl was quiet and nice and more or less fit in. "Have they told you where you would live?" Erica asked hesitantly.

"No. But I haven't really talked to them."

"When do you need to let them know?"

"I don't know."

"Don't you think you need to get on that?" Erica asked, a ripple of urgency marking her tone. "At least find out the deadlines?"

"Probably."

"Because you are coming back. Right? You just said that's the plan."

There was a line in one of my father's poems that I tried now to recall. It was about how we work to reject the realities right in front of us. It wasn't a great poem, but it was better than most of them. It was one that I believed should have been published somewhere. "Who would take care of my sister?" I asked Erica. "Who would take care of my dad?"

"Latchkey. Paige would thrive as a latchkey kid."

"No, she wouldn't. No one thrives as a latchkey kid."

"And isn't that your dad's problem?"

"Spoken like a true younger sister."

"Spoken like someone who's worried about her friend."

"I learned something this weekend," I told her, wanting to change the subject.

"Oh?"

"Remember when I told you about my mom's miscarriages?" It had been our sophomore year, one of those revelatory conversations I occasionally had with my close friends during finals week when we were taking breaks from the papers we were writing in the small hours of the morning.

"Yes," she said, drawing out the word expectantly, curious.

"My dad thought he might have been responsible for them."

"What did he say?"

"He didn't say anything. I was . . . oh, what the hell . . . I was snooping through my mom's computer. I was reading some of her e-mails. And I found a pretty recent one about a study he wanted her to read. It was about male chromosomal abnormalities. He said her miscarriages all those years ago might have been his fault because his little dudes were DNA-challenged."

"What did your mom say?"

"She said to let it go. My dad was just bouncing around an idea. But it made me sad that he was still thinking about that. Still feeling guilty. Based on the e-mail, it was something he had considered— something I guess both my parents had considered—as the reason for all those miscarriages between Paige and me."

"Your dad's sweet."

"He is. I'm worried about him."

"And I'm worried about you. There's something else going on inside you, I get it. You're not ready to come back to school now. I understand. But you will be ready in three or four months, I'm telling you that. And you need to plan for that eventuality now."

I nodded. "That makes sense."

"Thank you. So, you'll talk to the college?"

"I guess."

"You guess," she said. She sounded a little disappointed in me. "So, what are your exciting plans this week? Anything special?"

I almost confided that I was seeing a detective with ash-blond hair and hazel eyes twelve years my senior for lunch that day. But I stopped myself. Instead I said, "I'm going to vacuum. I'll go to the supermarket. You know, push a shopping cart with a crappy wheel that makes it slide into the shelves of potato chips. I'll buy lots of food with high-fructose corn syrup. I'll be a homemaker."

"This will pass, Lianna Ahlberg. I mean that: this nightmare will pass."

When I said good-bye, I thought of the word *nightmare*. An expression came to me: it was like a dream, but it was real. I couldn't recall who had said that and wondered if it was also something I had read in one of my father's poems. It was, I decided, an eerily apt summation for my life.

IT'S SO OBVIOUS a distinction, it's often overlooked: your eyes are open. But when you're dreaming—at least in the traditional sense, deep in a REM world without natural laws—your eyes are closed. And yet the wide-eyed sleepwalker is sometimes acting out a desire. Bringing to life something a bit like a dream. Instead of thrashing about in your bed, you're moving about in the world. And there is the problem. The big problem. You are bringing those desires or dreams to bear on a world that has laws— natural and otherwise.

And so sleepwalkers worry and fret, because we know what we dream. We know what we desire. And there always are consequences. The depth of our amnesia varies—some of us, in truth, know almost nothing—but we still know just enough to be scared.

Yes, our eyes are open. But only we know what we see.

CHAPTER SIX

THE NEWSPAPERS WITH their stories of my mother from those first days were still strewn on the far side of the living room. We couldn't throw them away, but we couldn't recycle them either. They sat like swatches of carpets for a makeover we had chosen to abort. When I finally picked them up, squaring their edges and piling them together, most of the ink that remained on my fingers was from photographs of my beautiful mother. I carried them up to the attic and placed them on top of the carton that held my kid sister's old Barbie dolls. Neither my father nor Paige ever remarked upon the fact they were gone.

☽

Tattered gray clouds blanketed the mountains to the east, and it was deep enough into September that the sun was too weak to burn them off. The autumnal equinox was later that week. If I weren't going to Burlington, I thought I might have started the first fire of the season in the woodstove in the den. I wondered if it would rain. We needed rain so badly.

Now, as I was finally getting dressed for the day, I stared long and hard at my sweaters, a little disgusted. If I had been at school and were planning to see a boy on what could only be construed as a date, I would have borrowed one of Erica's. I hadn't that choice here in Vermont. I considered a dress, and threw three possibilities on their hangers onto the bed. I toyed with a dotted shirtdress pulled extra tight at the waist with a belt, but that seemed a little too formal for lunch with a cop. It screamed *date* and *neediness* in ways that I didn't like. And so I wandered into my parents' bedroom to see what my mother had. She was four inches taller than me, so anything I found was sure to be a little big. But maybe I could find something that would work if I rolled up the sleeves.

And I did. I found a Norwegian cardigan that hung midway down my thighs, red and white and gray, buttons the size of checkers, and it would work well with jeans. It might be a little heavy for the first days of autumn, but I reminded myself that this was Vermont and it wasn't supposed to climb above fifty-five degrees that afternoon. I dressed up my jeans with a pair of black shoes with lace accents on the sides that Erica had christened my lingerie flats.

I was nervous as I was driving to Burlington, and a little relieved that I had nearly an hour to listen to music and steady myself. I hadn't had a boyfriend since the middle of my sophomore year, and even Carl—another kid who, like Erica, planned to change the world—had been more like someone to hang out with at parties and sleep with than a boyfriend. We'd spent the summer between our first and second years apart because he was an aspiring documentary filmmaker and was interning with the PBS affiliate in New York City, while I was working children's birthday parties across northern Vermont. I certainly hadn't ached for him. I was pretty sure that he hadn't ached for me. I presumed that was why we broke up just before Christmas that year. It had been almost eerily amicable, in hindsight.

And yet there had been a time when I was nineteen when I'd been quite sure that I loved him. Same with my boyfriend in high school.

I'd never been on a date before with someone older than me. I'd never been on a date before with—and the words caused me to smile and roll my eyes, even though I was alone—a grown-up.

I shook my head reflexively, trying to clear my memories of Carl. Of all my boyfriends. I told myself that viewing this as a date might be a stretch. I was, arguably, simply grabbing a bite to eat with a friend of my mother's. I reminded myself that I might even discover something interesting or important about her, and that this alone was sufficient justification. Still, I understood there was a reason for stealth.

$$\mathbb{D}$$

Rikert was already at the bakery when I arrived. He had a table in the back corner, beside the window. He was seated facing the door. For a moment I was surprised that he was dressed as casually as he had been at his niece's birthday party, but then I remembered: he had said it was his day off. He had a leather jacket draped over the back of the chair, the coat a shade of dark caramel.

"Oh, my God," he said, laughing, as he stood to greet me, "you're wearing your mother's sweater."

He was extending his hand, but I stopped and stood perfectly still, a little nonplussed. "You recognize it?"

"I do. Your mom loved it because it was warm and had pockets. But even she called it 'the spinster sack.'"

"Well, thank you. You really know how to make a girl feel good about herself."

He shook his head. "You're beautiful. Your mother was beautiful. But I'm a guy. I will always prefer what you were wearing as Lianna the Enchantress over Lianna the Spinster."

"It's too cold for a belly shirt."

"And harem pants. I get it. I'm sorry, it was just a reflex. I shouldn't have said that. I shouldn't have said anything. Let's start again. Lianna, lovely to see you. Thanks for joining me." He pulled out a chair for me and I sat down.

"That'll work," I said.

"Again, my bad."

"I guess I should be impressed that you remember the sweater. A lot of guys probably wouldn't even have noticed."

"Maybe not."

"On the other hand, you've been carrying a grudge against it for a really long time."

He chuckled. "*Grudge* is a very strong word."

I almost said something about the profound effect my mother must have had on him, but stopped myself. "This place smells pretty incredible," I said instead, inhaling the aromas of confectioner's sugar, vanilla, and maple. There were a dozen tables in the bakery, all but one taken, and the crowd was a mix of students and Burlington executives. People were chatting easily, laughing at some tables, leaning in attentively at others.

"It does. The secret is to make a decision: entrée or dessert. If you order a sandwich, you won't be able to restrain yourself. You will eat every bite. And then you won't have room for dessert."

"I am an eat-dessert-first girl. Life is short."

"Very wise. That's how you have to approach a place like this."

He nodded in the direction of the glass case with the desserts and the long blackboard with the lunch specials. "The way it works here is that we go order and then they bring it to our table. We should decide what we want so they don't kick us out."

☽

It wasn't especially nutritious, but I guessed the flourless chocolate cake was pretty low on carbs—which was a good thing because unlike Paige, I wasn't getting a whole lot of exercise those days. Vacuuming was as good as it got most of the time, and I really didn't vacuum all that often. The slice of cake was indecently large. The cappuccino I ordered had a cinnamon-colored heart swirled into the foam.

"So what did my mom eat when you two would come here?" I asked the detective. I was curious, but it was also among the most innocuous questions I could think of. "A big cupcake?"

"Usually a slice of the maple cake with vanilla icing and walnuts. And, like you, a cappuccino."

I nodded. "I'm not surprised. She loved maple. And not just maple syrup."

"I once saw her inhale a maple creemee."

"So you didn't just come here or the coffee shop."

"Busted. Yes, one time we went across the street from the hospital and down the road to the ice cream place for creemees."

"Okay."

"Would you like a list of every single place we ever went?"

"Maybe. Not today."

"Fair enough."

"What did you two talk about? Clearly it wasn't just sleepwalking and dreams."

He was eating a chocolate and peanut butter cupcake that had to be the size of a softball. He took a bite with a fork and murmured, "Most satisfactory." Then: "We talked a lot about you and your sister. I was serious when I told you how much she loved you two. I mean, she told me all about your magic and Paige's skiing. I gather the kid was practically skiing before she could walk."

"An exaggeration," I said, a sibling reflex that I regretted as soon as I had spoken.

"And she was thrilled about Amherst and so proud that you were going there."

"I was a freshman when you were transferred, right? When you two stopped seeing each other?"

"That's right. You had just started your junior year of high school when we met."

"My mom ever talk about my dad?"

"Little bit."

"But not really."

"That's correct."

"So she didn't, I don't know, exude love for him the way she did for my sister and me."

"Oh, I never doubted she loved him. It never crossed my mind that she didn't love him."

"Then why do you think she didn't talk about him?"

"Talking about your husband to another man implies the two of you are lovers or confidants. We weren't—at least not in that way. We were sleep confidants, and I mean *sleep* in the literal sense."

"It's still kind of intimate," I said carefully.

"Arguably."

"And, as you said, a woman having an affair doesn't talk much about her husband, either."

"Maybe. I've never slept with—excuse me, had sex with—a married woman."

I had about a third of the cake left before me, but put down my fork. I was pretty sure I would finish it if I were stoned. But now? I had eaten plenty. "I just want to make sure I understand the chronology. You saw each other eight or nine times over a year and a half and then, when you were transferred to Waterbury, you just stopped seeing each other."

He smiled a little boyishly. "Still don't trust me?"

"I trust you. I wouldn't be here if I didn't trust you. I just want to be sure I get this—this relationship you had with my mom."

"It was all about sleep and sleepwalking. We were sounding boards. We were our own little sleepwalking support group."

"I want to believe that."

"You can."

I thought about my mother's computer, which had been returned by the police. If my mother and the detective had simply grown apart because he had been transferred to Waterbury, why wasn't there any correspondence? Or, perhaps, why wasn't there evidence of a fight?

"See those two?" he was saying. He was pointing at a pair of uniformed police officers walking slowly but with great assurance down the street.

"Yeah."

"I know them. Two of Burlington's finest. And a baby step above felon. Both of them."

"Seriously?"

"A lot of cops are. For some people, it's a razor-thin line between good guy and bad guy."

"How did you wind up a state trooper?" I asked.

"Wondering if I could just as easily have gone to the dark side?"

"Maybe."

He sat back and told me. He talked for easily five solid minutes about what an incredible screwup he had been in high school and how lucky he was to have wound up at even a state college—and without ever having been busted for dope or speeding or any of the ridiculous things he had done when he was sixteen and seventeen years old. When he was a junior in college, he was still unsure what he was going to do with his life, but he wanted something that promised a little excitement—and would allow him to remain in Vermont. When he was home for Thanksgiving that year, a friend of his parents' who was a state trooper was regaling the family with what he called "idiots behind the wheel" stories, and Gavin grew interested. Soon after graduating, he was at the State Police Academy in Pittsford.

Outside the bakery it was starting to rain, a drizzle that was darkening the sidewalk.

"My God," I said, "it's raining. It hasn't rained since August, has it?"

"We're not supposed to get very much. It won't do much to ease the drought."

"Still."

"Still," he agreed.

I thought about what he had said at his niece's birthday party about the river. If the drought lasted long enough, the Gale might fall so low that my mother's body might emerge. It was ghoulish to imagine. I wanted closure, but I wanted hope far more.

"Is the job as exciting as you thought it would be?" I asked.

"It's not. Which is probably a good thing. It's like flying. Hours of boredom interrupted by moments of terror—but I might replace terror with intense interest. Trust me, I don't miss the time I used to spend pulling over high school kids in pickup trucks who think they're immortal and drive a hundred miles an hour. God, I used to be one of those kids. And I really don't miss the time I spent with their corpses. I like what I do now much more. It's cerebral. And it makes a difference."

I watched a woman in a khaki-colored raincoat pull up her collar against the rain and my heart skipped a beat. The woman's hair was the same incredible shade of blond as my mother's, and my mother had a raincoat just like that. But then she turned and I saw she was younger than my mother. She really looked nothing at all like her.

"You okay?" the detective was asking.

I turned back to him. "I miss my mom," I said.

"I know," Gavin told me. "I do, too." For a second I thought he was going to reach across the table and take my hand, but he didn't. I wished he had. "I do, too," he said again, and this time he sighed.

THE WORD POLYSOMNOGRAM *makes all the sense in the world when you break it down into its three-part origin:* poly *for "many" or "much";* somnus, *"to sleep"; and* gram, *from the verb* graphein, *which means "to write."*

When you have a polysomnogram, you have twenty-two wires and sensors attached to parts of your body—including a pair for your eyes. They measure movement (eye movement, too, of course), heart rate, and oxygen saturation. There are the wires along your scalp for the electroencephalography, which record the brain's electrical activity. A video watches you while you sleep.

You wouldn't think a person could ever doze off amid those wires and sensors. But we do. I did.

One of my videos, I gather, is pornographic.

CHAPTER SEVEN

PAIGE DIDN'T WANT me hovering while she swam her laps at the college pool that afternoon, and so I considered stopping by my father's office and saying hello, but I didn't want to disturb him if he had student conferences. And so I watched her bring her fingers to her toes at the edge of the water, compacting that small, athletic frame of hers, and then explode like a torpedo, elongating, flying, and finally plunging into the water and leaving a wake of bubbles and froth behind her. She was alone in the pool and I was alone on the tile. Her splash echoed inside the massive natatorium. I waved at her, aware that she wouldn't notice and wouldn't have stopped to wave back if she had, and wandered to the snack bar, where I thought I would have a cup of coffee and read the student news-paper. When I got there, instead I thought mostly about Rikert. Gavin. Even in my head I wasn't sure what I should call him.

When we had left the bakery in Burlington, it was still sprin-kling, but only slightly. Rikert had walked me to the car, which—just like the sweater—he had recognized instantly as my mother's SUV. He had apologized again for making fun of the cardigan and then asked me if I had any plans that Saturday night. There was a comedy club in Montreal that actually had a magician that eve-ning, and it might be fun to go see him. Montreal was a long drive from Bartlett—three hours—and so I wasn't entirely sure what he had in mind. Did he expect we'd spend the night there? And so I had agreed that I'd think about it, figuring if I said yes I could decide then on the ground rules: whether he had to drive me home or whether we could stay in Montreal. I'd also have to decide what, if anything, I told my father, and that might be the deal breaker for me right there. I wasn't sure I was prepared to fess up. I wasn't sure I was supposed to.

Just before I had climbed into the car, while we were standing on the sidewalk, he took my hands in his and gave me a very chaste kiss on the cheek. "A kiss in the rain is one of the few romantic fantasies that lives up to the hype—at least for me," he said softly. Now, in the snack bar at the college, I found myself running two fingers over the spot on my face where his lips had been.

☽

Driving home from the college, I recalled the woman in the khaki-colored raincoat with hair so reminiscent of my mother's, and thought of all the women I had seen that month who had inadvertently toyed with me. Given me brief, explosive bursts of possibility—*That's her! There she is! She's alive!*—and then left me only with longing and a dreamlike confusion. How many more times in my life would I glimpse women on buses, in the general store, or along the pathways of my father's campus who would tease me like that, and then leave my hopes scotched? If I lived to be fifty, sixty, or seventy years old, would I still see her, forever unchanged, racing through airport concourses or along the corridors of skyscrapers as the elevator doors slid shut and separated us once again?

☽

"And how was your day?" my father asked Paige over dinner.

Paige held the Mexican wrap from the Bartlett General Store in her hands and stared at it. "It was unbelievable," she said, "but Kenny picked up Jennifer's plate at lunchtime and licked some of her macaroni and cheese off it with his tongue. It was disgusting.

So gross. And he was already on bubble three." At the nearby middle school, where children from four different villages assembled, discipline was meted out via something called the Bubble System. When students misbehaved, they were placed on the bubble. When they reached bubble level four, they were sent to the principal, and a note would go home to their parents. They were guaranteed detention. Kenny Sheldon—Elliot and Vangie's little boy—lived on the bubble. I actually liked the kid—everyone liked him, even Paige, though she would never admit it—but he was a hellion.

"Did he wind up in Donna's office?" I asked, referring to the school principal.

"Not then, but only because Jennifer didn't tell on him. But he had to go when we started talking about the Shakespeare play." Every year, the sixth and seventh graders at the school performed a different Shakespeare play in the spring. It was dramatically abridged, but still impressive. They worked on it for months, and my father on occasion brought some of his college students to Bartlett to watch a performance. "You really haven't seen Shakespeare until you've seen it performed by twelve-year-olds," he once said.

"How come?" I asked. "What did he do this time?"

"He kept using a pointer as a sword. He said Shakespeare always needs swords." She swallowed the last of her milk and made a face: "I think the milk is just about to go bad."

"Oh, Shakespeare does not always need swords," my father corrected Paige. He sniffed her glass and shrugged. "But sometimes swords help. *As You Like It* this year, correct?" He smiled at my sister, his hands in his lap. His shoulders were sagging. I wondered how long it would be until his smiles weren't so beaten and sad.

"Uh-huh."

"There is at least one lovely reference to a sword—'I remember when I was in love I broke my sword upon a stone'—but, alas, there is no sword fighting. Kenny will have to soldier on without brandishing whatever sword he has as a prop." He turned his attention upon me: "And you, my dear?"

"Me?"

"What did you do today?"

I wanted to reward my father's attempt to rise above his despair and show some interest in life—in my life, in my sister's. But I couldn't bring myself to tell him that I had had lunch with the detective, especially given the murkiness of my mother's relationship with the man. I still had a feeling that this needed to be a secret. So I lied to him: "I read and watched it drizzle. It was kind of heavenly."

"You didn't leave the house?"

"Not until I picked up Paige after school and we went to the swimming pool."

He nodded, but said nothing more. In another life, he would have asked me what I was reading.

☽

"Are you dreaming a lot these days? Like more than usual?" Paige was asking me.

I was sitting at my desk and smoking a bowl. The nearby window was open an inch. I had carried our portable TV with the VHS slot up to my bedroom and was watching a video of a magic show I had been given at a magic "emporium" in Somerville. The store was actually what had once been a dining and living room in a rundown house in a once-proud neighborhood that was starting to grow seedy and tired. The shop was reminiscent of a dangerously overcrowded antique store, except instead of porcelain lamps and davenport desks, piled high and crowding the sofas and chairs were brightly colored wooden boxes and metal canisters—all with politically incorrect depictions of men and women from Asia and the Middle East—and top hats and wands. Dingy paper bouquets and worn silks, their once neon colors faded with time, cascaded from the shelves that climbed high on one of the walls. I used to go there soon after I started college in Massachusetts, making the pilgrimage whenever I was anywhere near Boston. The owner, a gentleman older than my grandfather with knobbly, age-spotted hands, had once been a rather successful performer who went by Rowland the Rogue. His real name was Lindsay McCurdy, and he was nothing like a rogue in real life. He was sweet and actually a little shy at first. My grandparents lived nearby in Concord, and on one of my family visits my sophomore year I had brought my parents and Paige to Somerville to meet him. Four of my illusions had once been his, and two of them he had given to me simply because I would have tea with him when I was in the area. Like most magicians, he was a wonderful raconteur, and he would regale me with tales of his late lovers, his partners, and his assistants. But unlike many magicians—and unlike most men of his generation—he was a really thoughtful and engaged listener. Although I saw him only seasonally, in some ways he knew as much about my life as anybody. I loved his emporium. I loved him. I had sent him a note two weeks after my mother disappeared, and he had written back using one of his old, elegant fountain pens with an italic nib. The letter was beautiful. It was not precisely a letter of condolence since my mother was missing, not dead, but it was at once realistic and deeply comforting. I considered now whether I should go visit him.

"Maybe. I guess I'm dreaming more," I answered Paige. I paused the cassette as the magician—a fellow in his midthirties, perhaps a half century younger than Rowland the Rogue—was striking a match and about to transform the flame into a live dove. Already there were two birds beside him. I wondered if I'd ever work with live animals. I had no idea how I'd care for them at college—assuming I returned to college (no, I told myself, I would, of course I would)—and then there was the whole animal rights dilemma. I was confident that PETA didn't approve of using birds and bunnies in magic acts. I was pretty sure that I didn't, either. But a live animal? It always left an audience awed. The rabbit in a top hat? It was iconic.

Out of the corner of my eye I saw Paige wave one of her hands theatrically, as if the room were awash in teargas. There was no point in snuffing the bowl now. I didn't like to smoke around Paige, but I was busted. I might as well finish it. My sister was in her pajamas and had appeared rather suddenly in the doorway to my bedroom. "Why do you ask?"

"Sometimes I worry I'm going to wind up like Mom."

Instantly I understood how the question was connected to our mother's disappearance. My kid sister's worries were crazy, but she still needed reassurance.

"I wouldn't fret even a teeny bit," I said finally. "Pardon the bad pun, but I would lose exactly zero sleep over that."

"A person who has a parent who sleepwalks is ten times more likely to sleepwalk than someone who doesn't."

I knew there was a genetic component because of those incidents I'd had as a little girl. But ten times? Clearly Paige had found the statistic on a website or in a library book. Maybe she had come across it in our own *Mayo Clinic Family Health Book,* the doorstop of choice for hypochondriacs everywhere. The number was meaningless, I presumed, and I was certain that I would still believe it was meaningless even if I hadn't lit up a few minutes ago.

"Well, then: I was the one who got it," I said, hoping this would be comforting.

"Yeah, right. How many times did you actually get out of bed? Twice? Three times?"

"It was more than that. Way more than that. At least that's what they tell me. I think it went on for two years."

"Mostly you just sat up in bed and didn't recognize Mom and Dad."

"Sometimes. Still an arousal disorder."

"A pediatric sleep disorder," Paige said. "Super common."

"I am guessing you found that expression on whatever website or in whatever book gave you that ten times number."

"It was very informative."

I took a last drag on the bowl and tipped the ashes onto the dessert plate I had brought upstairs to my room expressly for this purpose. Then I went to my bed and sat down. I patted the mattress, encouraging my sister to join me. I was actually a little surprised when Paige did. "You've studied probabilities in math, right? You know what probability means?"

"It means likelihood," she said. "Odds, right?"

"Right. It's when we try and get a sense of how likely it is—how probable it is—that something is going to happen. And here's why it matters: even if my arousal disorder was only a pediatric problem, it means that I inherited sleepwalking from Mom. And if I did, the probability falls that you did—or you will. And then there is this: Have you ever had an incident? No. Never."

She looked at me. "That's not true."

"Seriously? When? I think Mom or Dad would have told me."

"Well, you think wrong. I told Mom. I don't know if she told Dad."

I tried to clear my head and focus. "Tell me what happened," I said.

"One night in August—about a week before Mom disappeared—I think I went downstairs."

"You think?"

"My swim bag wasn't where I'd left it."

"Maybe you forgot where you put it."

"It was on the floor in the den by the TV set. I always leave it by the front door so I don't forget it." Paige was as meticulous about her swim bag—always packing a dry towel, a dry suit, and her goggles—as she was her ski gear. Sometimes her wet towel wound up in the back of the car on the way home if it was warm out, because she would walk from the pool to the car in her suit, wearing the towel like a skirt. But before leaving the house, she always double-checked that she had what she needed in that bag.

"So one time you just put it down in the den by mistake," I said. "Or maybe Mom or Dad moved it."

"Also, it was unpacked."

"Unpacked?"

"Everything was on the rug."

"What did Mom say?"

"She said I was worried for nothing. She said I just forgot to pack it. And even if I had gotten up in the middle of the night, she said it was probably a one-time thing."

"Okay, then. It sounds like the odds you were sleepwalking are pretty slim."

She took a deep breath: "But then this happened: last week, I woke up in the barn."

"Seriously?"

"Seriously. I was in Mom's car."

"At night?"

"Uh-huh. The middle of the night. And I don't remember walking out to the barn or getting inside. I don't remember getting behind the wheel. But there I was."

"You're sure?"

"Gee. Did I wake up in my bed or outside in the barn? Hard to be sure," she said sarcastically. "Of course I'm sure."

Paige had been one of those kids who'd always loved to sit on our mother's or father's lap and steer the car as a little girl. Now, though she was still a few years from even a learner's permit, our parents would let her back in and out of the barn. "Why didn't you tell me?" I asked. "Why didn't you tell Dad?"

"I didn't want to worry Dad. He's kind of a mess. And I'm telling you now."

I thought about this. "Well, thank you."

"I mean, I guess I should have made a bigger deal about the swim bag in August. But we were all freaking out because Dad was about to go to that conference. You know, his first big trip leaving Mom. I didn't want to ruin everything and prevent him from going. I guess Mom didn't either."

I understood completely, and I didn't want her to become any more alarmed than she already was. "I get it," I said. "At some point we should probably let Dad know. I really don't think it's a big deal, so you shouldn't either. But let's find a moment in the next couple of days when you or I can tell him."

"Okay," she agreed. Then she sat back against my headboard

and folded her arms across her chest. "So what do you think of your odds and probabilities now?" she asked me.

"I think you worry too much," I told her, smiling.

The image on the TV screen was still frozen where I had paused the cassette. The magician had just returned the second dove to the cage on the table beside him. For a long second we both stared at it. The magician had tattoos of the sun and a crescent moon on his neck.

"What do you remember about your own sleepwalking?" she asked me after a moment.

Like most sleepwalkers, I recalled almost nothing. I really had but one memory: waking up and my mother was sobbing. It was one of those horrific, perfect storms. It was ten at night and I was six. In my memory, my mother was writhing alone on the floor of the bathroom off the master bedroom, curled up almost in the fetal position beside the tub. She was wearing a white nightshirt and there was blood on one of her thighs. I was clutching a portable, plastic Barbie dollhouse. I had no idea how or why I had woken up, or what I was doing with the dollhouse in my arms. I had been oblivious to my mother's crying. My father had gone outside to bring the car to the front steps from the carriage barn. I had been terrified when I had woken and seen my mother in that condition, and I had dropped the dollhouse onto the tile, breaking off a part of the roof and the wall. A small, sharp piece of plastic had shot into my mother's face, nicking her just below her eye, and the blood had mixed with her tears, making the wound look far worse than it actually was.

Years later, my mother would explain to me what I had walked in on: the third miscarriage. It was starting and my mother knew the feeling, having endured it twice before. She was going to lose another baby.

"I don't remember anything," I told Paige. "I really don't recall anything at all." The last thing I wanted to do was share that nightmare of a recollection with my kid sister, especially when she was already feeling such anxiety. Our conversation had put a serious crimp in my buzz.

"Nothing?"

"Not a thing."

Paige seemed to think about this. "What are you dreaming about these days?" she asked. "You said you're dreaming more."

"I'm not one of those people who recalls her dreams."

"Can you think of anything?"

"Sure. I had a dream last night about a building on campus that—at least a part of it—has eight sides. It's called the Octagon. I've had two classes in there. It's an older building."

"What happened?"

"I wish I could tell you something interesting and amazing. But all I remember is that I was eating cigarettes."

"Eww. Gross. Why?"

"It's even grosser. The cigarettes were lit. I was doing a magic trick."

"Who was in the room?"

"A couple people. I have no idea who."

"You're right: that's not very interesting. It's only disgusting."

I smiled at her. "Okay, then. What about you? What have you been dreaming?"

"Joe the Barn Cat watched Mom leave the house."

"That's the dream?"

"Yup."

"Well, he probably did."

"I was with him—in the dream. We followed her."

"Where did she go?"

"That's the problem. That's what's so frustrating. All I remember is that Joe and I follow her downstairs. We follow her when she opens the front door, and we follow her when she goes outside. We follow her when she starts to walk down the street toward the village. She's walking on the yellow lines right in the middle of the road, but it doesn't matter because it's nighttime."

"Arguably, that's an even worse time to sleepwalk down the middle of the road."

Paige frowned in exasperation. "I just mean there aren't a lot of cars on the roads around here at night."

"Okay."

"Anyway, there's Mom and Joe and me. Mom is maybe twenty-five meters ahead of us. You know, the length of the college pool."

"Do you call out to her?"

"I want to, but I can't speak. I can't make my voice work. Dreams are like that, right? Then she disappears. It's so frustrating."

I thought about this. "Did you get as far as the general store? The bridge?"

"Nope. Then, poof, Joe and I are just home again."

"I'm really not an expert on dreams. But I think it shows how much you miss her. That's all."

"Duh."

"You asked."

She pointed at the television screen and the frame of the magician with his doves. "You're not going to get doves, are you?"

"No."

"Good. It would just be so sad when Joe ate them or they died."

"God, you can be ghoulish."

"I'm not," she said. "I'm just the realist in this house."

YOU MASTURBATE IN your sleep. So you are told. So it begins. And, for some people, so it ends. Self-stimulation. That's all.

That's . . . all.

But, alas, not for you. You swim through a nocturnal world of slow-wave non-REM stage-three sleep—a clinical term that is just metrical enough to sound like bad poetry—and experience an abrupt pseudo-awakening with your heartbeat a frenetic paradiddle in your chest. And your prefrontal cortex, which is dormant because you are asleep, can't help you. It can't rein in your hands as they reach down below your waist. Or, when that's not enough, as they reach for whoever's beside you. Or, when there is no one beside you, as you set out to find someone.

We see a Berlin Wall between sleeping and wakefulness, between the conscious and the unconscious mind. But that's wrong. Think a spectrum. Imagine a line.

And then imagine your limp surrender when you cross that line—the tremors, the unbidden release, the subsequent shame when you wake. And then imagine that you cross that line one time too many.

CHAPTER EIGHT

IT WAS A revelation as a twenty-one-year-old to push a grocery cart. I realized that despite having been in supermarkets easily hundreds of times in my life, I had never before taken a metal cart and guided it up and down the aisles. I had sat in them, of course. I had walked beside my mother or father as one or the other had pushed one, eventually with Paige in the seat. And I had shopped for myself at the grocery in Amherst and I had picked up things for my family right here over the years, but I had always used a plastic basket. Or I had balanced the cat food, the apples, and the heavy cream in my arms like a circus clown. And now I decided that I rather liked pushing the cart. I knew the pleasure would wear thin if this really were a weekly chore, but there was still an element of unreality to it—a sense that I was playacting. Twice when I was alone in one of the long, well-lit aisles, I had given the cart a little shove with the toe of my sneaker and watched it roll half a dozen yards ahead of me. I might have done it a third time, but my second push had sent it swerving like a bowling-alley gutter ball into a section of boxed cereals, and the impact had caused some of the cartons on the very top shelf to fall to the floor. Still, this task—grocery shopping—had exhumed some latent childhood happiness. There were the Saturday mornings before Paige was born, when my parents together would do weekly errands and I would wander these aisles with either my mother or father or both, and pick out the items that I wanted to bring with me to preschool or daycare, or I wanted packed in my lunch for school. How many of those very early memories were real and how many were manufactured from conversations with my parents or photos of me and my preschool pals at snack time I would never know. But the recollections from second grade? Precise. Same with the Uncrustable lunch phase. The peanut-butter-and-banana-sandwich phase (still one of my favorite sandwiches when I came home from college and craved comfort food). And, yes, the curried egg salad phase. (I was, apparently, a fourth-grade gourmand.)

But what did it matter if those first memories were, in fact, fabricated? It mattered not at all. The images in my mind were all as pleasant and reassuring as the supermarket recollections that I was confident were real: all those times after Paige had arrived when it would be only my father and me, because my mother would be home with my baby sister. Two aisles away from where I was standing right now, poised behind the back of the cart, was the bakery section, where my father and I had picked out the cake mixes and the icings and the sprinkles and the candles for my tenth birthday party cupcakes. (I smiled almost reverentially at the memory, and how I had wanted cupcakes instead of a cake, and how each one had to be decorated a little bit differently—and how my father had obliged. Paige was still an infant, and my father had done most of the heavy lifting at that birthday party. It was a sleepover on a Friday night. The next day, Saturday, after my friends had gone home, my father had taken me to Boston and brought me to a place called Club Conjure, the shabby second floor of a comedy club where magicians performed on the weekend. I was awed. By the time I was twenty-one, I had performed there twice myself, once with Rowland the Rogue in the audience. He brought me flowers.)

"Lianna?"

I awoke from the daydream and saw Marilyn Bryce was beside me. Marilyn was a friend of my mother's who tended to drive my father a little crazy. She was a painter in one of the hills beyond the village of Bartlett. Sometimes both of my parents joked about what my father called Marilyn's "peace, love, and tie-dye" vibe—

which was shorthand for the fact that her paintings all looked like album covers from 1967 and there was always the chance when you dropped by her studio that you would be offered some pretty serious weed—but her canvases went for thousands of dollars in galleries in Vermont and two and three times that in Massachusetts and Manhattan. It seemed as if her husband, Justin, was rarely in Bartlett: he was either at one of his bistros in Middlebury or Burlington, or visiting other restaurants that he thought might have something to teach him. Their son, Paul, was three years younger than me, and the sort of kid who smoked dope with his mom and had all the drive of a well-fed house cat. He was, I presumed, a freshman in college, and it embarrassed me now that I had no idea where.

"Marilyn, hi," I said, trying to focus.

The woman was wearing a black-and-purple peasant dress as a tunic over blue jeans. The dress had Arabesque stitching that reminded me of the designs on some of my magic tricks. She was tall and slender, her hair still a lush reddish brown: today it was in a long braid that fell to the base of her spine. She would have been beautiful if her eyes weren't quite so close set. She was standing behind her cart as if it were a podium.

"I keep meaning to stop by the house and check in on all of you," Marilyn said, and she shook her head and smiled in a way that at least hinted at self-loathing. Disappointment in herself. I hadn't seen Marilyn since the very first days after my mother had disappeared. Marilyn, like most everyone else, had moved on.

"We're okay," I said.

"I'm sure you are, but only because you don't have any choice but to be okay. When do you go back to school?"

"I'm not."

"What?"

"I mean, I'm not this semester. I probably will in January."

"God."

"It's fine."

"Tell me more: How is your father? And Paige?"

"Like I said, we're okay. Maybe a little shell-shocked. I mean, it sucks, but what are we supposed to do? Dad is teaching and Paige is going to school and swimming and I'm"—and I motioned at the cart overflowing with (among other things) paper towels and cat sand and coffee, cereal and cookies and beer—"I'm shopping."

"So, you're the glue."

"No. I'm just . . . here." I glanced briefly into Marilyn's cart but suddenly felt this was invasive. Carts were public, and yet it felt intrusive to peer in. I looked away.

"Are there any new leads?" Marilyn asked.

"No."

"How can a person just evaporate into thin air?"

"A person can't."

"Do you all need anything?"

I took a breath and thought about it. "Not really," I answered finally.

"You're sure?"

"I'm sure." Then, almost impulsively, I said, "Can I ask you something?"

"Anything, Lianna. Anything."

"Did you and my mom ever, you know, get high?" I had come across an article online that suggested marijuana might diminish a sleepwalker's tendency to get up in the night. Most physicians saw no reason to believe this, but I knew Marilyn liked to smoke and I pondered the lengths to which my mother might have gone to dial down her sleepwalking. Also? I was curious. I wanted to learn what I could about my mother.

"No. Okay, yes."

"You did."

"Once in a while. Maybe twice. One time right after she left that architectural firm up in Burlington and needed to chill. Another time when your grandmother was diagnosed with Alzheimer's."

"That's it?"

She looked around conspiratorially. It was as if she wanted to be sure we were all alone in the aisle. "I guess we did more than twice, in that case. Maybe three or four times. We also shared a bowl before you went away to school for the first time, and then again when Paul got into college last spring."

"You would light up before and after the life-changers," I said, and I smiled ever so slightly at the idea. "Those really big moments. The really big good ones and the really big bad ones."

"When your child is growing up and leaves home, it's good and bad. It's both. But mostly good. It's only bad because we're all a little selfish as parents, and we hate to see our babies move away. But, of course, we're also crazy proud. I mean, I'm living that empty nest right now with Paul off at school."

"Did my dad ever join you when you'd smoke? Or your husband?"

"So, is this what happens when our kids grow up? We talk to them about our dope?"

"Oh, come on," I said playfully. "I know you and Paul sometimes light up together."

"Well, there is that . . ."

"So, did my dad sometimes come over with my mom?"

"For a smoke? No. She wouldn't have wanted you and your father to know."

"Really? Not even my dad?"

"No way. Your father? He would so not have approved," she said, and she laughed once, an exuberant and unexpectedly big chuckle.

A thought came to me, and I wasn't sure whether to pursue it. But I also knew that I couldn't resist. "I guess not," I agreed. "Did my mom have any other secrets from my dad? You know, things she would tell you but not him?"

Instantly Marilyn stood up very tall, her whole body stiffening. She reached behind her head for her braid, as if she wanted to make sure it was still there. "What sorts of things?"

"I don't know. Girl things," I suggested, hoping to defuse the tension with a silly expression.

"Give me a *for instance.*"

"Her sleepwalking."

"That is so not a girl thing. There was nothing playful about her sleepwalking."

"I know."

"But, yes, it might have come up."

I waited.

"It scared her," Marilyn said finally. "That's why she went to the sleep clinic. I mean, when you pulled her off the bridge—"

"She told you?"

"Yup."

"I thought she was too, I don't know, ashamed to talk about it. I didn't know she had told anyone around here."

"She told me. She was really frightened."

"Did she ever discuss the sleep clinic?"

"Well, I guess she was pleased that they seemed to get the sleepwalking under control. At least for a while."

"At least for a while," I agreed. Then: "I didn't wake up that night." It was a reflex. I wasn't interested in Marilyn's sympathy or consolation, but I knew instantly it sounded like I was.

"No, it's not your fault, sweetie. You must know that. You have to know that."

I shook my head and went on, trying to bury my guilt like a seashell beneath beach sand. "Did my mom ever talk about anyone she met there?"

"At the sleep clinic?"

"Uh-huh."

"Why?"

"Just curious."

"Do you know something?"

"I'm just trying to figure out her life. What happened . . ."

Marilyn took a deep breath. "The detective talked to me, too. Obviously."

"So you know who I'm talking about."

"Garrett."

"It's Gavin."

"That's right. Gavin. He said he knew your mom from the sleep clinic."

"Did my mom ever talk about him when they met?"

"What are you suggesting?"

It was almost like patter, I thought to myself, the way Marilyn and I were dancing around the subject. It was a misdirection of sorts. And so I decided to speak as plainly as I could. "Do you think that my mom and Gavin were having an affair?"

Marilyn sighed. "No, not really. I believe it was more of an emotional infidelity."

"I think I know what you mean, but I'm not completely sure."

"You're young. I think your mom and Gavin were attracted to each other, despite the age difference. Your mom had a decade on him at least. But they were never going to act on those urges. Your mom was never going to cheat on your dad. She wasn't built that way. But she and Gavin shared something special."

"Their sleepwalking."

"Well, yes, but I didn't mean that. I mean they opened up to each other in ways that I'm not sure your mom did with your dad—or with me."

"Do you think she talked to Gavin about my dad? About their marriage?"

Another customer passed us in the aisle, an older woman in what I supposed was her husband's red flannel shirt. We all smiled at each other. When she was past us, Marilyn answered, "Maybe. I guess she talked about whatever people who have these sorts of friendships discuss. What's lacking in their life. What's missing. I think a person only falls into one if there's a hole in their marriage."

"There was a hole in my parents' marriage?"

"Oh, Lianna, not like that. But you had to know it wasn't perfect. You're a smart girl. But what marriage is?"

"Perfect."

"Yes."

"What was wrong with my parents' marriage—in my mom's eyes?"

"I don't know. I mean, I shouldn't even be talking about this. But your dad can't be the easiest man in the world to live with. He's—"

"Right now he's just completely overcome," I said defensively. "He's just wrecked."

"So you're all not okay. You're more than just shell-shocked."

"Of course we're not okay," I went on, angry suddenly for reasons I couldn't quite parse. But the combination of the way that Marilyn had deserted my family so quickly, the revelation that my mother and Gavin had had what Marilyn called an infidelity, and now Marilyn's attack on my father had all conspired to upset me. "We're not okay at all. How could we be?"

She took my arm. "You're right. I shouldn't have believed you. I'm a mother, I should know better. Can you come to my house for tea? I'd love to see you. It's so lonely with Paul at school. Justin is always out and about somewhere, and so the house and the studio are just so quiet."

I took a breath. "Yes. Sure."

"And while I see from your shopping cart that you're feeding your dad and Paige well, why don't I drop off dinner one day later this week?"

"Fine."

"I'll call you so we can coordinate. And Lianna? I'm sorry for anything I told you that I shouldn't have. I really am."

I extracted my arm from Marilyn's grasp and wiped at my eyes, which were starting to tear. "Don't be. I probably needed to hear it."

"No, you didn't," said Marilyn. We embraced, and I could smell weed on the woman's dress and thought of how Paige reacted when she detected the stench on my clothes. It made me feel even worse about myself. I presumed that tea meant grass—or at least would include grass—and wondered if I would have the willpower to resist.

⟩

I listened to the message that Gavin had left on my cell phone. At the time, almost no one called me on it. My parents had bought it for me "in case of an emergency." I viewed it more as a rescue flare than a phone. Gavin said he had gone ahead and gotten a pair of tickets to the magic show in Montreal, and that he hoped he wasn't going to be giving them to his mother and father to use. I had been gazing at my small bag of weed on one of the slate kitchen counters, tempting myself really, trying to decide whether I wanted to flush it all down the toilet or pick out the sticks and stems and pack a bowl. It was lunchtime and I was all alone in the house. I had unpacked the groceries and vacuumed the first floor. The midday sun was cascading in through the windows, and I guessed another day this would have cheered me, but at the moment all it did was illuminate the grime on the screens and the streaks on the glass panes.

I didn't feel like calling Gavin back, because at the moment his name alone evoked the words *emotional infidelity*. And yet my pulse raced a little faster when I thought of him. When I thought of his lips on my cheek. Marilyn seemed confident that my mother's relationship with the detective hadn't been physical, but how could she be so sure? And even if my mother hadn't strayed from my father, she had had a relationship with this other man that was meaningful and complex.

I decided not to flush the dope into the septic tank. But I didn't light up either, which meant that I wouldn't light up that afternoon. In a few hours, I had to pick up Paige after school and bring her to the college to swim. I tried not to drive when I was stoned, and I didn't want my sister to smell marijuana on me anymore. So, this really had been my only window. I made sure that the baggie was sealed and brought it upstairs to my bedroom.

When I returned to the kitchen, I picked up my phone once again. My mother had always taught me that it was best to get the difficult or unpleasant chores out of the way first. Just do them, she urged, because they don't go away. And why stew over them? She had offered this lesson in the context of a particularly vexing and disagreeable client; she said she used to call him first thing in the morning, so neither anger nor anxiety would scar the rest of her day. I recalled that advice when I thought about Gavin's message and the sound of his voice: a low thrum with irony always at the edges. I relaxed ever so slightly. I sat down on the barstool and listened to the message once more. I reminded myself that I had known even prior to my conversation with Marilyn at the grocery store that my mother's relationship with the detective was meaningful and, on some level, inappropriate. But I myself had met him now, and I liked being with him. I had liked the way my blood had leapt when I had stood before him in a midriff as Lianna the Enchantress.

In the end, I called Gavin back simply because I was incapable of not calling him back.

"You went off radar," he began. "I was getting worried."

"Oh, there's really no place for me to go, trust me."

"Of course there is. Montreal. You got my message with the details, right? I'm hoping we're still on."

"What time is the show?"

"Seven."

"Seven?"

"Well, there is a ten p.m., too, but then I'd have you back in Bartlett around three in the morning. And I'm working on Sunday."

I thought about this. I thought of my assumptions about what he had in mind—the way I had imagined a hotel and how I would have to decide whether I wanted to spend the night with him.

"So, it would mean an early-bird supper," he went on, "and that means you will be the youngest person in the restaurant by far. But the place I was thinking of has spectacular risotto and a chocolate mousse that will make that slice of cake you had the other day in Burlington seem like a Devil Dog."

"Hey, now. I like Devil Dogs."

"Just saying. I can make our dinner reservation for five. The wait staff will be condescending and self-important because they don't approve of people dining that early. But they'll also give us an excellent table because they'll want to show you off: A young person is here! We're not really an assisted living facility!"

"You make it all sound so appealing, how could I resist? Sure, I'm in," I said, and I walked with my phone to a spot by the living room window where the sun was streaming in like a spotlight and stood there, pretending the illuminated dust was a nimbus.

"Excellent. Why don't I pick you up a little before two?"

A thought came to me. "No. I have some errands in Burlington," I lied. "Why don't we meet in the parking lot of the mall by the interstate—exit 14. We could meet by the Sears. This way you don't have to come all the way south to Bartlett. It'll save you a boatload of driving in the afternoon and the middle of the night."

"Why do I have a feeling there's more to it than that?"

"What do you mean?"

"Let me guess: you haven't told your dad about me."

"Wow. That would be a very good guess."

"But you know what? I don't mind."

"Because you shouldn't have asked me out?"

"Nah. I told you it's a gray area. I mean, I'm always happier when I don't have to explain myself. Sometimes a little reticence makes everyone's life simpler, right? Mostly I just see your point about the driving. I feel a little unchivalrous, but what the hell? You're making my life a lot easier."

"So, we'll meet there at two thirty?"

"Perfect. You know, this is a first for me."

A couple of possible firsts passed through my mind: *Dating a younger woman? Dating the daughter of a woman whose disappearance you are investigating? Dating the daughter of a woman you may—or may not—have been sleeping with?* "And that is?" I asked simply, wondering if any trace of wariness had crept into my voice.

"A magic show in a club! Never done that!"

"Well, it should be way more interesting than what you saw at your niece's birthday party last week."

"More interesting than your show? Not likely. I kind of doubt the magician will be dressed like Jasmine."

"You are obsessed."

"Maybe," he said. "But only in all the right ways."

When I hung up, I guessed I was flattered. I know I was smiling and my face felt a little flushed. But I was also relieved: we each had our own reasons for keeping our date a secret. If I met Gavin in Burlington, I really wouldn't have to tell my father about him. I wouldn't have to concoct an elaborate excuse for where I would be on Saturday night. Any little lie would do.

☽

The other day, while Paige had been swimming her laps, I hadn't wanted to risk disturbing our father in his office. Today I decided I would. Marilyn's remarks about my father and Gavin—the first a man who couldn't be easy to live with, the second a man my mother had been emotionally tethered to—were no longer dogging me like bad dreams, and I attributed this to my brief conversation with the detective. In a few minutes he had managed to quiet the unease that Marilyn had triggered. But I still wished that I had pressed the woman for details about both men—probed to learn what Marilyn had meant. And yet how could I? I was Warren and Annalee Ahlberg's daughter; my instinct was to defend them. To believe the best about them both. Nevertheless, that afternoon while Paige was in the college swimming pool, I hiked across the campus to the limestone and marble monolith that housed the English Department. I wasn't precisely sure what I would ask my father (if anything), but I felt the need to be reassured that he was who I thought he was and my parents' marriage had been fine. Not perfect. But fine. Moreover, his office on an autumn afternoon might be the right spot to share with him Paige's fears that she may have had a sleepwalking occurrence—or two—and together we could figure out what to do next.

When I arrived, the door was open and a slender girl my age with lush, auburn hair was sitting beside my father. They didn't notice me, and so I leaned against the wall outside and listened for a few minutes as they discussed the student's vision for an honors thesis about Wallace Stevens. I wondered if I sounded that pretentious and that ridiculous when I was talking to my adviser. I hoped not. But there was also something intimate about their conversation. I was struck by the way she had pulled a chair around so she was seated on his side of the desk. When she left, I saw that she was wearing a tight retro T-shirt with a Russian cosmonaut on the front. I ignored her as she passed me and then collapsed into the other chair—the one across from my father. I reached behind me and shut the door.

"Well, this is a lovely surprise," my father said.

"I got bored at the pool. Do you have another student coming in?"

"Not for a few minutes. How's your day?"

"Weird."

"Elaborate."

"I ran into Marilyn Bryce at the supermarket."

"Oh?"

"Uh-huh."

"I used to love grocery shopping with you and your mother when you were little," he said, his tone pensive.

"Why?"

He sat back in his chair, an antique leather monster that shrunk him a bit, and rested his hands on his stomach. He was wearing a knit tie and a blue oxford shirt. His blazer was hanging from the wooden coat rack beside the door. "I was nurturing you and that always made me happy. The chore is all about feeding and comforting . . . and, one must admit, consumerism. And, of course, I was with you or with you and your mother. How could I not love it?"

"You know that Mom knew Detective Rikert, right?"

"That was abrupt."

"Sorry. It just came out."

"Yes. The detective told me the day I flew back from Iowa."

"But Mom didn't talk about him when she was . . ."

"When she was at the sleep clinic," my father said helpfully, finishing the sentence for me. "No, she didn't. Why?"

"I was just wondering."

"Why now?"

"I have too much time on my hands."

"Perhaps. Maybe you should volunteer at the elementary school. You like children."

"I like giving them magic shows," I corrected him.

"Do that then. Or read to them."

"Or crafts, maybe. God knows Mom taught me enough crafts."

He looked out the window and grew ruminative. "That detective," he began, and he paused. Then: "If I hadn't had an alibi, I am confident that in the eyes of that detective, I would have been more than *a* suspect. I would have been *the* suspect. If I hadn't been in Iowa, I am quite certain that Detective Rikert would have believed that I killed your mother."

The last four words reverberated in the room for me like a clap of thunder. My father had said them calmly, almost abstractedly. A sickening twinge of dismay—not quite fear, but a cousin—rippled along the back of my neck.

"Why would anyone think that?" I asked, my voice small and dazed.

"Oh, husbands are always the suspects in these things. Until they're not."

This was the moment, I decided, when I should tell him what Marilyn Bryce had said. In my mind, I heard myself speaking the sentence: *Marilyn Bryce said you weren't the easiest person to live with.*

But I couldn't do it. Instead I murmured like a small child, "But you two loved each other."

"We did."

I waited. He turned back to me and met my gaze. "But . . ." I murmured, trying to start a sentence for him.

"There were no buts," he said, and he sounded definitive.

"Can I ask you something else?"

"Yes. Of course."

"This is kind of random, but I keep thinking about all of Mom's miscarriages. She really, really wanted another child. You did, too, right?" I curled one of my legs underneath me.

"Absolutely. You and your sister are everything to me."

"Did you and Mom ever look into why she kept having them?"

"The miscarriages?"

I nodded.

"Yes," he said. "Of course. Your mother put up with ultrasounds, MRIs, a hysteroscopy. Her thyroid was examined. Her prolactin was measured. Her ovaries were tested. There were no chromosomal abnormalities in her eggs. Her uterus? First-rate. She had a model uterus. Utterly perfect, as far as these things go."

"Then why?"

"We'll never know," he said. "I'm not sure what put more of a strain on the marriage in those days: the miscarriages or the medical testing."

"And you never did find the cause."

"No. I can only speculate."

"Tell me."

"Well, maybe it was me."

"You?"

"Ten years ago, they didn't test men. They are only beginning to study us now. Molecular karyotyping. Perhaps the miscarriages were my fault."

"Did you and Mom ever consider adopting?"

"As I recall, we were just about to begin that process when your mother became pregnant with your sister. And this time—

miracle of miracles—the pregnancy had a perfectly wonderful happy ending."

"And Mom never walked in her sleep those years?"

"Oh, occasionally she did. But not like years later. She didn't leave the bedroom quite so often. She rarely got out of bed. Sometimes, it was more like a . . . a childhood arousal disorder. Still between the miscarriages—and my fears they were my fault—and the sleepwalking, I probably wasn't a perfect husband. I resented not traveling. I really did. I loved your mother, but I didn't handle the realities of her infirmity all that well. You were at college when I was chafing most at the bit."

I felt queasy. My father sounded tired.

"What . . ."

"Go on," he urged.

"What triggered it?"

"Your mother's sleepwalking? Hard to say. We really don't even know why it got worse. It could have been a sleeping pill. She was trying them when you were in high school. It could have been perimenopause. It could have been the idea you were growing up and would soon be leaving home. The parasomnia seemed to escalate your junior year of high school, when you were deep into the college process."

"But when you were with her, she'd sleep through the night." I wanted confirmation that my father had never had to wake my mother up in the midst of one of her episodes.

"That's correct. As far as I know, whenever she left the bed when I was with her—here in Vermont or on vacation somewhere— she was wide awake. Not sleepwalking." I noticed how carefully he had framed his response, how meticulously he had chosen his words. It was either the sort of answer an erudite college professor would offer, or the careful obfuscation of someone who had something to hide.

"Can I tell you something?" I asked him.

"Always."

"Paige thinks she may have started sleepwalking."

He sat forward and grew attentive. "Go on."

"She thinks she moved her swim bag one night in August. Last week she woke up in the barn. In Mom's car."

"The first may be nothing."

"And the second may be something," I added, finishing the thought. I told him why Paige hadn't said anything until now. I said she was worried.

"I'll talk to her tonight," he said.

"Should we be alarmed?"

"Alarmed may be too extreme a reaction. But after your mother's disappearance, we should be attentive. Concerned. I may call the sleep center."

"Thanks," I said.

He shrugged. "Oh, I wouldn't thank me. These days, I seem to be a study in ineffectiveness." Over my shoulder there was a knock on the door.

"Are you okay?" he asked.

"No. But I will be."

"You and I can talk more tonight, too." Then he motioned at the door. "Go ahead, open it," he said.

I stood up and went to the door. In the frame was another student, a beautiful girl with clementine-colored hair cut into a bob and plate-round purple eyeglasses. I had acquaintances who dyed their hair just like that. She looked like she should be working in a store that sold vinyl records or vintage clothes.

"Ah, Sam, as always you are right on time," my father was saying, his voice melodic and happy. "Lianna, this is Sam, a very gifted Elizabeth Bishop scholar. Sam, this is my daughter Lianna. Lianna is a very gifted"—and here he paused ever so slightly, and it left me feeling strangely insulted—"magician."

I said hello to the girl and motioned at the seat in which I had been sitting, but she was already melting into it, kicking off her clogs and curling her feet beneath her. I tried not to read anything into how comfortable she felt around my father, but of course I did.

Her socks were dainty; her jeans were tight. "You'll be home for dinner?" I asked my father.

"Yes. Mexican wraps?"

"I can do better."

He smiled. "You're doing just fine. I think you're doing great and I'm very, very proud of you."

SRV IS SLEEP-RELATED violence.

SBS is sexual behavior in sleep.

The charges in SRV include murder and attempted murder. In SBS, there is rape. Sexual assault. Assault with intent to rape. Sexual misconduct. Indecent exposure.

In one study in The Journal of Clinical Sleep Medicine, *the defendants who used sleepwalking as a defense for an SBS crime were acquitted nine out of ten times. The defendants who used sleepwalking as a defense for an SRV crime were acquitted four out of nine times—and the case was dropped in two others.*

You take comfort in these odds if all you care about is acquittal. But someone has still been assaulted. Or raped. Or killed.

CHAPTER NINE

"OH, BOY," SAID Paige slowly, her voice an absolute monotone. "A magic show in Montreal. Corny patter in French. Sign me up." It was Saturday morning and she was helping me put the last of the vegetable garden to bed for the winter. I was dumping the ruins of the tomato plants—long, stringy tentacles that reminded me of the remains of the dead man o' war jellyfish I had seen on a Florida beach as a little girl—into the wheelbarrow. I had told my father and Paige that I was going to the club with a friend from Amherst who lived in Montpelier. My father had asked whether this friend was a boy. He had seemed a little disappointed when I had said, no, it was a girl.

"English and French, probably," I replied, correcting Paige.

"Well, corny is a universal language," she went on, a study in sarcasm.

"You know, I don't make fun of the things you love."

"I love normal things."

"And so do I." I pulled from the earth another of the tomato cages. I was pretty sure that our mother had been all alone when she had pushed the prongs of it into the earth back in May. I would have been writing my final papers in Massachusetts and my father, most likely, had been at the college. He never helped with the garden. My mother usually planted it by herself. My mother usually did most things by herself. Even her job was far more solitary than not. It made me sad.

"How did you talk this girl into going with you?" Paige asked. She took the trowel from the wheelbarrow before it was buried completely by garden detritus and knelt in the dirt. She stabbed at the soil, rooting around for beets we might have missed.

"She was the one who suggested it."

"Is she a magician, too?"

"No."

"Just insane?"

"Paige, come on. Let it go. I get it. You don't like magic. Fine."

Paige found a beet and tossed it underhand into the grass. "Dad wishes you were going with a boy," she said.

"I know."

"I think he feels guilty you're stuck here—carting me around everywhere and making my lunch and stuff."

"What did he say?"

She shrugged. "He wishes you had a boyfriend who was taking you. It was random. You know how he is these days."

"Well, he shouldn't feel guilty. And neither should you."

"I'm twelve. My mom is gone and my dad's a zombie. I don't feel guilty about anything."

"Good. I really don't want you to feel bad about the fact I'm here. I want to be here."

"So it really isn't a boy?"

"It really isn't a boy. Why would I lie?"

"I don't know. Mom had secrets. Dad has secrets. Why wouldn't you have secrets?"

I stared at my sister, but Paige was on her knees, looking at the earth and not at me. "What do you mean?"

"About what?"

"Secrets. How do you know either of our parents had secrets?"

Paige took the trowel with both hands as if it were a spike and plunged it as hard as she could into the soil. "Die, Vampire!" she yelled. "Die!"

"I'm serious, Paige."

Still she didn't glance up from the ground. "Got him. The world of the undead just got a little smaller."

"How do you know they had secrets?"

"Because sometimes when I'd be playing Snake on Mom's phone, it would ring. We'd be in the car. She'd take the phone and tell whoever was calling that she couldn't talk."

"Maybe Mom was just being a good driver."

"She took calls from Dad or Marilyn when we were on roads that actually had cell service."

"Who were they from—the calls Mom wouldn't take? Any idea?"

She pulled out the trowel and studied it as if she were inspecting it for blood. "I don't know."

"The same number?"

"I told you, I was usually playing Snake. I didn't check. I don't think I even know how to check."

"You didn't ask?"

"Sometimes I did. She'd say it was nothing. She'd say it wasn't worth turning off the radio. She'd say she'd call them back."

"But it could have been just a client or something. Or her hairdresser."

"She took those calls. At least usually she did—like when she was building a ski house in Sugarbush or something."

"And this was during the last three years," I murmured, thinking aloud as much as I was speaking with my sister.

"It was. I mean, we didn't even have cell service in a lot of this area four years ago," she said. "So, yeah, it was this summer. It was this spring."

I thought about the detective and wished that I would simply trust Gavin. There was no reason to leap to the conclusion that some of the calls were from him and, thus, he had lied to me about when he and my mother had lost touch. But this was where my mind had wandered. And yet I was drawn to him, too: I wasn't sure any of the boys or younger men I had dated had left me with the sort of exquisite longing I felt as I anticipated Montreal. I could try and convince myself that I was seeing him because I was the hunter on the scent of details he might not otherwise share about my mother's disappearance, but I knew in my heart—truly, in my heart—that there was more to it than that.

"And Dad?" I asked finally. "What were his secrets?"

Paige had found another beet, this one a giant the size of a peony, and she rolled it along the grass as if it were a bowling ball. "A perfect strike—no bumpers needed!"

"Paige, you just said you think Dad had secrets," I repeated. "What were you talking about? Give me an example."

"I can't."

"Then why would you say he did?" I snapped.

"Don't get all bitchcakes with me—"

"And where did you hear that word? You're too young to use it!"

"I probably learned it from you. And as Dad says, words are just words. Some are better than others, but only because they are better at explaining what you mean."

"Dad was in professor mode when he said that. Not dad mode. You're too young to say *bitchcakes*."

"I'm in seventh grade. We say a lot worse. I could have called you a dick."

"Paige!"

"You're not my mom."

I thought my head was going to explode and took a deep breath to calm myself. "I'm as close as it gets," I said finally. "I'm sorry, but that's how it is. You can't use words like that, just like you can't smoke cigarettes or drink beer."

Paige didn't say anything in response. She rooted around and found a much smaller beet, this one the size of a grape. "We did a terrible job harvesting these," she said, holding the beet in her hand. For a moment I thought she was going to apologize. But then she continued, "Mom is in heaven going bitchcakes over the waste." For a split second we both waited, the air between us charged, but when Paige looked up, her eyes were wide and her smile was mischievous. I couldn't help but laugh. Then she put the beet in the palm of her left hand and flicked it at me with her right middle finger. She missed, but it was close—a testimony, I thought, to what an incredible athlete my kid sister was.

)

I drove to the Sears outside of Burlington, where I was meeting Gavin, confident that I had dodged a bullet and not overdressed, but worried (not for the first time) that I was not as beautiful as my mother. I had neither her height nor her hair, that incredible blond mane. My blond? Mousy and thin, I fretted. My mother was forty-seven the summer she disappeared, and her hair was as lush and luminescent as ever.

Originally I had chosen a pair of high heels, black with a strap around the ankle, but the temperature was supposed to flirt with the lower thirties tonight, and I didn't have the right tights to accessorize them. And so instead I had gone with my brown Frye boots, which meant changing from a skirt and a blouse to a white-and-gold wrap dress—the gold was fiddleheads and ferns—that fell almost to my knees, and my leather jacket. But in between my first and my final choice, I had run through easily a third of my wardrobe, scattering the mix-and-match ensembles on my bed and the floor. I had agonized for easily ten minutes on my lingerie, even though I had no plans to sleep with Gavin that night. But what if? I recalled my conversation with Paige. Our mother had secrets. Our father had secrets. I myself now had secrets.

When Paige had strolled past my bedroom and spied the disarray—the dresses waterfalling off the side of the bed, some still on their hangers, the underwear and shirts and socks rising like bread from the open drawers, the shirts and jackets now throw rugs on the floor—she had shaken her head and said, "Yeah, you're going to Montreal with a girl. Uh-huh." I had defended myself by saying that I was hoping I might have the chance to meet the magician after the show and needed to look professional and mature, but Paige was having none of it.

I arrived in the parking lot where I was meeting Gavin before he did and once again checked my lipstick and hair. The irony that I was checking them in the mirror behind the visor in my mother's car was not lost on me. I took comfort in the fact that today, unlike the last time I saw Gavin, I was not wearing one of her sweaters.

He arrived in a red Acura, the vehicle still dripping from the car wash, and hopped out quickly to open the passenger's-side door for me.

"I don't know much about cars," I said, "but I didn't expect a Vermont cop to drive an Acura."

"Entry level," he said, smiling. "But clean."

"And red. Isn't that a magnet for speeding tickets?"

"Only if you speed—or you don't have connections. You know, I still feel a little guilty about meeting you here. I really could have picked you up."

"That was so not happening."

"Still haven't told your dad about me?"

"Nope."

"Probably wise. I'll bet you haven't told anyone, have you?"

"Not a soul."

He shook his head. "Playing with fire. Isn't this how pretty girls disappear?"

"I don't expect to disappear," I told him, sitting down and adjusting my seat belt.

Once he was inside the car, I could see his eyes behind his sunglasses. He stared at me for a moment, appraising me, and then said, "Well, you look great. You look beautiful."

"Thank you."

"Next stop? Montreal. You'll love the restaurant."

And then we were on the highway, heading north, and I gazed up at the few clouds in an otherwise cerulean sky and at Lake Champlain when the interstate neared the water. I watched the mountains to our east and our west recede as Canada neared and the topography flattened. Most of the time, though not always, I was able to push from my mind sleepwalking and my mother and the questions I hoped I would have the courage to ask Gavin. I told myself that I was in the midst of a love story, not a mystery. Not a murder mystery. I tried to read nothing into his car or his relationship with my mother or the way he was attracted to me. The way I was attracted to him. I was—and the realization surprised me—happy.

☽

He ordered a bottle of wine, a Riesling he thought I would like, but he was still nursing his second glass when our entrees were cleared. I ordered the risotto he'd recommended, and I'd enjoyed it—just not as much as the wine. We'd each begun with a pear mojito, the glasses rippling with chartreuse and topped with mint leaves, and I had polished off mine with uncharacteristic zeal. I'd never had one. I wasn't sure I'd ever had any cocktail with juice other than a screwdriver. Over dinner, the waiter refilled my wine goblet three times, and now he was draining the last of the bottle into my glass. I was tipsy, I knew it, and I was aware that even my grin was growing a little sloppy. Though I was a girl who was, by any standard, expert at navigating the world stoned, I rarely got drunk. I rarely drank. This was different. It was less . . . cerebral. It was (and I understood what the word really meant) intoxicating. I felt wobbly and courageous at once.

I knew on some level that I should stop, but then decided it was too late. An expression came to me: in for a nickel, in for a dime. I was going to finish this last glass because I did indeed like the Riesling, and because I liked the permission the alcohol was giving me to lose a little of the control that had marked my world since my mother had disappeared. Had died. I blinked at the way my mind had made that alliterative jump. I vowed that I would not slur my words; I would think before I spoke; my pronunciation would remain crisp. Gavin might suspect I was getting drunk, but I didn't need to advertise the fact for him. We were sitting in a corner, nestled on an L-shaped settee, seated on adjacent sides of the table. He had been right about how the hostess would give us a lovely spot, but he had been wrong about it being a showplace table by the window. It was instead a nook that purred romance.

"So, you know nothing about this magician," he was saying.

"Not a whole lot. I hadn't heard of him before you suggested we come here, but I found out a little about him on the web."

"And?"

And he was handsome, I recalled, though I didn't say that. He was young, maybe thirty or thirty-five, with dark eyes and a Scottish accent. He was part of that newer breed of magicians who performed in skintight black T-shirts, had serious guns for arms, and did a lot of terrifying things involving knives and Sweeney Todd straight razors. He had tattoos. Watching him turned me on. "He isn't your mother's magician. He's pretty hip. Think David Copperfield with an edge," I answered.

"Maybe he'll escape from a cage."

"Not his thing, as far as I can tell. Expect a magician, not a gorilla."

"You know what I mean: like Houdini. Handcuffs, chains, underwater."

"We'll see."

"Think he'll saw a woman in half?"

"Oh, we are so over that," I told him, shaking my head. I meant to laugh ever so slightly, but in my head it sounded a little raucous. I imagined myself prone. In a box. Then a bed. I saw Gavin atop me. I knew how long it had been since I'd had sex.

"Levitate someone from the audience, maybe?" he asked.

"If someone from the audience is levitated, it will be a confederate."

"Southerner?"

"Accomplice," I corrected him reflexively.

He nodded. I realized after I spoke that he had been kidding. I found myself looking at his mouth. His smile. "Well, Jasmine will be a tough act to follow," he told me.

"Hah! I think you are about to be dazzled."

"Maybe. But I keep telling you: you were fun to watch. And the toughest act to follow will be dessert here."

"The chocolate mousse?"

"The chocolate mousse. We're not talking pudding."

"I like pudding."

"Pudding's for kids. This is adult."

"NC-17?"

"Depends on how you eat it, I guess. You want coffee? Cappuccino?"

I motioned at my wine. I had planned to just wave at it with my fingers and tell him I was fine. But did it really matter if I got a little rickety on my feet? I'd gone with the boots, not the heels. Boots. Not heels. I'd be okay. I was in Montreal with a guy who was, I remembered from the moment he had appeared outside my family's house that awful August morning, handsome. Hot. A hot cop. I chortled, saw him raise his eyebrows. And so I reached for my glass by its stem and polished off the last of the Riesling. Then I smiled and spoke: "Yes. Coffee would be perfect with the mousse."

When a busboy and the waiter once more had come and gone, clearing the table and taking our dessert order, he started to ask me something about etiquette in a magic show. Something about whether I would tell the performer I was a magician if he happened to ask me—no doubt, he added, the most beautiful young woman there—to come to the stage to be part of a trick. He was sitting back against the rear of the settee, his right hand on the cushion no more than four or five inches from my thigh. I was feeling adult; the wine had made me daring, desirous of doing something I'd never done before. I took his hand and placed it underneath the tablecloth in my lap, spreading my legs and pressing his fingers against me. Then I leaned into him and curled my lips over my teeth, sucking for a brief second on his earlobe. When I pulled his fingers from between my legs, I kissed them—locking my eyes on his—before returning his hand to the settee.

☽

The magician was too big and too good for the club, but I loved watching him work. There were seventy-five or so people scattered around the small tables, but there was room for at least twice that many. I hoped for his sake that his next show was sold out. The performer almost—though not quite—took my mind off the desire the alcohol had unleashed. I felt myself starting to sober up, and I didn't want to, and so I ordered a glass of wine, and then another one after that. I kept Gavin's hand in mine as the performer chewed up and swallowed Canadian and American paper money and restored the bills in the different owners' wallets, and as he put an ice pick through his forearm. I only released Gavin's fingers when we would applaud, which we did a lot. The guy was good. Inspiring. I knew how he did about two-thirds of his show, and probably could add half of that to my repertoire if I wanted. But it would take a lot of work and a lot of practice.

When we were walking to the parking garage, while Gavin was telling me that he still preferred watching Jasmine perform, I interrupted him. "I don't want to go home tonight," I said.

"Well, if you do go home, I'm driving you. There is no way I'm allowing you behind the wheel of a car."

I had hooked my arm through his, and now I stopped him in his tracks. "No, I wasn't just wishing or worrying about having had too much wine." I repeated myself, speaking as clearly as I could: "I don't want to go home tonight. I want to be with you."

He gazed down at me for a long moment and then, as I knew he would, he kissed me. He put his hands on the small of my back and pulled me against him there on the street and—his face almost grave, I thought before I closed my eyes—bent down and pressed his lips against mine, and the world around me went quiet. Except for my heart. When I opened my mouth and felt his tongue (a tentative probe at first, but then it was mirroring my own wanton playfulness and need), I heard my heart in my head. An idea came to me: This is why I am here. This was meant to be. This is really why I stayed home in Vermont.

☽

And yet we didn't make love that night.

I awoke alone in the morning beneath a quilt in his bed. At least I presumed it was his bed. I discovered I was still in my dress. I was still wearing my bra. My underwear.

My head was throbbing and my breath was toxic, even to myself, and I lay with my brow burrowed deep into the pillow, astonished at the disabling spikes of pain that accompanied just rolling my eyeballs. How was that even possible? Carefully I rubbed at my temples and pieced together what had happened after I had climbed into Gavin's car. Mostly, I realized, I had slept. I had fallen asleep—passed out, if I was going to be precise—and slept all the way home. Here. Not home. Here. I vaguely recalled parking in Burlington and the elevator to his apartment. The paneling on the elevator walls and the bronze plate from another era with the numbers for the floors. I called home, expecting I would just leave a message on the answering machine, but of course my father had picked up. I had lied—badly, I presumed—that I was safely at my friend's family's house in Montpelier. Had he said he was just glad I was safe? I thought so, but the whole conversation was fuzzy.

I saw on the clock on the nightstand that it was already noon and felt a deep stab of remorse. Serious guilt. I remembered my vow to smoke less dope, and told myself that white wine and pear mojitos were ill-advised substitutes. In a heartbeat I would have traded the superfund cleanup site that once was my tongue for mere cottonmouth. I took a deep breath to steel myself against the pain that loomed and then sat up in bed. Gingerly, with the care of the oldest woman in the world—in my mind I saw a shriveled but beatific woman eating yogurt in the Caucasus—I swung my

legs onto the hardwood floor and looked around. I saw my handbag beside the nightstand and pulled it toward me with my foot
because I was afraid to bend over. I reached for my compact and
looked at myself in the mirror, assessing the damage. I guessed I
had looked worse, but probably not by much. I popped a couple of
Altoids into my mouth.

The bedroom door was shut, and a piece of paper from a yellow legal pad had been slid underneath it. I walked gingerly there
and picked it up. Gavin had written that he'd left for work. He
explained where he kept the coffee in his kitchen and that there
was Advil in the medicine cabinet. He wrote the name of a friend
in the building and gave me his number, and said the guy would
be happy to drive me to the Sears parking lot so I could retrieve
my car. I sighed: I was the embodiment that morning of *high main-
tenance*. I was the definition of *hot mess*.

I reached for the door handle and saw it had a push–button lock
on the knob and it was pressed in. Locked. Had I locked him out
of his own bedroom after throwing myself at him in Montreal?
Didn't seem likely, but the idea caused me a pang of anxiety. I had
no idea if he had slept in the bed with me. It was possible he had
pushed the button before closing the door and going to work. I'd
have to ask him.

I opened the door and saw a short corridor to the living room
and the kitchen. There was a blue blanket and a sheet on the couch.
So, he had slept out here. Above the couch was a long black-and-
white photograph of a dairy barn in the winter. The snow was
fresh and the trees were skeletal. The apartment was sparse, but
clearly that way by design. The furniture was sleek and modern:
a lot of hard edges and chrome. The only clutter was his skis and
boots leaning near the front door, along with a pair of sneakers.

I found the bathroom and peed, popped a couple of Advils, and
drank from the faucet. Then I drank some more. I squeezed out
some toothpaste onto my finger, spread it onto my teeth and my
tongue, and rinsed. I would shower when I got home. I would get

some coffee at the nearby diner. Not here. And I wouldn't call his friend, I'd call a taxi.

I regretted both the way I had drunk too much and the way I had chosen not to ask him more about my mother's parasomnia—and, yes, about his. I couldn't do anything other than apologize about the former, but perhaps I could learn a little more about Gavin before leaving. Was it a violation? Of course. But that didn't stop me. I decided I would explore his apartment, but not ransack it. I understood it was a fine line, and I would try not to cross it.

His home was a one-bedroom on either the sixth or seventh floor of the Vermont House, an eight-story apartment in Burlington. The building was among the taller structures in the city, once the city's most elegant hotel before its conversion to co-op apartments, and Gavin's place faced the lake. I opened a random drawer on the credenza below the TV and saw it was filled with nothing but snapshots. I looked at a few, recognizing his sister from the birthday party, and gazing at one of his parents. He resembled his father: same iron cheekbones, same yellow hair. There were a few of him as a teenager or college student with a dog. A springer spaniel. Along an inside bedroom wall was a tall bookcase that was filled with military history tomes and police handbooks, and a couple of novels set in the midst of different wars. There were framed photographs of him fly-fishing, and with his mother and father at his college graduation. There was one of him with either a group of friends or a bunch of cousins—women as well as men—in bathing suits on three great boulders in the midst of a river I presumed was somewhere in Vermont. I peeked into his closet and saw a couple of blazers and a black suit. There were two coat hangers draped with neckties. The floor there was clearly where he piled his dirty clothes. In the back I saw a fly rod, a tackle box, and a hunting rifle. I imagined if I really searched the place, I'd find a handgun.

I went to the window to see the lake and squinted against the sun. Then I closed my eyes and backed away. Too soon, I thought, way too soon. But I had seen enough to know the view was lovely.

Romantic. The sunsets over the Adirondacks must have been glorious.

The kitchen was cleaner than I expected, but I wasn't sure why I thought it would be messy. My mother would have approved of the white cabinetry and slate-colored countertops, and I shivered at the very thought of my mom. Could she have been here, too? God, I hoped not.

I knew I should phone Gavin to thank him. I dreaded it, but wanted to get it over with. So I pushed the blanket and sheet onto one side of the couch, collapsed into the cushions, and called him.

"I am so sorry," I began when he picked up. "I am so embarrassed and I am so sorry."

"Don't be. I feel bad. I should have stopped you when you ordered that second glass of wine at the show. Maybe I should have stopped you when you ordered the first. I had a feeling that was the tipping point."

"Next time, feel free."

"I will. You know, I'm older, but I think I was afraid to advertise that. I think it would have felt too, I don't know, controlling to weigh in. I'm just glad you still want a next time."

"I do if you do. But I won't drink."

"I gather you don't drink much at college."

"No, I smoke a lot of"—and I remembered he was a detective and stopped myself.

"Dope," he said, finishing the sentence for me, almost laughing as he spoke. "Don't worry, I won't judge you or arrest you."

"Thank you. And thank you for last night. I had fun. I had a great time."

"Me, too."

"And thank you for, um, putting me to bed."

"It took about three seconds. I pulled off your boots and you were out like a light. Again."

"Again. Wow, I was just great company."

"You were."

"I gather I locked you out of your bedroom."

There was a beat I hadn't expected, a pause. Then: "What do you mean, you locked me out?"

"The bedroom door was locked. From the inside."

"Really?"

"Really."

"You know, I don't think you would have done that. I don't think you could have done that. I must have locked it by mistake when I was getting my clothes," he said, but something had changed in the tenor of our conversation. He sounded at once affable and false. But I couldn't imagine why he would lie.

"Okay," I said. I let it go, but I knew my curiosity and confusion about it were going to gnaw at me—like so much else that autumn.

"Have you called my buddy?" he asked. "He's doing nothing today but watching football. He lives in the building and he's happy to bring you to your wheels."

"I'll just take a cab."

"No, call him! It's all good."

"We'll see," I murmured. "I like your apartment," I told him.

"Thank you. I hope you'll come back."

"I will. But don't bother to chill a bottle of wine."

"I'll make a note," he said.

After we hung up, I called my father and told him that I was on my way home. In the background, I heard Paige singing "Drunken Angel" for my benefit. I folded the sheet and the blanket on the couch. Then I returned to his bedroom to retrieve my boots. I made Gavin's bed. There was a computer on a small, antiseptic black desk by the window—there it was, the digital knowledge free to be plucked—and for a long moment I stared at it. I knew I couldn't resist, and so I didn't even try. I turned it on and watched it spring to life: the cobalt blue of Windows and rows of square icons. One of them, I noticed, was for an art program that came with the operating system, and it reminded me of an armoire or clothing cabinet. Narnia, I thought: I was about to open the ward-robe. I told myself that I should turn the machine off before I had gone too far.

But I didn't. There was a document on the desktop, and I assumed by its name that it was a case file. I opened it and saw it was about a domestic abuse murder-suicide that had been in the news all week. An unemployed car mechanic in Newport had shot his wife and then himself. Gavin probably was working on it before leaving to meet me yesterday afternoon. I closed it and clicked on his e-mail. I felt bad, but I knew I wouldn't turn back. Not now. I resolved that I would do one search and one search only. I put my mother's name in the search bar and pressed the return key. And there they were: a dozen and a half e-mails from her. Maybe more. All were short, but all were clear.

> I'm designing a guesthouse on the lake out along Appletree Point. I'll be there on Wednesday. Up for a cupcake?

> No adventures. I slept through the night.

> Clonazepam dreams. Not for the faint of heart. You?

> Paige will be racing all day Saturday and Warren is entertaining some poet from Scotland. Any chance you're around for coffee?

> I'd love to see you. I need to see you. But I can't. Not this week. I'm so sorry.

> The coffee shop on Tuesday would be great. 11:30?

> Perfect. I'm actually at the sleep center that day. See you then.

I read through the chains that led to each final e-mail in the mailbox. There was nothing incriminating in them, though I stared long and hard at my mother's sentence, *I need to see you.* The tone of that one unnerved me. But most really were about nothing more than logistics: where and when they would meet. Gavin was more likely to bring up sleepwalking than my mother was, but always as a dark aside or deliberately bad joke.

Yeah, if I believed in God, I'd be a roamin' Catholic.

Surest cure for my sleepwalking? The night I walk off my roof.

I know there's not supposed to be a connection between our dreams and our parasomnias, but I think there is—which is why the sex dreams are the scariest. (Your Honor, my client was only in bed with her because of a very rare parasomnia.)

There were no e-mails in nearly three years. The last one from my mother was an apology of sorts that she couldn't see him after all, because that Friday was my first Parents Weekend at the college, and she and Warren and Paige would be in Amherst then. I found it reassuring to see that Gavin hadn't lied to me: based on the dates of the e-mails, at least, he and my mother hadn't met each other in a very long time. Less reassuring, however, was the realization that my mother must have been deleting the e-mails between herself and the detective as soon as she wrote and received them, which suggested she felt they were incriminating. Or they made her feel guilty. Either way, she didn't want anyone else to see them.

That is, of course, assuming that it was my mother who had deleted them.

Before I left the bedroom, I stared for a long moment at the lock on the bedroom door, and then tried to see if I could lock it by accident. In the end, I decided it was possible. But it wasn't likely.

FOR A WHILE, *I researched what great minds said about sleep. I learned that both Gandhi and Poe equated sleeping with dying.*

Then I collected amazing stories about sleep—about the incredible things people did in their sleep. It made me feel less alone. Less crazy. Less strange.

I only stopped when I realized I was better off alone.

CHAPTER TEN

I WAS FOLDING laundry on the living room floor Monday morning, listening to music as I worked, when I heard the doorbell. I saw it was the minister and ushered the woman into the house. I was relieved—no, I was downright proud—that the kitchen was clean: I had loaded the dishwasher and sponged off the counters after I had gotten Paige off to the school bus and our father had left for the college. Katherine Edwards had been the pastor at the church for at least twenty-five years, a little longer than my parents had lived in Bartlett. She was wearing khakis and a navy cardigan sweater, but her wire-rim eyeglasses still suggested "attorney" to me. The woman's hair looked a little more gray than some days, but her eyes had their usual sparkle. She was smiling, but all that did was remind me that I had been hungover in Gavin Rikert's bed yesterday morning when this woman was preaching at the church maybe a third of a mile away from where we were standing right now. I punched the stop button on the CD player.

"I just thought I would see how you're doing," she asked me. "Your dad home?"

"No, he's already off to Middlebury. Do you want some coffee or tea? I think we even have apple cider."

"I'm fine. I just came from a breakfast meeting. Your dad called the other day, and I said I'd drop by."

I was almost incredulous at the idea of my father phoning the minister, but kept my surprise to myself. "What about?" I asked simply.

"Your mother—of course."

"Of course." I motioned at the front hall behind me. "Want to come in? I was just finishing the laundry. My very exciting life."

"I will, thank you." She started to slip off her pumps, but I told her that wasn't necessary. The pastor took one of the barstools around the kitchen island, and I took another.

"You're a good egg," Katherine said. "You're taking wonderful care of Paige and your dad, I can tell."

"I guess. Who knew I was such a nurturer?"

"I gather there's no news about your mom. That was the impression I got from your dad."

"Can you tell me more about why he called? I mean, was it something specific about my mom?"

"Oh, it was a very brief conversation."

"I'm sure."

"You have a magic show next weekend, don't you?" she asked, instead of answering the question.

I nodded. "Eliza Bowen's birthday party. Thank you again for that lead."

"Do you know her?"

"Not really. She's three years younger than Paige."

"Well, be warned. She's a hellion in Sunday school, I hear. Her teacher dreads class some mornings. So . . . don't thank me for the lead just yet."

"I'll be fine."

The woman gazed at me a little more intensely. "Tell me honestly: What do you need? What can I do? What can the church do?"

I looked away; I couldn't meet her eyes. "I don't know."

"I must admit, I feel the deacons haven't done enough, I feel I haven't done enough. My husband definitely doesn't feel any of us have done enough." Her husband was a therapist, but I wasn't sure where his practice was. They had twin sons a few years older than me. One, I knew, was in grad school. The other? I had no idea.

"I'm being totally serious: I don't know what I need. I don't know what we need. I just don't. I mean, we don't even go to church. I'm surprised my dad called you."

The minister shrugged. "Is that it?"

"No. But I feel bad."

"This isn't about that. No quid pro quo, I promise."

"Do you think there's any chance she's still alive? Is it crazy to hope?"

"You're talking to someone who spends her Sundays telling people to have faith . . ."

"I hear a *but* coming."

"But I don't think it's likely. I'm sorry, Lianna."

I looked at the stack I had made of my sister's folded shirts. "So she's in heaven," I murmured.

"Yes. Absolutely. No *buts* there."

"Even though we don't really go to church."

"Again: no quid pro quo."

"I had an interdisciplinary course last year about heaven. Philosophy and religion. There were some versions of heaven where my mom would have been much happier than others."

"Well, heaven on earth for her was always you and your sister. I hope you know that. Your mom once said you were the most good-natured little girl on the planet. It was after one of her miscarriages. She told me she felt guilty about wanting another baby so badly."

I thought about this. My mother certainly knew Katherine, but I couldn't recall the two of them ever speaking about anything of consequence. Had she actually reached out to the pastor? "My mom told you about the miscarriages?"

"Yes. A miscarriage isn't a state secret," she said. Her eyes went soft and she took one of my hands in both of hers. "It's nothing to be ashamed of. And one time I happened to be at the hospital visiting someone else and I saw your mom was there. She had four?"

"Five," I corrected her. God, it was just so many, I thought. So very many.

"Anyway, she did talk to me about it. About them. She said she'd loved being a sister, and wanted you to have a sibling. And she really enjoyed being a mom. But I think she always wanted to be sure that you knew how much you were loved, too."

"I never doubted it."

"How many times did you save her life? Twice? Three times?"

"That's how rumors get started. It was just the once—that night on the bridge. And maybe I just saved her from a broken leg."

"Rumors are awful things," said the minister, and she sounded a little exasperated. She released my hand and sat back on the barstool. Something about her tone caused me to tense.

"What rumors are out there about my mom?" I asked. I wasn't sure what she was referring to, but I assumed the stories involved my mother's sleepwalking.

"It's all just gossip. It's all meaningless."

"Nothing that's awful is meaningless. If something is awful, it has power. It doesn't matter if it's true. It still has power."

Katherine folded her arms across her chest. "You are a very wise girl."

"Curious, mostly."

"You've probably heard this," she began, her voice hesitant, "but some people think she was meeting someone the night she died."

"Yup. I know there are rumors out there that she just ran off— you know, left Dad and Paige and me—which is crazy."

"Those ones are crazy, I agree. Just think of how much she loved you and Paige. And while the idea she was meeting someone is unlikely, I can see why that one has legs. There's no sin as much fun as adultery, is there?"

"Are there any names?"

"No."

"Really?"

"Really."

I didn't believe her. I had the distinct sense that either she was shielding me or was simply unwilling to gossip. "What about my dad?" I asked, trying a different tack.

"What about him?"

I shrugged, hoping it would make my question seem more casual. "Are there any rumors about him?"

She shook her head and dropped her gaze for a fleeting second. Then she looked up and sighed. "Fine. If you must know, there's one story swirling around that your mother was with a woman from the college the night she disappeared. Supposedly, your father was having an affair and the woman just showed up at your house. Didn't know your father was out of town. She knocked on the door in the middle of the night, and something happened."

"God," I mumbled, and then added quickly, "Sorry." I had never considered that my mother might have been challenged by another woman. *The* other woman. I thought of the Elizabeth Bishop scholar with the clementine-colored hair. Sam. Samantha. I recalled the girl in the cosmonaut T-shirt on my father's side of the desk. Did he flirt with students my age? Of course he did. But until I had watched those other girls make themselves at home in his office, I would have presumed an affair would have been with a woman closer to his age than mine. Perhaps I was wrong.

"It's okay," Katherine said, and she smiled. "But don't believe it. It's just a story."

"I guess."

"Your mother would be very, very proud of you. I hope you know that. She'd be very proud of all you're doing for your dad and Paige."

"She'd also be frustrated that I wasn't back at school. She'd be feeling guilty about that."

"Maybe."

"So, why did my dad call you?"

Katherine smiled a little enigmatically, and then nodded. "We're back there, aren't we?"

"It can't be any weirder than the stuff we've already talked about. It just can't."

"Your father is looking for closure. He's not sure what that means, which is why he wanted to talk."

"Closure?"

"At some point, it may be time for a memorial service—with or without your mom's body. That's what your dad wanted to discuss. He wanted my opinion about timing. About when. About when—"

"My dad is not real religious," I snapped, cutting her off and surprising us both with my vehemence. But the idea of a memorial service irritated me. The word *closure* annoyed me.

"No, he's not," she agreed, responding to my pique with unflappability. "I believe he was thinking about the community. About her friends. About your grandparents. Your aunt. About you and Paige. He was thinking about how none of you have been allowed to grieve."

"She hasn't been gone all that long. It's been a month and three days."

"You're right. And I didn't mean to suggest that your dad had given up hope. All hope. I probably shouldn't have said anything. He just wanted to start a . . . a dialogue about when it might be time. You need to mourn. You deserve to mourn. You need to heal." The woman was saying more, trying to explain what she was thinking and what my father might have been thinking, but I was no longer listening. I looked out the kitchen window at the trees behind our house. It was only the twenty-fifth of September, and already this year a few were as bare as the middle of winter. I wondered if it was because we'd had so little rain.

☽

An idea had begun to form in my mind when the minister had alluded to the rumors and innuendo that had followed my mother into the night: I needed a gossip. I needed someone who, unlike the pastor, lacked any sort of filter—someone who talked to a lot of people and would have no reluctance to share with me the hearsay that Katherine wouldn't. And that person existed behind the deli case at the Bartlett General Store, the woman who had made for my family all those Mexican wraps that autumn. Her name was Peggy and she had a son in the marines and a daughter in the navy, and she absolutely loved to chat. She wasn't mean-spirited, but neither was she especially circumspect.

She was, as I hoped, alone behind the deli counter making sandwiches and wraps when I stopped by the store later that morning. The owner, a woman my grandmother's age who had bought the store with her husband well before I was born and still showed no signs of slowing down, was behind the front register, laughing with a pair of linemen for the power company.

"I don't think I've ever seen you this early in the day," Peggy said, smiling, when she saw me.

"A first, right?" I agreed.

She was slicing tomatoes and stopped to ask if I wanted the usual. I said sure and watched her go to work on the wraps. As she did, she asked if I'd had a nice weekend and how my father and Paige were doing. I said they were hanging in there and then volunteered that I had gone to Montreal to see a magic show.

"With your sister?" she asked.

"No. I was with a friend from school."

"Boy?" she asked hopefully.

"No. Just a friend."

She looked disappointed and it seemed this was my moment. I leaned in and said conspiratorially—lowering my voice—"Can I ask you something?"

"Why, yes."

"Have you heard any stories about my mom in the last month or so?"

"Like what?"

"You see people. You know people. People talk to you," I said, hoping to flatter her.

"They do. People will say anything here some days."

"I'll bet they do," I agreed.

"They always ask me if we have any news about your mom. You know, because we have a police scanner." I nodded. Of course they did. The store was the communications hub for the village. Prior to cell phones and the digital age, we would actually leave messages for each other at the front register. Even now, in the year 2000, if you had to leave town in a hurry and needed someone to milk your three-hundred-pound llama, you dropped by the store. If you simply had to know why the fire engines just left the station, you gave the store a ring. And if you wanted the very latest on that missing Annalee Ahlberg, here was the source.

"Things like sightings?" I asked.

"Oh, sure. And everyone who was out looking for her that first day wants to know if we've heard something. Anything. They feel sort of an investment. Especially Donnie."

"Donnie Hempstead?" I asked. "Why Donnie?" I recalled that he was among the first people my father had asked me to call after I'd told him that my mother was missing.

She looked around uneasily. "I don't really want to go there, Lianna."

"Why?"

"No."

"Please?"

"You really don't know?"

I waited. Finally she shook her head, self-conscious, and fiddled with the tie of her apron. "There are stories—none true, I am quite sure—that your mother was meeting him."

I was stunned but tried not to show it. "You mean the night she disappeared?"

"Uh-huh."

"Because people think the two of them were having an affair?"

"Some people. Not me," said Peggy. "I know it's ridiculous. It's just crazy."

When I thought of Donnie now, I thought first of the tall, athletic fellow with a trim beard in blue jeans and a white T-shirt, a radio on his hip, the day my mother disappeared. He was a volunteer firefighter, too, and some sort of money manager by day. He had a couple of boys, one in the elementary school and one in

Paige's class in the middle school. He traveled a bit, I believed, but he worked mostly from his home. My mother liked him; she liked his wife, Erin, too. The three of them were on the same schedule at the gym. She had designed the aqua solarium addition to their home: a dome big enough to house three chaise lounges, a glass table, and a heated saltwater pool a dozen feet in diameter.

"They were just friends," I said.

"Of course they were. And she was just friends with Justin Bryce. But there are rumors about him, too."

"That's ridiculous."

"I know."

"His wife, Marilyn, was one of my mom's best friends," I reminded her. I didn't add that I couldn't imagine my mother with a balding foodie who thought French fries in a blue cheese sauce was haute cuisine.

"I remember."

"My mom was a sleepwalker," I said, hoping I sounded definitive. I regretted coming here; I regretted what I had begun. This had been a mistake. "The parasomnia occurred when she was alone—when my dad was away. My dad was gone that night in August and she went sleepwalking. We both know that's what happened. That's all that happened."

"I agree, Lianna. I agree. But you asked me. People like to talk. I probably shouldn't have said anything," she said, and she stared down at the ingredients on the cutting board in front of her.

"Do the police know about these rumors?"

"I guess so."

"Did you tell them?"

She looked up and met my eyes. "They never asked me," she said, and she sounded disappointed.

When I got home, I took the three wraps she had made for me and threw them away. It would be a long time before I would be able to bring myself to return to the store.

☽

"I'm too old to go trick-or-treating," Paige said to me as we drove home from the pool Monday evening. She had been trying to stuff her wet towel into her swim bag, and had just given up and tossed it into the backseat.

"You're twelve," I reminded her, though I understood that seventh grade was about the last year that kids in our community took the night seriously. I had been suggesting costumes. I recalled how two years ago our mother had worked with Paige to transform the girl into a tombstone angel. I had been at college, but our mother had taken lots of photos. The costume demanded what must have been vats of gray acrylic paint, because it had to smother an ankle-length white dress—gathered to look like a robe—an iconic drama mask (tragedy), toy store wings, and a wig. Annalee Ahlberg had loved Halloween, and I recalled fondly all the years my mother had taken me trick-or-treating, and all the costumes she had designed. I had been an octopus one year and a spider the next, the great papier-mâché legs recycled from the previous year's sea creature. When I had been Artemis, my mother had sewn the costume herself and found me a spectacular bow and arrow from a client in an archery club. One year, when I was in first grade, the two of us went out together on Halloween night as mother-and-daughter devils. I was six, and it was only from the photos I would study later that it dawned on me that my mother had been having fun with the idea of a hot mom: the mama devil costume was skin tight and sexy as hell.

"I just don't feel like it," Paige grumbled.

"Well, it's not even October first. You might in a few weeks."

"Nope."

"Is it that I'm not Mom?"

"No."

"Because I can help you come up with something awesome. I mean, obviously I'm not Mom. Halloween was kind of her thing. But I'm not a moron."

"You'll just put me in a belly shirt like a harem girl."

"God, you sound like—" I stopped myself midsentence.

"I sound like who?"

"I wasn't going to say anyone in particular. I was going to say you sounded cranky. That's all." I kept my eyes on the meandering two-lane road up the hill into Bartlett, the asphalt paralleling the Gale River, but I felt Paige staring at me. My sister didn't believe me. "How much homework do you have tonight?" I asked, changing the subject.

"Not much. Can I ask you something?"

"Sure."

"How come you haven't been smoking marijuana the last couple of days? Did you get super high in Montreal? Is that why you didn't come home? Or have you stopped?"

"I didn't get high in Montreal, but I wouldn't say I've stopped. I just haven't the last few days. No big reason."

"I haven't smelled any on you."

"I would think that would make you happy."

"Is it me?"

"I don't know. Maybe."

"Well, you don't have to stop because of me. I feel bad enough as it is that you're stuck here."

"I told you the other day: don't feel bad. I'm not just here for you and Dad. I'm here for me. I'm not ready to go back to school."

"Would you do me a favor?"

"Probably."

"My coach was telling me that it's time for me to go away in the summer, so I can keep skiing. Swimming is good, but it's not skiing. He thinks two of us—me and Lucy—are ready for Chile. We would spend part of next summer there training."

My first reaction was that Paige would be thirteen next summer. In Chile. I thought of all those little girl gymnasts in Russia and Romania and, I guessed, the United States who had no childhood because they were always in training. I wondered who the adults would be who would be caring for the kids like my sister.

"Would Coach Noggler be there?"

"Of course not! It's not like he's my private coach. It's, you know, a summer camp. It's just a summer camp for really good skiers."

"So, what do you want from me? What's the favor? Do you want me to lobby with Dad so he lets you go?"

"He'll let me go. He won't care."

"Of course he'll care! What are you talking about?"

"He loves me, I get it. I just meant he's in la-la land. I need you to help me do stuff like get a visa and fill out the forms."

"How long is the camp?"

"Either two weeks or four weeks."

"Wow. A month in Chile. Not shabby."

"Think of how easy your life will be."

I shook my head. "You don't make my life hard."

"Yeah, right."

"I'll talk to Dad," I said. "I'll bring it up at dinner tonight. And maybe after dinner you can show me the website for the camp so I can get the full scoop. And I'll call your coach tomorrow."

"Thank you. And one more thing."

"What?"

"We need to make sure I'm not sleepwalking by then."

"I talked to Dad. I told him."

"I know, he talked to me, too. But he didn't seem that worried. And my appointment at the sleep clinic isn't for, like, six or seven weeks."

I was relieved. I hadn't realized that our father had scheduled an appointment. "Have you had another event?" I asked.

"No."

"Okay, then. You'll have seen someone at the sleep center months and months before Chile. All good."

"When's yours?"

"When's my what?"

"Your appointment."

"I'm not going to the sleep center. Not an issue in my life."

"You know that's not true. Dad told me it once was. He said you were the sleepwalker before Mom. He wants you to go to the sleep center, too."

"He does?"

"Uh-huh."

"He's made me an appointment?"

"I think so."

"Well, that's news to me," I said, but I made a mental note to talk to our father about this. I hoped he was merely trying to make Paige feel less singled out and alone, but I felt jittery inside. In truth, I knew very little about my own personal history with parasomnia.

"So, you'll keep your mind open about Halloween?" I asked, mostly to bring the conversation back to a topic that didn't cause either of us anxiety. "I don't want you to be disappointed when you wake up on November first." I glanced at her and decided that she was at least considering the notion. Then she reached for the radio and scanned the stations until she found a song we both liked.

☽

After dinner, in the dark, I walked toward the streetlights in the center of Bartlett. I had cleared the table, as I did always, so neither my father nor Paige would have to. My sister could do her homework and my father could read or watch TV and sip at his scotch until he dozed off. But then I had a change of heart and decided I would clean up later: I left the dishes in the sink and on the counter, went to my bedroom for my dope and my pipe and one of my college hoodies, and I started off toward the village. At dinner I hadn't mentioned that the minister had come by, though I had told Katherine that I would let my dad know. Nor had I confronted him about what the minister had said about closure; I hadn't asked him why he hadn't spoken to me first. I didn't want to have this conversation in front of Paige. I wasn't sure I wanted to have this conversation at all. A memorial service? It was too soon. It angered me that my father was giving up so publicly. First Paige. Now my dad. Didn't he have an obligation to carry the torch the longest?

Instead I had brought up Paige's sleepwalking over dinner, and her appointment at the sleep center.

"Yes," my father said. "It's not for a little while, but I believe we have Dr. Yager's very first opening."

"And me? Paige said you thought I should go, too."

He looked embarrassed, and he reached for his scotch to stall. I couldn't decide whether the issue was that he had forgotten to tell me that he honestly believed I should be tested, or that he had forgotten to tell me that he had offered Paige a white lie to make her feel less uncomfortable with the process.

"Yes," he said after taking a sip. "I've talked to our health insurance company. They'll cover you both."

"But why me?" I asked, strangely and unexpectedly alarmed by the idea that he had spoken to our health insurance provider about me already.

"Oh, only because you are your mother's daughter. I love you girls, and I want to be sure you will both be safe when you sleep. No mystery. No mystery at all." He smiled, trying his best to recover. "And while a sleep study sounds unpleasant—I know you've both heard about the wires all over you, the monitors, the camera—everyone manages to fall asleep."

"So we're both going to do it?" Paige asked.

"Yes," he said. "The very same day. But, again, I'm not all that worried about either of you. I'm just not. Remember, Paige, you've really only had one event."

Paige corrected him, reminding him about the swim bag. "That was far more likely your mother or me being absentminded," he replied. "The testing will give us all closure."

Closure. The word came to me again as I walked alone to the bridge. First the pastor had used it when she had come by that morning. Then my father had used it at dinner. It rattled me.

I hadn't thought much about the specifics of my mother's funeral or a memorial service—what it would look like. Feel like. Who would speak and what we would sing. I tried to think of hymns and realized I only knew Christmas carols. Yes, my mother was gone. Probably she was dead. But only probably. Not definitely. I myself was still dazed. We all were. And I was still reeling at the world of adult secrets that swirled about me like fallen leaves in an autumn windstorm. I wondered if I was keeping secrets from my father for the simple reason that I believed he was keeping secrets from me. But then I chastised myself: Was he keeping secrets from me or shielding me as a parent? There was a big difference. There certainly were things I didn't tell Paige because my sister was twelve.

When I got to the bridge, I walked to the exact spot where I had found my mother and parked myself on the sidewalk there. I leaned on the concrete parapet, my elbows roughly where my mother's bare feet had been, and looked down at the Gale River. I reached into the hoodie's kangaroo pocket for my dope and packed myself a bowl. And then, for the first time in a week, I allowed myself a small buzz and tried to relax.

My mother never told me what she recalled from the walk that had led her here that night, naked and alone. There were so many things I would never know about her and so many things I would never understand. In the days that followed that somnambulant journey, when—always so tentatively—I had asked her what she remembered, my mother mostly had blushed. She had been evasive. Were the recollections that taboo? My father apparently thought so. My mother, I believe, was ashamed.

It seemed unfair to me to be ashamed of your dreams. We can't control our dreams any more than we can control the weather or the tides.

My mother never mentioned what she recalled—if anything—

from that night when she had spray-painted the hydrangea, either. At least she hadn't told me. She never shared with me where she went in her dreams.

Because, technically, she hadn't been dreaming. She had been sleepwalking. I knew the difference.

I tapped out the ashes and did something I hadn't done in ages. I packed a second bowl.

I inhaled deeply, holding the smoke in my lungs, and closed my eyes. Another word came to me, *suicide,* and I wondered what it would be like to stand on the balustrade as my mother had. I thought it was interesting that no one devoted much energy to the possibility that my mother had killed herself. Certainly I hadn't. But why would we? Annalee Ahlberg loved her daughters. Her depression had never been debilitating. And hadn't it been under control? I thought once more of the spectacular energy she had put over the years into her girls' Halloween costumes. Sometimes into her own.

Still, one night the woman had come to this bridge and nearly hurled herself off it.

There was a bright half-moon tonight. There were no clouds. I looked down at the water, which was lower than I could ever recall. The water here was so clear that during the day a person could look down and see the rocks beneath the surface. Now, at night, I could see only the boulders that broke the plane like icebergs. Some were the size of Volkswagen Beetles; some were bigger still.

I guessed I could walk across the river without getting my hair wet in this section. The riverbank sloped farther than usual because of the drought. It was a long drop from here on the center of the bridge, and with the water so low, longer than usual.

I had been to funerals before. Although my mother's parents were both still alive, my father's parents had passed away: my grandfather when I was in kindergarten and my grandmother two years ago. Had those services helped my father? I supposed so. They hadn't really helped me. The truth was, I had been saddened by the death of each of my grandparents, but not overwhelmingly so.

They had each been sick awhile before they died. They had each been in pain. They had each, my father had reassured me, been ready.

I watched the small constellation of stars emerge in the bowl when I took one long, last drag. I blew the smoke straight into the air and thought, *I am a dragon*. The idea made me smile inside. I placed the pipe on the balustrade.

Almost as if daring myself, I climbed onto the parapet, first kneeling and then, ever so slowly, climbing to my feet. It was perhaps four feet high and little more than a foot wide. It was not as ornate as the ones on the bridges that span the Tiber or Seine, but it had a series of spindles below the balustrade that were rather elegant for the Green Mountains. I spread wide my arms to steady myself, prepared to jump (or fall) back toward the asphalt on the bridge if I felt myself losing my balance. When I was standing up, I allowed myself a glance down at the water. The elevation here was high enough that most likely I'd die if I landed in any manner but feet or legs first. And then I'd wind up crippled. A paraplegic, I guessed. Maybe even a quadriplegic. It wouldn't be pretty. It would be painful.

No, I'd die that way, too: I'd drown because I wouldn't be able to swim to the side.

I stared up at the moon, my arms still spread like wings. I craned my neck and liked how it felt. I stretched my fingers and recalled how my mother had stood here with her arms at her sides. My naked mother. That naked angel. Her skin had struck me as especially pale that evening, the alabaster of renaissance statuary. I wondered what it would feel like to stand here, a nude at night, alone with the moon. Had my mother been howling inside or was she as serene as the seraphs spanning the Tiber or Seine?

I had an idea; no, I was experiencing a craving. Here was the difference between a want and a need. This was not something I could do; this was something I had to do.

I made sure of my footing and then pulled my hoodie over my head and tossed it behind me onto the sidewalk. I unbuttoned my flannel shirt and carefully slipped that off, too. A part of me thought, *I am stoned and I am out of control,* but it didn't stop me from reaching behind me and unclasping my bra. I watched it fall and was disappointed that it didn't drift like a kite. Shouldn't lingerie float to the earth in slow motion?

I heard a vehicle in the distance, the growl of a pickup. I wondered if the truck was coming this way. I ran my fingers over the goosebumps on my arms, and I blinked at the tears that for reasons I couldn't fathom were starting to pool in my eyes. Perhaps somewhere nearby was my mother's body. Or had its final journey begun downstream of where I was standing now—near where the shred of her nightshirt had been discovered?

I unzipped my jeans. I unbuttoned them. It was only as I was starting to pull them down below my hips, taking my panties with them, that I remembered I was wearing my sneakers. I couldn't take off my pants without first taking off my sneakers. This was . . . logic.

I started to kneel so I could untie them, planning to begin with my right foot, but suddenly the toe of my left foot was slipping on a stone or thick twig—no, it was my pipe, my goddamn pot pipe—and I was falling. For a second I was suspended, tottering, a tightrope walker losing her balance and about to plummet from high above the circus ring, the audience gasping, but it was only a second, because although I was stoned I was able to think *street* and hurl myself toward the sidewalk instead of the river. I landed hard on the asphalt—beyond the sidewalk—palms out, and rolled onto my side. Instantly I felt the road burn on my hands and my shoulders, but somehow I managed not to crack my skull on the ground.

On the road perpendicular to the bridge the pickup rumbled by, and I felt the bridge shudder, but the driver didn't notice me. I collapsed onto my back, breathing heavily with relief and disgust. I was topless, I was stoned, and (now) I was crying.

Slowly, carefully, I sat up and checked myself. My hands were bleeding, but not horrifically so. Same with a long scratch on my side. Mostly my wrists hurt, but the pain was not incapacitating. I rolled my eyes as if someone were actually present, and patted myself down: I was not merely checking for broken bones (which I thought were unlikely), but actually reassuring myself that I was alive. That I was fine. I hadn't fallen into the river and died instantly by smashing my head on a rock. Or in minutes by drowning. When I stood, I saw my pipe on the ground near my feet. Near my clothing. I reached into the sweatshirt for my baggie and opened it, sprinkling the dope into the river, though I guessed most of it would waft in the night breeze into the brush along the banks. Then, even before getting dressed, I reached down for my pipe and hurled it as far as I could into the Gale River. Somewhere downstream I heard a small *thwap* as it parted the plane of the water.

I ONCE HAD a lover who didn't mind the sleepwalking. It was the sleep sex that was the problem.

And I once had a lover who didn't mind the sleep sex. It was the sleepwalking that ruined our relationship.

For me, the trouble always was this: I knew what I had done.

CHAPTER ELEVEN

THE NEXT MORNING, in the fifteen minutes between when Paige left for the school bus and my father left for the college, I confronted him in the kitchen. He had a stack of student compositions in one hand and a glass of orange juice in the other. He was about to head out the door.

"Why do you really want me to go to the sleep clinic?" I asked him point-blank.

He stared at me, but I couldn't decide whether his gaze was angry or defensive. Clearly I had caught him off guard. "So Paige feels less frightened," he said finally. "Frankly, I think she's being a bit of a worrywart. A drama queen. I'm really not all that concerned."

"Don't you think you should have asked my permission?"

"Your history is actually far more extensive than hers."

"So you just went ahead and made an appointment? You should have checked with me."

"Why? Because your calendar is so busy?" he asked, in an acerbic tone he rarely (if ever) used on me.

"What does that mean?"

"It means nothing," he said, softening. "I'm sorry. I know you're struggling—like me. That's all I meant."

"Honestly, how worried are you about her—about either of us?"

"Honestly? Not in the slightest. This is all just a precaution," he said, and then he put his glass in the sink and pushed past me. I wasn't sure I believed him.

☽

It wasn't lunchtime yet, but already I viewed the day as a small victory: apparently, neither my father nor Paige had noticed the scrapes on my hands over breakfast. My right wrist was sore, as were my ribs, but neither was incapacitating and I had gotten dressed. Most importantly, no one had witnessed my debacle last night on the bridge. Now I was sitting across from Marilyn Bryce in her home on one of the hills high above the village. Marilyn's painting studio was in an old sugarhouse behind their home, near a pond the Bryces had constructed some years ago. It was just the two of us, and we were sitting in the family's living room with its spectacular view of Mount Lincoln, one of the few four-thousand-foot massifs in Vermont. I was on the couch and Marilyn was on a burgundy pouf. She had set the tea service between us, on a round table fashioned from an antique milk jug and a dark marble saucer the size of a manhole cover. I watched in silence as she poured what she called the oolong tea from the special red clay pot she had brought back from China; the tea had been steeping inside it for precisely three minutes. The woman had used the timer on the oven.

It was clear to me that she had been smoking before I arrived: the living room reeked of weed, and her eyes were a red I knew well. I almost offered her the Visine I had in my shoulder bag. If I had any doubts, they were obliterated by what she said next: "This pot has been well seasoned over the years. It has the flavor of a thousand cups inside it."

Only someone who was stoned could say something like that with conviction.

"I'm impressed," I answered because I couldn't think of anything else I could say that would sound in the slightest way earnest. Moreover, I wasn't a big fan of tea. The few times I had drunk it, I had simply dropped a bag in a mug filled with tap water and nuked it in the microwave for a minute.

"You'll detect a hint of jasmine in the flavor," Marilyn told me affably.

"Jasmine," I repeated. The word was everywhere these days. It was, I decided, a sign—though I had no idea what the sign meant.

"And lily," Marilyn added. I reached for the mug—a local potter's own hypsiloid-shaped, thunder-head-colored creation—and took a small sip. The woman was watching me intently. It wasn't coffee, but it was drinkable. I was pleasantly surprised.

"Delicious," I told Marilyn.

"I'm so glad you like it!"

"This is what you served my mom?"

"Absolutely. She was a fan."

I nodded. My mom drank coffee at home and when she worked, so clearly she wasn't a big fan. "I've been thinking a lot about what you said about my parents at the supermarket."

"Oh, you should probably forget I ever said anything. I don't know what I'm talking about."

"You said that my mom was very close to the detective and my dad was a pill. That was the gist of it."

"I didn't say he was a pill, did I?"

"You said he was difficult to live with."

"Children don't need to know their parents' secrets. I was just babbling."

"I do need to know my parents' secrets."

"Why?"

"Because my mother is missing."

She blinked and held her eyes shut a long second. I knew that maneuver. She was trying to will her buzz away. It never worked. "And your father had nothing to do with that," she said after a moment, her eyes open and veined as ever.

"I know."

She sipped her tea and savored—or pretended to savor—the

experience. I sensed she was stalling. "Then why?" she asked. "What could I possibly tell you?"

"What sorts of things did my mom say about my dad?"

"She wasn't playing Mrs. Robinson with that detective, if that's what you're thinking."

"I believe you. But what might she have been sharing with Gavin Rikert that she wouldn't tell my dad? I mean, was it as simple as she was making fun of my dad's poetry? Or was it something more important?"

"I doubt she was making fun of his poetry. I think she respected his work."

"Then what?"

Her shoulders sagged ever so slightly and she put down her mug. "You know how much I loved your mother," she said, her voice a little soft and soapy because of the weed. "You know how much I miss her."

I believe that in Marilyn's own way she had indeed loved my mother and now she did miss her; but I had not for one moment lost sight of how quickly she had moved on—the speed with which she had forgotten my father and Paige and me. I wasn't moved, but I pretended to be; I sensed it was the best way to wear Marilyn down. She was close to telling me something, and she was just stoned enough that she might. "I do," I said. "And I know she felt the same way about you."

"We were a little like sisters."

"Absolutely."

"Absolutely," she agreed.

Half a dozen turkeys were wandering through Marilyn's yard. At first I thought they were aimless, but then they stopped beneath a bird feeder on a low branch in one of her sugar maples. They were like a family. Another time, I might have watched them until they moved on, and it would have made me happy.

"So, my mom and Gavin," I said. "Was it just the sleepwalking that connected them—when they first met?"

"Pretty much."

"Pretty much? There's more."

"No. Not really."

"What aren't you telling me?"

She looked away.

"There's something else," I pressed.

"Oh, Lianna, you must know." When I said nothing, she went on. "Your mother said something to me once that gave me the impression you did. Maybe you walked in on your parents and your mother didn't stop—because she was asleep."

"Walked in on them doing what? Having sex?"

"God, I've said too much."

"No, this is important. Go on."

She put her forehead in her hands and shook her head ever so slightly. When she looked up, I thought she was on the verge of tears. "Sleep sex," she began. "It sounds fun and maybe it would have been okay if your father had been, I don't know, less uptight. Hell, Justin would have been thrilled if my thing had turned out to be sleep sex. That's part of what I mean about how your dad could be difficult. The right sort of man . . . the right sort of attitude . . . what's the big deal? But maybe I shouldn't judge. We all have our demons, right? Look at me. I can't hold my dope, and I'm telling you things I shouldn't. I just shouldn't."

I sat back against the couch cushions. I hadn't heard the term *sleep sex* before, but its meaning was evident in the context of my mother's parasomnia. I recalled what Cindy Yager had said at the sleep center: *They have sex in their sleep.* "No. You're right to tell me," I said simply, hoping that Marilyn hadn't detected the way the short sentence had caught in my throat.

"So I haven't spoken out of turn? Really, I haven't?"

"You haven't," I lied.

"I mean, she was a different person. They all are then, I guess. When they're asleep."

"They?" I suspected I knew who she meant—what she meant. But she made them sound like werewolves, so I asked her to elaborate.

"Sleepwalkers. Sleep sexers. It really freaked your dad out. It made him feel like he was inadequate. It made him feel like he wasn't satisfying her. And your mom was already so humiliated. She shouldn't have been, but she was. She was. And he just made her feel even worse. The things she would do . . . the things she wanted. For years their sex life was just a minefield." She gave me a small, sad smile: "It's a miracle their marriage worked as well as it did. It says something really powerful and lovely about both your parents."

I felt queasy, and put down my tea. "My dad said he didn't know why my mom only went sleepwalking when he was gone. But he did know why, didn't he?"

"Of course he did. When he was in bed with her, she'd have sex with him. Or try and have sex with him. Sometimes she'd just, you know, finish herself. But he was the warm body her sleeping self needed."

"And when he was gone . . ."

"She'd try and find someone else. And the key word is *try*. It's not like she ever did—at least around here. Maybe if she was alone at a hotel she found someone. She fears that once happened at an architectural conference of some sort—back in the days when she worked for that firm in Burlington. What was it called?"

"Lewis, Fowler, DeGraw," I reminded her.

"Yes. She traveled for them. She saw people at night. But, God, what was she going to do around here in Bartlett? Knock on Nick McClellan's front door at two in the morning and ask him to come out and play? Walk over to Donnie and Erin Hempstead's? Come here to my house?" She snorted and shook her head. "It goes without saying that Justin would have been fine if she'd ever come here and tried to get in bed with the two of us. I'm kidding—but only sort of," she added.

"So you knew the sleepwalking didn't begin just five years ago?"

"I did. It just got a lot worse five years ago. A lot more frequent. And it changed. Suddenly she was leaving the bed and going to the bridge and painting the tree. Suddenly she was . . . you know, more often."

"And you think my mom used to talk to Gavin about it? She used to talk to him about her . . . her sleep sex?"

"Of course!" she told me. "That's what the two of them had in common: Sleep sex. That's his parasomnia, too!"

☽

"I'm a mess," I told Gavin. "I'm way more of a mess than you realize. Than I realized." We were sitting at a bar on Church Street in Burlington, though both of us were sipping decaf coffee: by then I had learned that he drank very little alcohol because of his sleepwalking. And me? I had no desire for wine or beer after our evening in Montreal. I had driven to Burlington after having dinner with my father and Paige because—rather like my mother, I guess—I needed to speak to someone. I needed to speak to him. I wanted to tell him I knew.

"You have every right to be a mess," he said. "It's okay. It might be worse if you weren't a mess."

"I almost fell off a bridge. I almost jumped off a bridge," I told him.

At this he looked alarmed. He was still wearing the blazer and tie he had worn to work that day, but at some point he had loosened the knot below his neck. He pulled it a little farther now from his throat, opening the collar of his shirt, and gazed at me intently. I recounted what I had done the other night—what I almost had done—and when I was through, he looked at the bartender, and I expected him to order a beer. He didn't. He just asked for more decaf.

"And I know way too much about my parents' sex life," I went on. "Way. Too. Much."

"You got rid of all that dope, right? There's none left in another baggie?" he asked, still on the bridge story with me.

"Yes."

"Good."

"Why? Are you afraid I'm going to do something that stupid again?"

He nodded. "A little. But mostly I'm just worried it was laced with something. PCP, maybe. It happens, even here in Vermont."

"I just smoked too much."

"Either way, it's gone."

"It is," I assured him. Then: "And I almost wish I hadn't talked to my mom's friend. It was awful enough remembering my mom on the bridge or spray-painting the hydrangea. Now? Now I can't help but imagine her as some predatory sex zombie."

"It's not like that. Not always."

"Gavin, I did my homework. I always do my homework. You locked yourself out of your own bedroom the night I passed out because you were afraid you'd attack me in your sleep. Am I right?"

"I'd had a drink and a glass of wine at the restaurant, and another hours later at the magic show. I wasn't drunk. I wasn't even buzzed. But I couldn't take the chance. Alcohol is one of those things that can trigger an event."

"An event. I love that. Nice euphemism, Detective."

"But we're not zombies."

"I didn't realize there was a politically correct term for it."

"Just saying: we're not the walking dead. At least not always."

"Could my mom's disappearance have something to do with sleep sex?"

"It could. It was something we were exploring in those first days. But it's not likely. You know exactly what I think happened: I've told you. I believe your mother walked into the Gale River in her sleep. I believe it was a more traditional parasomnia occurrence."

"I remember you said that you and my mom were your own little sleepwalking support group. I'm not angry, but it might have been helpful if you'd said you were your own little sleep sex support group."

"That day in the cruiser? Hours after your mother had disappeared? I disagree: it wouldn't have been helpful at all for you to hear that."

"Well, then, maybe you could have shared that little bit of news with me any day since then. You've had plenty of chances."

"I would have told you. Eventually. And certainly before our relationship had progressed to someplace where it might matter."

I thought about the word *relationship,* and I realized I liked how it sounded on his lips. "So, we have a relationship?" I asked.

He sat up perfectly straight and folded his arms across his chest. "Arguably, yes. We've been on two dates. This might count as a third. My hope is there will be more."

"Then tell me now. Tell me all that you can about your sleep-walking. Tell me the sorts of things that you told my mom."

☽

And he did.

He told me of his past. He told me of the girl who had accused him of sexual assault when the two of them were sixteen-year-old counselors at a summer camp in central Vermont, and how close he had come to the sort of criminal record that would have dogged him forever as a sex offender. He confessed that this was actually why he had gone to a nearby state college: he wanted to live at home. He thought it would be safer for everyone. He shared with me that since then he had had girlfriends who, in the end, could not bear the man he became some nights in his sleep and some who, for a time, thought it was an interesting kink in their sex life—but only for a time. The novelty grew thin. Some relation-ships, he said, simply can't endure that sort of nocturnal murk.

The sleep center had dialed down his sleepwalking; they had failed to rein in the sexually voracious golem he occasionally became in the night.

I did not return with him to his apartment that evening. But what does it say about me that I considered it, that I wondered if I should try and meet his other, stranger self? Would it suggest that

I was kindhearted and giving—a girl who thought I could cure or comfort him? Or would it convey only a wanton sexual adventurousness? Either way, it would have been a gesture that Gavin Rikert would have refused. I was not merely a mess that night; I was naïve and he was not going to take advantage of me.

And so I went straight home from the bar. Paige and my father were asleep when I got there, my sister in her bedroom and my father in the chair in the living room. I woke him, turned off the television, and put his scotch glass in the dishwasher. Then I went to bed, too.

It would be late the next morning when my father would call me from the college. It seems that the detective had phoned him with news. My mother's body had been found.

☽

Annalee Ahlberg's body floated and sank, and then refloated and sank again, as it decomposed in the cooling waters of the Gale. In the first moments after my mother hit the river, water supplanted the little air that was left in her lungs—a palace coup in the alveoli she was by then powerless to stop—and her body grew heavier and drifted to the bottom. Over the following weeks, however, as above the river the leaves began their phantasmagoric autumnal transformation (dying, too, in truth), her body's decomposition continued. Microbial-induced putrefaction. Microbial-induced bloat. Microbial-induced stink. Gases lifted her body back to the surface—rather like a blimp, except even inflated with the miasma of death Annalee Ahlberg was no dirigible. There was little fat on her at all, and lean bodies can stay at the bottom with the ease of catfish and hermit crabs.

But eventually, the gases win out. The currents win out. My mother was dragged in death nearly three miles along the Gale River, sometimes along the bottom and sometimes along the surface. Her body would most often drift in that classic pose known as the dead man's float, a lowercase *n,* because that is how dead bodies move in the water: her fingers and forehead and knees showed the expected abrasions from scraping against pebbles and sludge.

Some days, her body would remain where it was, her leg lodged beneath the trunk of a dead tree that had rolled underwater, or beneath the lip of a boulder. Snails and crayfish and brookies would gnaw at her. The animals would eat the juiciest parts.

What would propel it farther downriver? Either the current or the accumulation of the gases would trump the tree or the rock: it would glide or it would rise. In either case, it would move. It would carry with it the muck and the growth from the river bottom. My mother would wear algae like jewelry and body armor.

And in its movement, her body would be pummeled further, the integrity of its frame and its shell further violated. No: savaged. There were, in addition to the ineluctable deterioration that occurs because a body is dead, the rock surfaces that would grate the epidermis like cheese, peeling the skin from my mother's thighs and breasts and the right side of her face; there was—and here, in truth, I am conjecturing—the rusting wrought-iron gate that had been lodged into the silt for decades that tore off her left arm, and the hubcaps, the metal mangled now into jagged throwing stars, that sliced off great swatches of tissue from her lower back; and, of course, there were the innumerable rocks and dead branches that battered all of her body as the waters dragged it over and upon and into them.

By the time it reached the intake grate at the penstock for the small, long-dormant hydroelectric plant near Atkins Falls, it was but a mephitic bag of jelly and goo, jostling around bone. The navy-blue nightshirt was history. Her tendons and skull were exposed to the world with pornographic cruelty. The power plant was an antique from the early part of the twentieth century; the remnants existed almost entirely underwater now. The powerhouse with its generator and transformers was long gone. But the turbines, primitive though they were, were still there. So were the scaffolding and the stanchions.

The body's last great movement had been over the falls that

neared the plant. Imagine a kayak taking on the white water there. Whether it had careened over the cascades days or weeks after disappearing into the water was anyone's guess, though the search teams assumed it was days. They believed they would have found it near the LPS—the last point seen, a dot on the map selected from a strip of a nightshirt—had it remained upstream for any length of time.

And, of course, they didn't find it. A dog did. And mostly she smelled it. She was a great, leaping, playful mutt that was part yellow lab named Lola. She belonged to a photographer from across the lake in Au Sable Forks who was in Bartlett, Vermont, to chronicle the fall foliage. And he was artistically relentless. Unstoppable and talented. And he was so entranced by the colors of the trees that he waded into the chilly waters of the Gale to capture a copse of red maples in their death throes from a very specific angle. Lola joined him and was drawn to the ripe stink of the corpse. Went right to it, splashing and dog-paddling her way there, sixty-plus pounds of canine exuberance and wonder and joy.

Would she have seen it without the drought? Would she have smelled it?

Unlikely.

Certainly the photographer would have missed it. But the days and then weeks without rain had dropped the water to its lowest level in years. In decades.

Still, without Lola he most likely would have captured the shot of the trees and climbed back up the steep bank from the water. A body that has been in a river or lake that long is difficult to see. My mother was hard to distinguish from the slime that enshrouded her. But Lola was adamant, and there my mother was: all that was left of Annalee Ahlberg, half submerged in the shallow current, bobbing like rotting wood against the penstock grate. Had there not been a drought, had the reeking cadaver not been spotted by Lola, it is likely that eventually the body would have oozed through the bars like apples through a cider press, disappearing in pieces into the turbine, and then through the outflow and back into the Gale.

But there was a drought. And so, in the end, my mother's body was found. It was recovered and gently laid inside a mesh bag (for drainage) and then a zippered body bag, and transported to the morgue at the hospital in Burlington—where it was given its own cooler, one reserved specifically for bodies that pungent.

My mother's dental records were already at the morgue: they had been there for weeks, in the event that her body was discovered after hours and no one could reach her dentist. There it was autopsied.

And it was from there that the Vermont state medical examiner, a trim physician with a graying beard who biked to and from the morgue when the weather cooperated, surprised us all by announcing that the cause of death was not likely the Gale River. It was not likely that Annalee Ahlberg had drowned.

Which is where this story would begin anew.

PART TWO

ON MAY 23, 1987, Kenneth Parks—husband and father of a five-month-old infant—rose from his bed and drove fourteen miles to his in-laws' home. There he stabbed his mother-in-law to death and nearly killed his father-in-law with a tire iron. Then he drove to the police station and turned himself in. He was acquitted of both crimes because the jury agreed he was sleepwalking.

Melissa Toms of Scotland would emerge from her bed, her husband asleep beside her, and meet college boys from the nearby university. The Tomses lived at the edge of the campus. At first she met them at the hall in which the students resided. But then, for reasons no one can quite recall, the boys started coming to her house, where they would be waiting for her in her front yard. She would have sex with three and four of them at a time there, though always on her terms. She hardly spoke. It only stopped when her husband found the condoms scattered in the wood chips along the front walkway. To this day, she insists she has no recollection. Two of the college boys have admitted they were quite sure when they were having sex with Melissa—or as one said, "she was having sex with me"—that she was sound asleep.

In January 2009, Timothy Brueggeman of northern Wisconsin walked in his sleep from his house into the nearby woods in only his underwear and froze to death.

James Currens, seventy-seven, once walked in his sleep into a pond full of alligators in Palm Harbor, Florida. He survived because he had been *sleepwalking with his cane, which he would use that particular night to keep the animals at bay.*

I collected stories like these like stamps. I hoarded them the way some people amass matchbooks, postcards, or old coins.

In them I saw deviance and strangeness, but also the raw power of the id. I saw its absolute independence.

And, of course, I saw . . . me. And I knew I was not alone.

CHAPTER TWELVE

I CLUNG TO my memories of Annalee Ahlberg that autumn and tried to focus on the mother I knew. It was impossible to ignore the thrum of words and the sexual werewolf they conjured—*parasomnia, sexsomnia, sleepwalking, sleep sex*—but our home was a museum to the singular woman she was. Even the footlocker with the magic tricks I had outgrown but was unable to bring myself to resell could resurrect her for me in my mind.

When I was ten and Paige was still a baby, my father had a conference at Columbia University, and my mother joined him and brought her girls to Manhattan. (And, in hindsight, we always were *her* girls: not *their* girls and not *his* girls.) While he was uptown at the university, she took me to my favorite store for magic tricks on Broadway and Twelfth Street. It was near the Strand Bookstore, where we would also spend hours on that trip, and a restaurant that specialized in chocolate. (I had honed my appreciation for decadent chocolate desserts long before my mother would die and I would meet Gavin Rikert.) The store was on the second floor of the building, and on that particular visit we took the elevator, rather than the stairs as we had in the past, because Paige was against my mother's chest in a robin's-egg blue Snugli.

Like Lindsay McCurdy—a.k.a. Rowland the Rogue—the gentleman behind the counter was from another era, but otherwise he was nothing like the dapper and rather elegant old magician I would meet when I was in college. This fellow was crusty and brusque. He had a paunch reined in ever so slightly by suspenders, unruly topiaries growing from his ears, and a thick shock of salt-and-pepper hair it seemed he hadn't washed or combed in a very long time. I saw men like him in magic stores or in how-to videocassettes about magic all the time. His hands were awash in tea-colored sunspots, but I loved watching him use them to demonstrate tricks for us. They were smooth and fast. And like a lot of the magicians of his generation, he tolerated a girl like me—but just barely. My mother and I were the only customers in the store that morning.

He was showing us a trick called the magic pan, a silver skillet perhaps four inches deep with a silver lid. You show the audience it's empty, cover it, and then whisk off the lid to reveal an overflowing mound of sponge balls, flowers, or silks. I liked it, but I worried that if I couldn't produce something more solid— something not easily compressed in the hidden panel—the trick would lack dazzle. I was imagining hard candy: a great big, colorful pile of hard candy. Then I would toss it to my classmates or the really little kids who, back then, were my audience. My mother and I were discussing this possibility with the salesman, and my mother was asking him if he could disclose the size of the compartment. It was right about then that Paige awoke and started to fuss. My mother gently lifted her from the carrier, unbuttoned her own blouse, and pulled the lone chair in the small showroom up to that counter. And then she sat down and began to nurse my baby sister. Instantly, Paige settled down.

I never thought twice about my mother nursing in public in Vermont in 1989. I might not have thought about it in Manhattan that day. But the old magician said to my mother, "If you'd like, you can do that in the storeroom." His eyes were on the corner of the floor behind us. It was as if my mother's breast, even shielded by a rapacious infant's mouth, was the sun.

My mother smiled at him, momentarily surprised by his discomfort. Soon, however, she was relishing it. "Oh, we're fine," she said. "You were about to show us the panel. The secret panel. I'm guessing it's in the tray, and when you lift the lid, you release it—and then it becomes hidden in the top. True?"

He glanced down at the trick. He eyed me. He was going to gaze everywhere but at my mother. "Look, you really need to do that elsewhere," he said finally, speaking straight into the glass display case. "What if another customer comes in here?"

My mother shook her head. "They won't care," she told him, losing none of her equanimity. "I think you might. But most men your age have seen breasts, and I know every woman has. Now, one of my daughters is hungry and one is interested in buying some magic tricks. I think between the two of us, we can make them both very happy. Why don't you pay attention to Lianna here, and I'll pay attention to this little one. That way, everyone will get what they want."

The salesman knew he had lost. He saw my mother's logic; he respected her intensity. And so he said nothing more to her while Paige snacked, and a few minutes later, when Paige was sated, he welcomed my mother back into the conversation.

And when the three of us returned to my aunt and uncle's later that day, I had with me in a big paper shopping bag the magic pan, as well as a trick deck and a spring bouquet I could stash inside a hollow wand or up my sleeve. The salesman had given me the last two items.

Make no mistake: my mother was a lioness with a ferocious love for her cubs. I recalled how she had gone to battle on my behalf when my high school guidance counselor had insisted that certain colleges were beyond my reach, and how she had gone nuclear when a boy drove me home from a party when I was in tenth grade and she could see (and smell) that he'd been drinking. She'd driven him to his house in her car and presented him drunk to his parents.

Yes, I had lost her earlier than I should have. Paige, of course, had too. But something inside me changed when her body was found, something inside me grew up. I understood once and for all that my courageous mother was never coming back, and I vowed to stop sleepwalking through grief.

☽

My mother was probably as good as dead by the time her body broke the plane of the Gale River. There was water in her lungs, but little indication of active respiration; her injuries suggested she was going to die even on dry land soon enough.

Cause of death? A skull fracture and an acute subdural hematoma. Blood had pooled between her brain and her skull, suggesting a violent head injury prior to her body hitting the water. It seemed that someone or something—and when my father and I were informed of the autopsy results, I envisioned a wooden baseball bat—had caved in the back of her skull. My college roommate Erica, however, told me later that day when we were talking on the phone that my imagination had run wild: Who carries around a baseball bat as a bludgeon? she had asked.

It was also possible that my mother had had consensual but violent sex (which led me to wonder privately if there could have been consensual but violent sleep sex). Still, that was merely conjecture, too. The medical examiner could catalog the contusions near my mother's genitalia, but how was he to know for sure the bruising was not the result of the rocks and logs and debris against which her body—naked but for the tattered remnants of a navy-blue sleep shirt—had been colliding for weeks? She had a pelvic fracture, but the M.E. said that the injury may have occurred postmortem. In the water. Her corpse (what was left of it) was a ragged, gelatinous, stringless marionette. Entire strips of sinew, muscle, and tissue had washed away. After so many days in the Gale River, her skin was the texture of cottage cheese and the fathomless brown of a swamp.

The pathologist examined her vaginal walls with a speculum; he combed her pelvic girdle for foreign hairs. He found none. He might have aspirated fluid from her vagina, searched for semen and blood, but the Gale had performed its ablutions: any liquid residues from a sexual encounter had long since washed away. Still, he swabbed what he could. He found nothing.

To perform the toxicology report, he squeezed the spleen: spleen blood is less costly to test than brain or liver tissue, and he was saving taxpayers a little money. We would have to wait a few weeks for those results, but no one expected any surprises.

And then, of course, there was this: that small strip of fabric that was found on the dead twig of a dying maple.

The investigators returned to that patch of the riverbank, hoping for a miracle. A clue. A trace of someone else's DNA.

They found none.

$$\mathcal{D}$$

Neither my father nor Paige wanted breakfast the morning of my mother's funeral. I wasn't hungry, either, but I drove to the bakery in Bristol and brought back a dozen maple scones and then brewed a pot of coffee. My grandparents—my mother's parents— were staying with us for the funeral, and I figured when they awoke they would want something. They did. My grandmother, falling deeper almost daily into the fog of Alzheimer's, had gotten lost in the second-floor bathroom. But she loved the scones, and food seemed to ground her with us in the moment. My grandfather offered to scramble some eggs to go with them, but the idea of eggs made me nauseous. I passed. Our father was going to give the eulogy, and he was alone in the den, editing and rehearsing his remarks. My aunt and uncle and my younger cousins—two rambunctious blond boys, one in the fourth grade and one in the first—were staying at a country inn in Middlebury, but they were already at our house for breakfast, too. Paige rather liked them both, because (like all boys, I had already decided) there was no sport involving a ball that did not interest them. Like my sister, they were energetic and competitive; they traveled that autumn with a soccer ball and a football.

It had been a week since the body was recovered and three days since the medical examiner had determined that Annalee Ahlberg hadn't drowned.

I had laid out on my bed three dresses I was considering, all appropriately dark and all inappropriately summery, revealing, or cheerful, when Paige came into my room. She was already wearing the black dress our aunt had bought her the day before in Burlington. She sat down on the edge of the mattress beside the clothes.

"I think you should say something," she told me.

"You mean at the service?"

"Yes."

"Dad will be way more articulate. And I don't think I'd be able to keep it together up there. I'd be a disaster."

"You'd be fine. But I wasn't even thinking about what you'd say."

"Then what?"

"I was thinking about what you'd see."

I paused and said nothing. I didn't understand what she was driving at. When I just looked at her, she went on, "You could see people's faces in the pews. Their reactions. You might be able to see who did it."

She was absolutely serious. "Who do you think you are, Cam Jansen? Nancy Drew?"

"Don't you think it's possible that whoever killed Mom will be in the church?"

"Not for one single second."

"Criminals always return to the scene of the crime."

"They don't."

"And they're never as smart as they think they are. In the end, they always do something stupid."

I knew what she was referring to: Gavin's boss, the head of the Bureau of Criminal Investigation in Waterbury, had said essentially that to the media after the medical examiner's findings were released. He'd said if Annalee Ahlberg had been murdered—and even the head trauma did not definitively support that hypothesis—

it was likely that whoever had killed her had made a mistake at some point. I was less confident. Gavin was, too. I had only seen him once in the last few days, and I missed him. But it was difficult for me to get away with my grandparents and aunt and uncle and cousins in town. Moreover, the state police had been energized by my mother's corpse. They were looking once more at my mother's clients and friends and—it was clear to me—my father. They insisted that none of us needed to be afraid, though how they could be so confident that whoever had killed my mother had no interest in the three of us sometimes left me perplexed. In any event, Gavin himself was busy, though he had told me that he would be at the service.

"Usually they only do something stupid in the movies," I said to Paige.

"Or around here. Some of the dumbest criminals in the world live around here."

"I'll give you that," I agreed. A few weeks earlier, a guy my age had tried shoplifting a couple of hunting knives from a sporting goods store near Burlington. He had hidden them, unsheathed, under his shirt. When he was running from the store, he had tripped and stabbed himself in the stomach. He'd nearly bled to death in the parking lot.

"So you'll do it? You'll say something about Mom?"

"No. I told you, I'm not capable. I'm just . . . not. But I will see who's there, okay?" I tried not to sound patronizing.

"I will, too," she said, nodding. Then she reached for one of the dresses beside her on the bed. "Wear this one," she suggested, holding up a black pullover with embroidered flowers along the bodice that fell to just below my knees. I always felt like a flamenco dancer when I was wearing it.

"It's not too, I don't know, frivolous?" It was a testimony to how out of sorts I was that season that I was even considering the fashion advice of my kid sister.

"No. Besides Mom liked it."

"Mom did."

Our father had had our mother—or, to be precise, what was left of our mother—cremated. The small urn with her ashes was going to be buried after the service in the Bartlett Cemetery. My father and Paige and I had picked out a spot on a hill that got a lot of sun. It was in the newer section—the original cemetery had plots dating back to 1785—but there was a hydrangea nearby and we all liked the irony.

I heard my grandfather's heavy walk on the corridor and then on the stairs. He wasn't a big man and he wasn't an especially old man. He was only seventy-six then. But he had outlived his daughter, a tragedy no parent should have to endure, and he had aged worse than any of us that autumn. Twice I had found him crying softly in our house. My grandmother was usually oblivious, which may have been a blessing for her, but it was devastating for me to witness. She was seventy-four and, it seemed to me, extraordinarily beautiful. Like her daughter, she was tall, though her hair by then was a lush alabaster mane that fell to her shoulders and that my grandfather brushed in the morning and evening. She was slender, and her eyes remained electric—undimmed, despite the way her mind was failing. She was, I had deduced as a very young girl, the source of my mother's charisma.

"I will keep my eyes out at the service," I reassured Paige. I had no expectations that I would learn anything, but I felt a deep pang when I looked at her, and I wanted her to know I was listening.

☽

Before we left the house, I found Paige and brought her to our parents' bedroom. I waved my arm theatrically over our mother's dresser and the jewelry there, as if I were a genie who had just made a small mountain of precious stones appear in the desert.

"Take something," I said. "For the funeral—and, I guess, forever."

"We can't just take Mom's jewelry," she said, uncharacteristically aghast.

"Why not? Eventually Dad will just divvy it up between us. Besides, the seriously valuable stuff is in the safe deposit box at the bank." To show her that I meant business, I took the cable bracelet with the blue topaz and cuffed it over my wrist. "I view this as a tribute."

"I view it as theft."

"Oh, please."

She looked around the room as if she wanted to be sure that no one was watching us, and then reached for the charm bracelet. "Everyone will know it was hers," she said.

"That's exactly the point."

I had to help her with the clasp that first time, but over the following weeks she learned to do it by herself. She didn't really have places to wear it, but she liked having it with her. She kept it in her swim bag some days and in her school knapsack on others. And then there were the days when she just wore it around the house, an amalgam of mourning and dress-up.

☽

I did keep it together at the funeral. I cried silently, as did Paige. Our father was handsome and stoic, and his voice never broke. The autumn sun gave the stained-glass windows a phantasmagoric glow.

And I did scan the sanctuary, despite the reality that I expected to learn nothing. Moreover, I understood that everyone present— and the small church was indeed packed—wanted to look at my father and Paige and me. (Of course, they wanted to see only the backs of our heads; none, I knew, really wanted to have to make eye contact with any of us as we sat in the front pew.) But I turned around and examined the crowd row by row whenever we stood and sang, and whenever Pastor Katherine Edwards welcomed another speaker to the pulpit. My father. Marilyn Bryce. My aunt. I watched Donnie Hempstead, wondering if it was possible that he and my mother could have had an affair. I decided it wasn't. They hadn't. But I was basing this solely on the way he stood beside his wife, Erin, and the proximity of their bodies. The way Erin discreetly held on to his elbow with her slender fingers with their impeccable nails. He was tall, like my father, with chestnut hair that showed no signs of either thinning or turning gray, and that immaculate beard. He was one of the few men in the church in a suit. A magnificent red-and-yellow necktie against a crisp white shirt. I recalled how different he had appeared the day he had been among the search parties out looking for my mother: the white T-shirt, the jeans, the way exhaustion and worry and intensity had all marked his face as he had stood beside Paige and me on the porch. In my mind, I saw my mother working with Donnie and Erin as she designed their aqua solarium. I imagined them in her small office in Middlebury or standing around a beautiful kitchen island, looking at plans. I envisioned the couple in their bathing suits, submerged to their shoulders in their hot tub. I saw my mother alone with Donnie in that tub. There she was sleepwalking to him. There he was taking advantage of her.

But this was groundless. I knew that.

And Justin Bryce? Again, unlikely. My mother would never have betrayed Marilyn. Besides, I'd read the jokes she had shared with my father about him. I rather doubted that Justin was her type. The same probably went for Donnie Hempstead with his nut-brown beard. If my mother had a type and it wasn't Warren Ahlberg, I had a feeling it was probably a man like Gavin Rikert. Arguably—and this gave me pause—my mother's type was my type.

I studied my father's female friends from the English department at the college, the other scholars with whom my father might have been sleeping. And I concluded they were either asexual or settled in marriage. These, I told myself, were not the randy, erotically alive poets of Bread Loaf, the slender women who would take you by the hands and melt with you into the dew, the rugged men who would take you on the porches and Adirondack chairs beneath the nighttime August sky—though, in all fairness, I also told myself that I might be wrong. What really did I know of midlife sexuality? Or monogamy versus polyamory? Of extramarital relationships? I knew nothing.

Toward the back of the sanctuary I saw some of my friends from Amherst, including Erica, and at the very edge of the pew, beside the students he must have just met, was another traveler from Massachusetts: Lindsay McCurdy. The old magician had made the drive, too. I was moved.

And I spied Gavin: he was standing between the most distant of the stained-glass windows and the heavy door to the narthex. When our eyes met, he nodded almost surreptitiously so that only I would notice.

I listened carefully to everything my father and my aunt and my mother's roommate from college said about her, wondering if I might find a bit of evidence in their eulogies.

But there were no revelations; there were no clues. Other than my father, no one spoke of her sleepwalking, and my father only used it poetically, expressing his hope that his wife's ever-restless soul might now be at rest. No one spoke of her occasional bouts of depression. No one spoke of the bombshell from the Office of the State Medical Examiner.

Instead, people rather accurately captured Annalee Ahlberg's eccentricities and talents and her creativity: her ingenuity as an architect and her inventiveness as a mom. Her friends would smile at Paige and me and tell us how much she loved being our mother. We had never doubted it: We had worn the Halloween costumes. We had felt firsthand the power of her embrace. And so we nodded at the stories, most of which we had known or had lived, and occasionally we even laughed through our tears. For most of my life, I had only heard Katherine Edwards speak in this church on Christmas and Easter. I decided that I had underestimated the pastor; maybe I had underestimated religion. Katherine made me want to come back on a regular Sunday.

At the end of the service, as I exited the church, I asked Gavin if he would be at the reception back at our home. First, however, my family—and only the family—was going to watch the mahogany box with Annalee Ahlberg's ashes be placed into its spot in the cemetery. He reassured me that he'd be waiting at the house when we returned in half an hour.

$$\mathcal{D}$$

One of my father's poems compared wedding receptions with funerals. When I first read the poem, I had misunderstood it, assuming it was a predictable (and uncharacteristically puerile) dismissal of marriage. At my mother's funeral, however, some of the couplets came back to me, and I realized that the poem was actually a rather astute appreciation of the unfair velocity with which time moved at these rituals for the immediate families. There were too many people for too little time. I would have two- and three-minute conversations with guests and mourners that really went nowhere, and we were all saying the same largely meaningless things:

Your mother was amazing.
Yes, she was.

You're holding up well. She'd be proud of you.
I guess.

I miss her.
Yeah. I do, too.

I kept trying to inch my way across the house to get to my friend Erica, because here was a person I missed and whom I actually wanted to talk to. But it didn't seem possible. It was too crowded and I was, as Annalee's older daughter, too in demand.

And then there were the exchanges that were surreal and left me stupefied by the utter strangeness of the world. At one point I saw my elderly magician friend Lindsay McCurdy and Donnie Hempstead chatting like old pals with their backs to the breakfront in the living room, each holding a sweating bottle of beer. Lindsay's Bengal tiger cravat was as striking as Donnie's red-and-yellow necktie. I worked my way through the throng to them just in time to overhear Donnie saying, "It was Sonny and Cher, right? I was a kid, but now that you mention it, I know I saw you on TV. I remember it really well!"

Lindsay nodded. "Mostly I was supposed to be a foil for Cher. A lot of jokes, I recall, about making Sonny disappear."

I was vaguely familiar with the show, associating it in my mind with other programs from before my time, such as *The Ed Sullivan Show*. "They had magicians on Sonny and Cher?" I asked, inserting myself into the conversation. "I wish you had told me you were on it, Lindsay!"

"I was on it just the one time. It was more of a comedy show than a variety show," he said. "I did a little magic that night and we all stood around gaping at whatever costume Cher came out in."

Donnie waved a finger in the air. "Oh, you did much more than that. You were great! You were like a hypnotist. You did some trick you called 'The Sleepwalker.'"

Instantly he went silent. He stood there, embarrassed, and then mumbled an apology. Meanwhile, Lindsay looked contrite, as if he had been caught speaking badly of someone behind her back.

"It's okay," I said to Donnie. Then, more because I was deeply curious than because I wanted to smooth over an awkward comment, I said to Lindsay, "I never think of you as a hypnotist. What was the illusion?"

"I levitated a woman," he said slowly and without enthusiasm.

"And then she walked around?"

"She walked around first . . . like she was asleep."

"An assistant?"

"Yes. An audience plant."

"Did you have her do anything else?" I asked.

Donnie and the magician glanced unhappily at each other—Donnie remembered what came next, I could tell—and then down at his impeccably shined black wingtips.

"Tell me," I said.

"I levitated her above a glass-walled tank of water. You know the trick, I am sure. I covered her with a sheet on a couch, rose her high above it, and then guided her sleeping body—still prone—over the tank. When she awoke, the audience expected she would fall in. The live audience and the TV audience all assumed it would be a little randy because she was pretty and her clothes would be sticking to her, and it would be a little cruel: what a horrible way to wake up! Remember, I was Rowland the Rogue. Instead, however, it was Sonny—who was standing on a trapdoor on the platform above the tank—who got dunked. When I whisked off the sheet, the girl had vanished. I summoned her back on stage from a wing, where she walked—still asleep and under my spell—to my side. Then, at my command, she sent Sonny into the water."

I could understand why they didn't want to share the story with me, but I had envisioned my mother sleepwalking or in the Gale River so many times by that afternoon that a magic trick called "The Sleepwalker" and a woman suspended above a water tank was not going to unsettle me. "Can you really hypnotize people?" I asked Lindsay.

"I could. I doubt I can now."

"Well," Donnie said, clearly wanting to move the conversation to less spongy ground, "Annalee told me how much she liked meeting you last year."

I wasn't sure what I found more curious: the idea that Lindsay had never told me that he had once been a hypnotist or that my mother had told Donnie Hempstead she had met Rowland the Rogue one day in Somerville. The more I learned about people, including my late mother, the more they surprised me.

☽

I was unexpectedly nervous when I was finally able to speak with Gavin in my home. Despite the crowd on the first floor of our house, I always felt that my father or Paige or even Marilyn Bryce was watching me when I chatted with the detective. I understood this was paranoia; there wasn't a soul in our living room or kitchen or den who knew I had said a single word to the detective since the day my mother had disappeared. (Even now, I still view August 25 as the day my mother disappeared, rather than the day she died. But, of course, it was both.) He was sipping coffee from a mug with a silhouette of William Shakespeare that I had put in my father's Christmas stocking years ago and leaning against the walnut sideboard in the dining room when I asked him to tell me everything he could. I wanted to know what the police had learned since redoubling their efforts, and whether he had noticed anyone at the funeral who might have murdered my mother. Did I sound to him the way my sister had sounded to me that morning? Naïve and silly and rather childlike? Perhaps. But I asked anyway. The truth is, I had always viewed my younger sister as smarter than me.

"Here? Seriously?" he said, his tone a little incredulous.

"I didn't just ask you to have sex with me on the dining room floor," I told him.

"It's not the time or the place to talk about the investigation. Are you around later today? We could go somewhere and talk then."

"No. I'll be here. I want to be with my family. My dad. My sister. My grandparents. You know, the whole crowd."

"Good. That makes sense. What about tomorrow?"

"Sure. But at least tell me this: Did you see someone here who's a suspect? A person of interest?"

He smiled at me. "Spoken like someone who's seen one too many cop dramas."

"I don't watch cop dramas."

"But you have a pop culture implant. You know the terms."

"And?"

He sighed. "I promise you, there is no one here you should worry about."

"How do you know that?"

"I just do."

"So you have absolutely no new leads?"

He shook his head. "But we'll talk more tomorrow. Can I take you to dinner?"

"Okay. I'd like that."

"Can I pick you up?"

"No."

"Got it. I'm still a secret."

"I honestly can't tell: Are you offended or relieved?"

"Neither. You have your reasons for not telling your dad, I have my reasons for not telling my boss," he answered. But then, in a gesture that felt oddly threatening, he took his coffee and went to the living room to say hello to my father. I scanned the room for Paige and saw her. She was with two of her friends from the ski team, and I could tell that she had been watching me from the corner of her eye.

SOME MEN DON'T *mind when their lover has sexsomnia. They view it as a little something something—an unexpected sexual bonus. Others are threatened: they fear they aren't sexually satisfying their partner if they wake up and the person beside them is masturbating or reaching for their penis in the night. And still other men? They're merely annoyed that they're being woken from a sound sleep at one or two in the morning.*

It's different for a woman whose man has sexsomnia. Occasionally, especially if they're young, it's a pleasant extra. Again, a bonus.

But most male sexsomniacs aren't especially giving lovers. They're not known for their gentleness or sensitivity. They get in and get out and then continue on their descent to serious REM sleep. Their partner's pleasure? Irrelevant. (Certainly this is true for female sexsomniacs, too, but men— especially young men—rarely complain when sex is offered. Recall those students in Scotland.)

Moreover, what if the woman once was sexually assaulted or raped, or was abused as a child? A sexsomniac, male or female, doesn't take no for an answer. For those couples, therein lies the greatest sadness of all.

CHAPTER THIRTEEN

A MEMORY CAME to me the night we buried my mother, unbidden and forlorn, as I was trying (and failing) to fall asleep.

My bedroom didn't share a wall with my parents' bedroom. The way our house was laid out, only the guest bedroom did. But before my freshman year of high school, that August, my mother and I together repainted the ceiling and hung new paper in my bedroom. The wild stallions wallpaper had been perfect when I was six, but that summer we replaced it with a floral design rich with shades of orange and peach. And so I was sleeping those days in the guest room. I was awakened in the middle of the night by the sound of my father's voice. He was speaking firmly, as if talking to a recalcitrant child.

"Annalee. Annalee. Stop it. Annalee."

I was on my side and sat up so I could hear more clearly. "Annalee. No. I can't perform like that."

A moment later I heard their bedroom door open and close, and then I heard my father going downstairs to the den. I wondered if my mother would follow him. She didn't. By the time my father returned to their bedroom—if he did return that night—I had fallen back to sleep.

For years, however, I had been haunted by that one sentence: *I can't perform like that.* In my mind, it was suggestive of my father's sexual inadequacy: his emasculation. I had been mortified and had tried to forget it. I couldn't. Clearly it had colored so much of my view of him.

The night of my mother's funeral, knowing what I understood now of my mother's parasomnia, I felt guilty that I had thought less of him—and now that haunted me, too.

☽

The next day was the first day that I volunteered at the elementary school in Bartlett. I had taken my father's advice and called the principal—the same woman who had been running the school over a decade earlier when I had been there—and offered to spend a few mornings a week wherever they needed me. The school had exactly one classroom for each grade, kindergarten through five, and fewer than twenty kids in each room except for the second grade. The Bartlett sixth graders left the village for the area middle school. I offered to do a magic show, but the principal was more interested in having me work with the second graders, where there were twenty-two kids, making it the largest grade in the school.

As I walked through the hallways, the adults I would pass would grow somber. The custodian, a kind man whose hair was now white but whom I remembered well from my years there, wasn't sure whether it was appropriate to hug me and finally decided that the best thing to do was pat me awkwardly on the shoulder. He murmured how sorry he was. The teachers who had arrived since I had left a decade ago looked at me gravely and nodded, as if we were privy to a very special secret. The teachers who I knew told me how special my mother was and asked that great, wholly unanswerable question: How was I doing? I would shrug and lie. *I'm fine,* I said over and over that day. *I'm fine.*

But mostly that morning I helped the children iron leaves under wax paper. I recalled doing it myself years ago with my mother, just the two of us working one afternoon on the counter of the kitchen island. I was terrified the kids were going to burn themselves because at any given moment I and the teacher—a woman in her late twenties who insisted the kids call her Hailey—had six hot irons going. She may have been no more than seven or eight years older than me, but she knew what she was doing: she had brought in a heavy-duty, six-outlet power strip with a fifteen-foot cord precisely for this project. She had lined up the irons on one long table—the pressing station, she called it—and the night before had shorn hundreds of sheets of wax paper from once-thick rolls. No one got hurt. We were an assembly line.

At one point a tiny girl named Dakota was showing me the fan of neon-yellow ash she had brought in from home, the seven leaves still attached to the thin branch. Most of the other students had maples—so many maples, some sugar, some red, all phosphorescent—so her ash was a lovely change of pace. Together we carefully snipped the leaves where their stems met the branch, dried them, and sealed them in the wax paper. As we were surveying the last one, I sat down. The final step would be trimming the wax paper, shaping it with scissors. Suddenly Dakota climbed into my lap, wrapping one arm around my neck and just plopping her head against my chest.

"I don't know what I'd do if my mommy died," she said.

I saw Hailey watching us—watching me—her eyes a little wide with worry. I nodded at her. I was okay. I was grateful for the child's warmth.

"You would do just what you're doing this second," I told the girl. "You'd hug people. And you'd be really happy when people hugged you."

☽

The sky was perfectly clear that night, a Friday, and so after dinner Gavin and I walked from the restaurant to the Burlington waterfront. I buttoned up my jean jacket and tightened the scarf around my neck, and was comfortably warm. He took my hand as we walked and only released it when we stood by the railing not far from where the ferries docked. We looked at the sickle moon over the Adirondacks.

"I wish I had understood my parents' marriage better," I told him.

He shrugged. "I know your mom loved your dad and I know your dad is an amazing person. Really loving. And really patient."

"But you guys were looking at him again as a suspect."

"You have to be thorough."

"How did he do it if he was in Iowa?"

"Strangers on a train. Paid hit man. Who knows? It's why we nose around. But he was never a serious suspect in my mind. He's not now."

"Is he a serious suspect in anyone's mind?"

"Maybe."

"Some days, I think he's just so clueless. Such a total basket case. And then other days, I wonder if he's sleeping with one of his students. Some wannabe poet my age. And then I'm furious with him."

"Cut him some slack."

"I do. I guess mostly I just worry about him."

"I heard him speak in the church. He'll be okay."

I watched the way Gavin laced his fingers together on the railing. "If my mom's death had something to do with sleep sex, was she out looking for someone? Someone in particular?"

"You mean, she wasn't just sleepwalking? It's possible. Obviously I've gotten out of bed any number of times and looked for . . . someone. But never someone in particular."

"Did it scare her?"

"The sleep sex? A little. She knew what she was capable of. But mostly it embarrassed her. It shamed her. It shames us all."

We gazed for a long moment at the lights from a passenger jet as the plane began its final descent over the water and toward the Burlington airport.

"So who killed her?" I asked.

"If she was murdered," he corrected me.

I acquiesced. "If."

"I don't know."

"Broadly speaking. What sort of person?"

"Use that cultural implant of yours," he said. "Why do people ever kill people? Anger. Jealousy. Money. Love. And then, of course, there are the psychopaths: the serial killers."

"And in Vermont?"

"Domestic violence. That's our dark and dirty little secret. The majority of our homicides are women in very bad relationships. The rest? Drugs."

"So, my mom was the exception."

"Yes."

"No one seems to think my dad or Paige or I are in danger."

"Why would you be?"

"I don't know. Maybe someone has something against my family."

He wrapped his arm around my shoulder and pulled me into him. "No one has a vendetta against your family."

"Okay . . ."

"You don't sound convinced. You should be."

"I guess I am."

"Good."

"Can I ask you one more thing about my dad? I don't know where it fits in, but I keep thinking it does . . . somewhere."

"You can ask me anything you like. No guarantees I can or will answer it."

"Okay. What do you make of my dad e-mailing my mom articles about miscarriages as recently as this past summer?"

"Are you wondering if the miscarriages are somehow connected to her death?"

"I'm honestly not sure what I mean."

He sighed. "It's an ongoing investigation, Lianna."

"So you're not going to tell me."

He shook his head. But I wondered if in my unfiltered questions, my random associations, I had tugged at a thread of some consequence for Gavin. It felt as if I had hit a nerve.

☽

Was it the reality that I had, finally, been forced to say good-bye to my mother? Perhaps. But it may also have been the way his fingers had felt against the small of my back, the welcome pressure, or the way the sides of his face had felt against my fingers when we kissed. So warm. I felt the color rising up along the nape of my neck and the most exquisite tingling just below my waist. We fell upon each other the moment he had shut the door to his apartment, undressing on his living room couch, that sickle moon still agleam in the sky beyond his window. He knelt before me on the floor and I spread my legs, opening myself to him, losing myself to the wondrous, wet recklessness of the moment. His mouth. His tongue. Later, when he was inside me in his bed, he whispered how he had never been with a woman as beautiful as I was, and how he had never been happier than he was that moment. The whole world went away. It really was just the two of us.

☽

And yet later, when I was lying with my head against his chest, warm beneath his sheets and listening to the waves of his heart, he urged me to leave. He said that was safest. I told him no; I told him I wasn't going home. And when I refused, he said he would sleep once more on his living room couch, locking me safely in his bedroom. I said he would do no such thing. I insisted he remain in his bedroom with me because I could not bear to have him leave me that moment. It took us both a long time to fall asleep, though Gavin was more worried than me. I was twenty-one, and mostly I was curious. I watched him. I watched him so much, I made him uncomfortable, and so we made love again. But eventually we did fall asleep. Both of us.

And he slept through the night. As did I. It was lovely.

☽

I had called my father and told him that I was spending the night with Heather Prescott at her apartment just off the UVM campus. By then my grandparents had left. My aunt and uncle and my cousins had returned to Manhattan, as well.

On my way home Saturday morning, I drove past Heather's place and considered dropping by. I was looking for a reason not to return to the strange, sad emptiness of the red Victorian. I could explain to Heather that I had used her as an alibi if it ever came up. She'd like to be complicit in a lie about a lover. But if she were home—and awake—she'd want to know who I had been with the night before. She'd ask who this new man was in my life. And I wasn't prepared to discuss Gavin. Moreover, she'd probably want to smoke a bowl, and I would have to defend my resistance, my rather sudden aversion to dope.

And so I returned to Bartlett, but I did make one stop there before going home. I dropped by Marilyn Bryce's and found the woman in her studio. She was standing before a canvas the size of a queen mattress in a pair of jeans and a well-worn and impressively stained sweatshirt, her hair pulled back in a tight bun. She was listening to late Beatles on a boom box and staring at the kaleidoscopic waves of neon that rippled across the painting. I had expected the room to reek of weed—and wondered briefly what it said about me that I had passed on one stoner and wound up with another—but there was only the tiniest hint of skunk. She seemed so focused on her work that I considered whether I needed to take her more seriously.

She suggested that we go inside the house for a cup of tea, but I said I only had a couple of minutes, so she motioned for me to take one of the two wobbly, paint-splattered ladder-back chairs in the corner, and she took the other. We discussed the funeral and I reiterated how much I appreciated what she had said about my mother—which was true. But then I asked her the question that was on my mind, the reason why I had come here: "Did you and my mom ever talk about her miscarriages?"

"Oh, of course. How could we not?"

"Did she ever, I don't know, speculate why?"

"Why they happened? As in a meaning of life, spiritual thing? Or why they happened biologically?"

"The latter."

"Well, she knew, didn't she? They did all those tests. Wasn't it something to do with your dad?"

"I don't know," I lied, curious where this was leading.

"It was," she said. "Your mom was quite sure."

"And my dad?"

"Well, he had to know, too, didn't he? If it wasn't her, it had to be him. Right?"

I thought of the e-mail from him I had discovered. I recalled what he had said to me in his office. "I would think if my father knew, he would have felt horrible. He would have felt pretty bad."

"I'm sure he did. But after Paige was born, none of that mattered now, did it?"

"But all the years in between?"

"What about them?"

"How did it affect their marriage?"

"It added stress, I guess. How could it not? But I don't know what you're driving at. I have no idea where you're going with this, sweetie."

"I'm not sure, either."

She scrunched up her face and looked at me intently. She sat forward on her chair and leaned into me. "Are you worried that Paige is, I don't know, just your half sister? Because that's insane. That is seriously kooky talk."

I was stunned, and yet at the same time I understood this was precisely what, on some level, had been dogging me. Marilyn had verbalized what had been gnawing at me for weeks, but had not yet been exhumed from deep inside me. "Yes, that is what I'm thinking," I admitted, and I could hear the utter tonelessness in my voice. "Do other people think that?"

"No!"

"Do you?"

"Of course not! It's just . . ."

"It's just what?" I pressed.

"Fine. You and your mom and dad all have light hair. I mean, your mother? Good Lord, she looked like a Swedish model. And the three of you have blue eyes. But Paige? Black hair. And those magnificent dark eyes. And she's such an . . . athlete. She is just so different from the rest of you."

I nodded to myself. She was actually corroborating the notion. "And yet in your opinion, she is"—and I had to think for a moment to phrase this question properly—"my father's daughter."

"Yes."

"And you're positive this isn't a rumor around here?"

"Completely. People don't know about the miscarriages. Only I do."

"Katherine Edwards does."

"Okay, some people know. But *rumor* is too strong a word. So is *gossip*. Maybe *joke* is better. I mean, your mom used to make them, too."

"Jokes that Paige isn't my father's daughter?"

"Yes! She was kidding, of course—and always just because Paige is so unlike you. She is so unlike your father."

"Then who is she like?"

"Are you asking who people speculate is her father?"

"I guess."

"No one! It was just a joke. Paige is your sister. Warren Ahlberg is her father, just like he's your father."

I recalled what she had said a moment ago about my father being the cause of the miscarriages and the idea that the reason might have been his chromosomal abnormalities. If other people questioned the paternity of my younger sister, then certainly my father did.

"Look, twice everything worked just fine," Marilyn continued. "Two times. What more could you ask for?"

"So when you and my mother talked about the miscarriages, she never mentioned a lover?"

"Never."

"Or, I don't know, a sperm bank?"

"Of course not!"

"Does Paige suspect anything?"

"There's nothing to suspect, Lianna. And even if she did, wouldn't you know better than me?"

"Probably," I agreed.

She tilted her head sympathetically and smiled. "I know you want answers to what happened to your mom. We all do. But I just don't see us ever getting them. I'm sorry, sweetie. I really am."

When I left, I was unmoored, as baffled by the world as I had been at any moment since my mother had died.

☽

That afternoon, I spent hours with our collection of photo albums and searched for old pictures of my aunts and uncles and grandparents. I had never really thought about what they had looked like when they were young. My cousins' hair was light and my aunt—my mother's sister—was a strawberry blonde. But what had my grandparents looked like before their hair had gone gray? What had my father's aunts and uncles looked like forty years ago? I found some images from a family reunion in one of our oldest albums; I was a toddler. I was always, it seemed, in either my father's or my mother's arms. I was wearing a floral pink smock dress with ruffles and clutching a small stuffed bunny in a similar outfit. Her name was Bunny Jo; I still had her. She was in the unmade piles of sheets and blankets on my bed that very moment.

Most of the people in the photos had Scandinavian hair and Scandinavian cheekbones. But not everyone. The reunion had been held at my mother's parents' house in Concord, Massachusetts—the reunion was for her side of the family—and there in the group photo was the man I was confident was her uncle Arvid. Uncle Arvid had cocoa-colored hair. Yes, he had blue eyes, but I took a Mendel-like satisfaction in the proof that deep in the recessive genes on my mother's side of the family existed the DNA for Paige's dark hair.

Next I pulled out my parents' wedding album so I could look at the Ahlberg side. Again, there were individuals with brown and black hair, though how many were guests and how many were Ahlbergs I couldn't say. But there were people with dark eyes. There were yet more people who could have been the genetic precursors to my kid sister.

Nevertheless, that afternoon as I practiced for a magic show I had the next day for one of the kids in the Sunday school, I found myself hugging Paige the two occasions when, bored, she put her head into my bedroom to see what I was doing. I think she found me more maddening than usual.

☽

My father suggested that the three of us go see a movie that Saturday night, and the two choices at the theater in Middlebury were a film about aging astronauts and a tale of competitive cheerleading. We went with the astronauts. But we had dinner at an Italian restaurant beforehand, where our father could get a scotch and Paige could have pizza. We had a booth, and after we'd ordered, I asked my father about his parents. My grandmother had only died two years earlier, and so I had known her well. I had loved her Swedish meatballs and Swedish pancakes with lingonberries and maple syrup. She had been a lawyer for an insurance company in Manhattan before she retired; over the years, she had taken me to wonderful, glamorous lunches in restaurants on Park Avenue

South. At least twice she had taken both my mom and me out after we had been shopping for magic tricks on lower Broadway.

My grandfather, however, had died suddenly when I was in kindergarten, and so I had never really gotten to know the man who had raised my father. He had been an advertising executive, though precisely what he did was beyond me.

"Oh, my parents are a very broad topic," my father said in response to my question. He was sitting across from Paige and me, leaning back against the wall of the settee with his arms folded across his chest. "What would you like to know about them?"

"I don't know: tell me about the time you introduced Mom to them. What was that like for you? For them? How did they respond?"

"Well, there's probably what actually occurred and then there's the way I massaged my recollections over time. That's how it is with everything, isn't it?" my father answered.

"Lianna's clearly about to bring someone home for you to meet, Dad," Paige said. "It's why she didn't come home a couple of nights the last few weeks."

I glared at her. "Nope. I was just crashing at friends' houses in Burlington and Montpelier."

My father didn't seem to acknowledge Paige's supposition. "Your grandmother had her mouth filled with an indecent-sized scoop of chopped chicken livers on a cracker when I brought your mother home to meet her. She had just gotten home from work and was starving. She was hoping to snack quickly before we arrived. She didn't hear us come in and we surprised her in the kitchen. She was standing in a blue suede gaucho skirt, with one hand on the counter above the dishwasher. Your grandmother's bite was so big—so marvelously and uncharacteristically gluttonous—that she couldn't speak for easily thirty seconds while she chewed. She gave your mother a half wave."

"Were you embarrassed?" Paige asked. She took a sip of her soda and frowned. "I think they gave me diet soda by mistake."

Our father nodded and looked around for our waiter. "Again,

who's to say it really happened quite that way? But that's how I recall it," he said. Then: "No, Paige, your grandmother never embarrassed me."

"Did she ever sleepwalk?" I asked.

"No."

"Your father?"

He took a sip of his drink and shook his head. "But did your mother's parents?" he asked me in response, ever the professor. "That would be a far more interesting and practical question."

"Did they?"

"No. The question is more interesting than the response. I'm sorry. Lianna, tell me why you just asked me about sleepwalking: Have you had an incident?"

"No."

"Good. You girls really shouldn't fret, in that case. The doctor at the sleep center is looking forward to seeing you both, but she really isn't alarmed in the slightest. Neither of you should be worried."

Paige looked across the restaurant at the large chalkboard with the specials and shrugged. I had to restrain myself from reminding the two of them that I really didn't need to see Dr. Yager at all—at least not as a patient.

"I was looking at your parents and Mom's parents in lots of old family photos today," I said instead. "I also looked at a lot of the family reunions. Wedding pictures. Our family has some of the worst hair on the planet," I went on, unsure how far I would take this line of inquiry with Paige sitting beside me. "With the exception of Mom, there is just so much mousy blond. So much thinning hair."

"I seem to be the only one who got stuck with black hair," Paige said. She sounded disgusted, and instantly I regretted what I had begun.

"You have the best hair," I said. "I would kill for hair as thick as yours."

"No, you wouldn't. I'm this weird black sheep. We all know that."

"You are way prettier than the rest of us," I tried to reassure her.

"I used to think I was adopted."

My father, I noticed, seemed to pay a little more attention. "Why in the world would you think that?"

"Because I don't look anything like you and Mom and Lianna the Enchantress over here. And because I'm nothing like the rest of you."

"What does that mean?" I asked.

"I've seen you on skis. You're a spaz. I saw Mom on skis. She wasn't exactly Picabo Street. And Dad, no offense, but you're not an Olympic athlete, either."

"No offense taken," he said, smiling in acknowledgment. "But, first of all," he added, "it wouldn't matter in the slightest if you were adopted. You're my daughter. You were your mother's daughter. Second, you weren't adopted. Lianna and I can assure you of your mother's pregnancy. I was in the delivery room when you arrived—dark hair and rosebud mouth and all."

"So who in our family do I look like? Who am I most like?"

He sniffed and thought. He was stumped. Finally he said to Paige, "Your mother's uncle Arvid was a very good Nordic skier, I understand."

"And he had your color hair," I added, recalling the photo and trying to be helpful. But our father corrected me.

"No," he said, "it was brown, but it was light brown. Maybe it looked darker in the photograph. It certainly wasn't that lovely raven's black of yours, Paige."

" 'Raven's black,' " my sister repeated. "Seriously? That's what people think of when they think of my hair?"

"The world needs more goth ski racers," I said, hoping to reassure her with a small joke.

"Dad?"

"Yes, Paige?"

"Do you think the police will ever find who killed Mom?"

"If someone killed her? I hope so."

"But do you think they will? Do you believe they will?"

I could tell my father wasn't at all confident, but I could see the acute need he felt to reassure Paige. He met her gaze so deeply that she stared down at the menu before her. "Yes, my dear," he said. "I believe that."

She didn't look up. "And then what will happen?"

"There will be more media coverage. There will be negotiations between the state's attorney—the lawyer on our side—and the defense attorney. There may be a plea deal of some kind. Maybe the person who did it will plead guilty. Maybe not. And so there may be a court case. A trial. If so, there will be yet more media attention and interest. Newspaper stories. Television stories. It will seem to be opening old wounds, but in reality it will be healing them. It will be giving us justice."

"Whoever killed her will go to jail?"

"Yes. Whoever killed her will go to jail."

Paige said nothing more. She kept her attention on the long list of pizzas and salads. I couldn't tell if she found this likely sequence at all comforting. I know I didn't—though it would still be a while before I would understand why.

I WANTED TO tell someone—at least a part of me did.

But the bigger part of me couldn't bring myself to admit it. To speak the truth aloud. To share what I thought I had seen. What I thought I remembered.

Some days I managed to convince myself that I was simply imagining the worst because I knew what I was capable of in my sleep. You have no idea how many hours I spent online researching the probabilities, especially as I grew older and more research became available on the Internet.

But over time, the reality grew inescapable. The truth.

Yes, sleepwalkers usually recall very little. Unfortunately, I always recalled more than most.

CHAPTER FOURTEEN

BEFORE MY MOTHER'S body was found, the mystery surrounding her story had revolved around her disappearance. After an exuberant dog and a determined photographer had discovered her corpse, the mystery focused instead upon the cause of her death and whether she might actually have been murdered. But when the state police could find no clues—there were still neither suspects nor motives, the toxicology report revealed nothing, and no one seemed to worry that my father and Paige and I were in danger—even that puzzle failed to hold anyone's interest. Once again the media and the detectives moved on. The last of the leaves died and fell, and the autumn rains commenced. The drought became a mere meteorological footnote. We no longer spotted the great well-drilling trucks as they rumbled along our shady, narrow roads or discussed whether the ski resorts would have sufficient water in their holding ponds to make snow. My sister would be back on the slopes right on time.

By the third week in October, once more my father and Paige and I had settled into a routine. At least it looked like a routine on the surface: I would get the two of them off to work and school respectively, keep house, and make dinner. I would cart Paige wherever she needed to go. I would visit my friends in Vermont or call my friends at Amherst. I still hadn't decided whether I was going to return to college in the spring, but the deadline was nearing: I had until November 1. If my father was aware of the date, he never mentioned it; looking back, I like to believe that he presumed all along that I was returning, because the alternative— that he expected me to remain indefinitely in Bartlett—makes him seem selfish and a little dislikable. He was neither; he simply wasn't coping, I told myself. He was grieving. That was it.

And, of course, I would visit my secret vice, a cop twelve years my senior, at least every second or third day. On a Friday or a Saturday, depending upon his work schedule, I would even spend the night in his apartment. Never once had there been any sleep sex. But Gavin insisted it would happen someday, and he worried that I didn't comprehend what I was signing up for. I assured him I would be fine. I was falling in love.

$$\mathbb{D}$$

About a week before Halloween, I was almost finished with the application for Paige's ski camp in Chile and her visa to visit the country. Our father had signed the permission forms and written the check for the down payment. A little after nine o'clock in the evening, I put my head into her bedroom and told her that I had two quick questions to wrap it up. She was lying on her back in bed in her pajamas and playing with her Game Boy.

"I'm not sure I feel like going anymore," she told me.

I was shocked; she'd given me no hint that she was having second thoughts as we'd driven day after day to the college swimming pool. "Why not?"

"I just don't want to." She still wasn't looking at me; she was focused entirely on her video game.

"You have to have a reason."

"I have to go to school. I have to breathe"—and here she made an exaggerated gasping sound—"but I don't have to go to Chile."

I sat down in her desk chair. "Why did you change your mind?"

"I just did."

"Did you have a fight with Lucy or one of the other kids who are going? Did you and Coach Noggler have some sort of falling out?"

She tossed the Game Boy onto the mattress beside her and rolled so she was facing the wall. "No. If I don't go, Lucy will be disappointed and Coach will be pissed off."

"Have you suddenly lost interest in ski racing?"

"I don't know."

A part of me wanted to scream at her, *Why have I been driving you to the swimming pool almost every single day if you're not interested in ski racing anymore?* But I restrained myself. It wasn't like I was so busy.

"No, I still like racing," she went on. "I'm still looking forward to the season."

"Are you worried about being away from home for a month? I mean, that is a crazy long time and Chile is crazy far away. Maybe you could just go for two weeks."

"Look, it's not like you've been so brave and gone back to college."

"That isn't quite the same thing," I told her. "But tell me: Are the second thoughts because of all that time away from Vermont?" It dawned on me that Paige had never even gone to a sleep-away camp. I'd been a Brownie; Paige hadn't.

"Can we talk about this some other time? The forms aren't, like, due tomorrow."

"No," I agreed. "They're not."

"Thank you."

"Have you done your homework?" I asked.

"Yes."

"Are you going to go to bed soon?"

"I'm in bed right now."

"Let me rephrase that: Are you going to go to sleep soon?"

"I guess."

"Good."

"You know what I wish?" Paige asked.

I waited.

"I wish I were a cat who didn't have to think about grades or Chile or dying or even whether your dad was ever going to be okay again."

"I don't think you have ever in your life lost any sleep over grades. You get A's without breaking a sweat." I focused on the grades because it seemed the most innocuous and unreasonable of her anxieties. I understood I was avoiding the bigger issues. So, I am sure, did she.

"You don't know that," she murmured.

"Well, I know how smart you are and how together you are. Okay? You're way smarter than I am. And I'm not just saying that. Try not to be such a goofball worrywart."

She rolled back over so she was facing me. I realized she had been crying. I went to her, but as she did whenever I tried to comfort her, she batted my arms and pushed me away. "I'm fine," she said, sniffing and wiping her cheek with the back of her hand. "I'm fine. I'll go to sleep." She tossed the Game Boy onto the floor, and as I sat helplessly by the side of her bed, she turned off the standing lamp beside it.

☽

"Paige has always been a wild card," Heather Prescott told me late that night on the phone. I called her to talk about my kid sister because we had been friends forever and she had known Paige since she was a baby.

"What does that mean?" I asked.

"All that downhill craziness: you have to be a wild woman to be a ski racer. And there was her determination to find your poor mom back in August and September. You told me she was out there all the time looking for clues. And Zach always said there was no one like her when they'd be playing kickball or soccer in elementary school. That no sliding rule? She ignored it." Zach was the youngest of Heather's three siblings. He was in Paige's grade at school.

"Well, then: her deciding not to go to Chile doesn't exactly fit that profile."

"She's kind of acting like you. You don't want to leave home at the moment. Neither does she. Frankly, I can't blame either of you."

"She said the same thing."

"There you have it."

"But she was the one who initiated this whole Chile ski camp a couple of weeks ago."

"Because her coach brought it up."

"So I shouldn't be wigging out?"

"No, you shouldn't be wigging out. I mean, at least don't wig out about Paige. There are plenty of other perfectly good reasons to wig out, beginning with the fact that your mom is gone."

Gone. The word was one of those euphemisms that some people used instead of *dead.* It sounded less harsh. It was closer to *out.* Here was the spectrum, I thought: Your mom is *out.* Your mom is *gone.* Your mom is *dead.* But I said none of that. People meant well. Heather meant well. She was a good friend.

"Okay," I agreed simply. "Can I ask you a question that might seem kind of random?"

"Sure."

"Do you think my dad might have been having an affair?"

"Why?"

"I don't know. I've just been wondering lately. There must be so much temptation."

"Because he's a college professor?"

"Yes."

She laughed. "Have you ever actually wanted to fuck one of your professors?"

"No."

"Neither have I. They think we are way hotter than we think

they are. I mean, I guess it happens—girls sleeping with their profs. Girls interested in older men. But I just don't see the attraction, do you?"

I said nothing. I reminded myself that Gavin was only twelve years my senior, not two or three decades.

"Are you asking because you think he might have had something to do with your mom's disappearance?" Heather went on.

"She didn't disappear," I told her. "She's dead. For all we know, someone killed her."

"God. Doesn't that sentence freaking terrify you? My parents actually bought an alarm system for our home after it happened. I'm not sure they used to bother to lock the doors before then. And Ellen's mom? I gather she won't even leave the house at night."

I thought about this. "Everyone tells us we have no reason to be scared," I said. I recalled how Gavin had reassured me.

"But your mom was sleepwalking when she left the house, right?"

"Right," I said. But something clicked as I spoke. We didn't know that now, did we? All we knew for sure was that she had left the house in her nightgown.

"So, something happened to her when she went outside in the middle of the night," Heather was saying. "If she didn't sleepwalk, she'd still be alive."

An idea hovered, hazy and embryonic, just beyond my reach. But it was out there. I got off the phone as quickly as I could. I called my secret vice. The next morning I met him for breakfast.

☽

"The name of the firm was Lewis, Fowler, DeGraw," I told Gavin. The two of us were meeting at a diner in Waterbury near his office, and we had both ordered waffles for the simple reason that we wanted maple syrup. The waffles themselves, he had warned me, would taste a little like paste. They did.

"I know," he said. "We've talked to people there. We've talked to her former clients from that period in her life. There is absolutely no reason to believe that anyone there would have wanted to hurt your mother."

"I figured you'd talked to them. That's not where this is going. Sorry."

"No, don't be sorry."

"Here's what I was hoping you could find out. Paige is twelve. Her birthday is March eighteenth. She was born March 18, 1988. But she was premature. She was due a month later—the middle of April. So she was conceived the previous June. My mom was still working for Lewis, Fowler, DeGraw then. I want to know if she was on any business trips early that summer."

"Because you don't believe that your father is Paige's father?"

"Maybe he is," I said. "But maybe not—because of the chromosomal abnormalities I told you about. I mean, look at the timing. My mother has a decade of miscarriages. She suddenly gets pregnant. She leaves the firm and stops traveling."

"And so you think that Paige's father is a man she met while on a business trip."

"I'm just saying it's possible. Perhaps my mom had a sleep sex encounter in a hotel and that's how Paige was conceived. Have you investigated that?"

"I can't say that we have."

I smiled. "Chalk one up for the novice."

"How does this connect to your mom's death?"

"Maybe she was meeting Paige's father the night she was killed."

"So she wasn't sleepwalking."

"That's right."

He made a pyramid with his fingers, his elbows on the table, and leaned into his hands. "Your theory is that your mother left the house in the middle of the night in her nightshirt, barefoot, to meet a man she had had sleep sex with in some hotel far from Vermont thirteen years ago. And then he killed her and threw her body into the river."

"It only sounds ridiculous when you say it out loud."

"Sorry." He looked at the silver bracelet on my wrist. "Is that new?"

"No. It was my mom's." I was relieved she hadn't worn it around him.

"It's pretty. The blue matches your eyes."

"Tell me," I said, afraid he was trying to change the subject, "did my mom ever say anything to you about Paige and sleep sex? The chronology just makes so much sense. And she told Marilyn Bryce that she thought she might have had sleep sex at least once at a hotel when she was still traveling for work."

"Okay, this is going to sound way more dismissive than I mean it to be. Forgive me. But you are really cute, and I think you have way too much time on your hands."

"You're not answering my question."

"I shouldn't because this is an open investigation. And I shouldn't because it's not fair to your mother to share with you those sorts of confidences—the things she told me in our little support group."

"But you will," I said, smiling.

He pulled his hands apart and sat back. "No," he said. "I won't."

"Will you look into my theory?"

"That Paige is a sleep sex baby?"

"God, there's a term for it."

"There's a term for everything. You're Warren Ahlberg's daughter. You know that as well as anyone."

"And is Paige his daughter, too?"

"Absolutely. Whether she has his DNA is irrelevant."

"Is that a hint?"

"No. I promise you, it's not. Whatever your mother did or did not do in a hotel in 1987 had absolutely nothing to do with her death. Nothing."

"How can you be so sure?" I asked, my face growing hot.

"Because I am."

"But how? Why?"

He took a breath and looked at me as intensely as he ever had. "Let this one go, Lianna. It's not making you happy, and it can't be good for your mental health. And it's all just a dead end. I've done this long enough that I can say that with confidence. So, please, let it go."

The waitress came over at that moment and topped off our coffee. It only took ten or fifteen seconds, but it was enough. Neither of us completely relaxed, but the thunderheads rising up between us dissipated harmlessly. When she left the table and Gavin suggested we go to a movie that Friday night, I agreed. I didn't stop thinking about whether Warren Ahlberg was really my sister's father, but I didn't bring it up for the rest of that breakfast.

And while I might have raised the issue again when I saw Gavin that weekend, I didn't. I didn't before the movie because I was just so happy to see him. And the next morning? I didn't because the night before I had finally met the sexual ogre he could become in his sleep.

And then, far worse, I had found the first of his lies.

"I KNOW YOU. I know what no one else knows about you.

"I know what you did.

"You are a coward. You are despicable. And I loathe you. I know just how much hurt you have left in your wake."

For a while, that's how I would begin my day. I would stare at myself in the mirror and say exactly those words aloud.

CHAPTER FIFTEEN

I AWOKE IN the night on my side, my back to Gavin, and felt his hands on my rear. He was prying apart my cheeks with his fingers. His police academy T-shirt, which I was sleeping in those days when I was staying at his apartment, was up over my waist. In the haze that brackets sleep, for a moment I assumed he was awake, too. The room was black. I whispered his name and he said nothing. His breathing was a guttural rustle, a moan uninterested in a response, and I understood. This was his other self. His sleeping self.

I said his name again, louder this time, planning to wake him. (Looking back, I find it revealing that I had been so irresponsible about sex. I was on the Pill and so I wasn't worried about getting pregnant, but it never crossed my mind to insist that Gavin—or any of my lovers while I was in college—wear a condom.) But then I went quiet. I was curious. I was interested to see what he would do, what this would be like. I told myself I had no reason to be frightened because this was Gavin. I could, I decided, just get out of bed if he became too rough and let him finish himself off. Apparently he had done that in the past. He might follow me, he had warned, but he had said he might not. He never knew what would happen, and he certainly couldn't control it. As a last resort, I guessed I could wake him. At least I thought I could. The issue—and now its reality gave me pause—was that he was stronger than me. He could hold me down. He might, if I couldn't rouse him, hurt me.

But he didn't.

He wasn't gentle, and he was utterly oblivious to me as a person. The novelty of the experience had me moist, and that helped. But he never bothered to roll me over, and he didn't care at all about my pleasure: he just pounded hard against me, his hands on my hips. (If there was pain, it was on the skin there, the intensity with which he was grasping my flesh; I tried to pull his hands off me, but they were epoxied there. In the morning, I would have two small, circular bruises from two of his fingers.) It wasn't violent sex, but neither was it tender. It just . . . was. And then I felt him shudder, and he pulled out and fell back into his pillow. His breathing went silent as his semen rolled down my thigh and onto the sheets.

It was odd: I didn't feel as if I had been violated. I felt it was more degrading for him than it had been for me. But I did not feel like I had been a partner—even a person—in the enterprise. It was nothing at all like when we would make love when he was awake. I also had a sense that this was, given his history, a rather tame assignation; the next time might be considerably more violent.

I wondered if tomorrow Gavin would know what he had done. And I pondered this: When it happened again—and I knew it would—what could I do to make it work for me?

☽

In the morning, I woke before Gavin. I wanted to shower. As I was passing his desk, I noticed his pocket calendar. I had seen him remove it once or twice from his blazer pocket but thought nothing of it. He had never before left it sitting, as it was right now, on his small desk beside his wallet and keys. What drew me to it that moment? Most likely it was the sleep sex. It was the connection to my mother. And so just as I had read his e-mails and my mother's e-mails, just as I had gone through their computers and drawers, I opened it. My mother had disappeared on Friday, August 25. I folded back the weeks, seduced as I was then—as I am now—by that date. What had been on his calendar that day? A haircut? A staff meeting with other detectives? A dinner with friends? On two facing pages, the calendar showed the week beginning Sunday, August 20.

And there they were, the two words. *Annalee. Bakery.*

He had written her name in that Wednesday, the twenty-third, two days before she would be killed. He had met her—or at least planned to meet her—for lunch at twelve thirty. I recalled the day. My mother had said she was meeting a possible client in Burlington about a lake house he was contemplating. But that almost certainly had been a lie. She had been meeting Gavin.

I closed the datebook and took a step away from the desk. Even if he hadn't seen Annalee Ahlberg that day—even if for some reason either he or my mother had canceled, and my mother had done something else that afternoon—they had been in contact. His insistence that he hadn't heard from her in years? An absolute lie.

And it seemed to me, if you are capable of one lie, you are capable of two. Or three. Or many. The first lie is the hardest. The rest, I had learned myself since I had started dating Gavin, came rather easily.

I turned and watched him sleeping. I thought of what had happened last night and what he had told me of his history. How much of it was the truth and how much of it was fabrication? It occurred to me that he and my mother might in fact have been lovers, a realization that sickened me, but far worse possibilities crossed my mind as well. I recalled what the coroner had stipulated as the cause of my mother's death: A subdural hematoma. A violent head injury.

I told myself that I needn't be frightened. I had been alone with Gavin a lot since we had met. But I was scared, I couldn't deny that. I went to shower as I had planned, hoping to clear my head there and decide whether to confront him with what I had learned. When I closed the bathroom door, I locked it.

☽

I dressed in the bathroom. When I emerged, he was in his kitchen making coffee; it smelled heavenly. He was wearing an old rugby shirt he liked and a pair of baggy gym shorts. He turned to me and looked a little sheepish. The sky out the window was a flat sheet of gunmetal gray. The lake was choppy.

"I woke up and was . . ." he began, his voice trailing off awkwardly. "Did something happen last night?"

I nodded.

He put the black plastic scoop back in the canister. He wrapped his arms around my waist, pulling me against him. I let him, but I was reserved. I could tell he thought it was because of the sleep sex. "I am so sorry," he murmured. "Was it awful?"

"No. It was strange. You were a little rough—"

"But only a little?"

"Maybe a little more than a little."

"Tell me the truth: Did I hurt you?"

I thought of the bruises I had noticed in the shower, but I answered, "Not really. No."

"Can you talk about it? I need to know what I did. I need to know how upset you are."

"Why?"

"Well, because I care about you. I don't want to lose you."

I pushed him away and took a step back.

"If you had to testify under oath in court," I said, speaking carefully because I knew how much I was risking, "could you honestly say you had not seen my mother in years?"

"What in the world does that have to do with last night?"

"Nothing."

"Then what's going on here? Was I talking in my sleep, too? Did I say something about her?"

"No. You were only moaning."

"Well, I guess I should be relieved. But clearly you were pretty disgusted. You are pretty disgusted."

"You left out your datebook," I told him.

His face went a little blank for a moment while he tried to understand what I was referring to. Then he leaned back against the counter and shook his head, annoyed with me. He knew what I was talking about. He knew what I had seen. "Do you make it a habit of going through people's things? Did you rifle through my wallet, too?"

"No."

"Kind of a violation, don't you think?"

"Kind of a lie, don't you think?"

"Yes."

"Why?"

"The fact I saw your mother two days before she disappeared is part of the record. Everyone who needs to know knows. I told them."

"But not me."

"Nope."

"Why not? Explain. Haven't I earned that?"

"Earned that? This isn't about recognition or achievement. It's not like you're back at college and you've passed some test."

Does anyone ever fight reasonably? Perhaps. But I've never met that person. It would have been reasonable for me to respond by reminding him that we were lovers or we were dating or, maybe, that I had a particularly vested interest in the status of the investigation. A reasonable person wouldn't have risked her life by antagonizing him. But the combination of my love for my mother and the fact he had lied to me trumped all of that. I was almost delirious. "You fucked me last night without my permission," I hissed.

"We're back there now, are we? Are you going to play the consent card? Claim I raped you? Or is this really about why I didn't tell you that I saw your mother two days before she died? Pick one and let's begin there," he said, exasperated.

"All right, why did you lie to me?"

"Because it's an ongoing investigation and you're not a cop.

I told the people who are involved. But you and me? We're not partners in this, Lianna. It was—and I am being brutally honest here—none of your business."

"Why? Because you were fucking her, too? Did you have some kinky sleep sex club? Was 'bakery' a creepy euphemism for fucking?"

"Why are you using that word?"

"Because it's violent and nasty. Because I'm really pissed off. And because you lied to me."

He went to me, his arms extended, and I batted them down. He tried again and I pushed him away. "Stay away from me," I ordered. "Don't touch me."

He stretched out his arms, palms open. "I'm unarmed," he said, trying to dial down my rage.

"Tell me why you lied."

"I just did. Because it's not your concern."

"That's not what I mean. Why did you see her the Wednesday before she disappeared?"

"Because she called me and wanted to talk."

"Why?"

"Fine. You win. Your father was about to go on a business trip, and your mother was frightened. She was afraid that what did happen might happen."

"So you met her at the bakery."

"Yup."

"How many times have you really seen her the last few years?"

He turned around and went to his bedroom. I was unsure whether to follow him, but he was gone only a moment. When he returned, he tossed the pocket calendar onto the kitchen counter beside me. "Just that one time. But if you don't believe me, thumb through it. Have a ball."

"Are you bluffing?"

"Only way you'll ever know is if you read it. Go ahead."

And so I did, while he resumed making the coffee. My mother's name appeared but once. When I put the datebook down, he said to me, "Shall we now turn our attention to what happened last night?"

"What did my mom say when you met that Wednesday?"

He took a deep breath and he told me. He shared with me her anxieties that without my father beside her, she would rise and she would roam. She might feel for a body with her fingers or legs, find none, and leave the bedroom. She would leave the house. She insisted that she hadn't had any incidents in years, but then Warren had always been in bed beside her.

"When she was done, I advised her to tell your father to stay home," he said. "I told her he should cancel the trip. I reminded her that we're never cured. Exhibit A? What I did to you last night. I said she should say to him, pure and simple, 'Don't go.' But either she convinced herself that she was worried for naught or she decided she couldn't bring herself to ask him to give up that conference."

"Which?"

"No idea. But if you made me guess, I would pick the latter. In any case, I don't believe she ever asked him to stay home. I don't know that for sure, but your father is on the record that she never asked."

I watched the coffee drip and listened to the machine's gurgle. "I think I should go," I said.

"You don't want to talk about last night?"

"No. Not now."

"Can I call you?"

I shook my head. I pulled on my boots. I went home.

☽

That night my mother came to me in my dreams. It was the first time since she had died. She gave me no clues as to what had happened to her, no insights in which I could take comfort. We were grocery shopping. The only twists my subconscious offered?

We were shopping at a supermarket that sold swim fins beside the fresh peas and carrots, and magic tricks in the same aisle with the Juicy Juice. She was wearing an ink-blue pencil skirt that was among her favorites when we were visiting Manhattan, a white blouse, and black stiletto heels. She was overdressed for a Hannaford's supermarket in rural Vermont, but in the mystifying world of a dream her attire made all the sense in the world and no one seemed to notice. Certainly I thought nothing of it. Mostly I was just happy. I was happy with the normalcy and I was happy to see her. Neither of us commented on the fact she was dead, because neither of us remembered.

And so when I awoke, I was weeping. I recalled Gavin's observation in the cruiser the day we had met back in August: at that moment, alone in my bed, I couldn't imagine anything worse than the sadness we feel when we understand an utterly perfect dream was only a tease. My mother was still dead and I was still a mess.

☽

How many times had my father looked at Paige and thought to himself, *Whose eyes are those?* Because they looked nothing like his and nothing like his late wife's. And the child's athleticism? Wholly foreign to either him or his wife. Did he ask himself about that, too?

I pondered those questions that autumn, and I decided he was too smart not to wonder. I thought about them on Halloween night, as Paige and I gave out candy to children from a front porch strangely and uncharacteristically bereft of jack-o'-lanterns. (Our mother would not have approved.) Paige did not go trick-or-treating; if one of her friends had a party, she never told me. (She said none of the seventh graders had dressed up as Al Gore or George Bush, but one group of girls was decked out in long black tunics and sunglasses à la *The Matrix*.) The questions were with me as the first snow fell on November 1 and the deadline passed to tell my college I was coming back. I wasn't. At least not in January.

I thought about the mysteries of sleep and conception when my sister's ski coach called the house, looking for our father, and asked me why my sister was having second thoughts about Chile—why suddenly she wasn't going. He wanted to see if our father could change her mind and rekindle her interest. And, yes, I thought about them when I listened to the messages from Gavin Rikert on my cell phone, none of which I had returned. I missed him, and the sound of his voice could make me at once wistful and giddy. But I wasn't sure I could trust him. The fact is, there was a part of me now that feared him.

Erica continued to beg me to please phone the registrar at Amherst, insisting it wasn't too late. Gavin continued to beg me to please call him back, trying to convince me that I was over-reacting. And my father? He asked for nothing. I made my family breakfast and dinner, and I drove my sister to the mountain, where now they were making snow, instead of to the swimming pool at the college. I made sure that my father had his scotch and my sister had batteries for her Game Boy. I cut cards and talked to myself, pretending it was patter. I voted for the first time in my life, using a pencil and a piece of paper in a three-sided wooden booth because this was a small village in Vermont that had no need for voting machines. Occasionally my mother's friends or the pastor would phone the house to check in, and I would lie and say we were fine. Sometimes my own friends would call and plead with me to join them for a movie or a drink or to get high. They wanted to talk about the election and Florida, and how a presidential contest could become such a disaster. But always I passed. Mostly those weeks I read and I dozed, and I would lie on the floor before the wood stove and beside Joe the Barn Cat. Sometimes he would get up and wander upstairs to the guest room with my mother's drafting table and computer, where he would sniff at her handbag and a scarf on the credenza, and then curl up on her chair. It broke my heart to see how much he missed her, too.

OTHER DAYS I would say, "Forgive yourself. They would. They will."

But I couldn't. I can't. It's one of those things, like losing weight or being patient or following through on any New Year's resolution, that's just so much easier said than done.

CHAPTER SIXTEEN

TWO WEEKS BEFORE Thanksgiving, my father announced that Grandpa Manholt, my mother's father, had invited us to Concord for the holiday. In my family, Thanksgiving had always been a movable feast with three rotating locations: our home in Vermont, my aunt and uncle's apartment in Manhattan, and my grandparents' majestic (and rather mannered) colonial in Massachusetts. It was technically our turn, but no one expected the Ahlbergs of Vermont to be capable of hosting a family gathering. Moreover, my grandfather could no longer care for my grandmother, and so he and my aunt had decided it was time for my grandmother to move into an assisted living facility that specialized in patients with Alzheimer's. That would occur at some point before Christmas, and so this was a last hurrah of sorts: another sad landmark in a season that was crowded with them. But Paige and I told our father that we were fine with the idea of one final Thanksgiving with everyone gathered at Grandma and Grandpa's; the three of us would drive down the day before and spend a few days in the Boston suburbs. My father suggested we could all go into the city on Black Friday and face the madness and the crowds on Newbury Street. I had expected Paige to resist, since that would mean she wouldn't be skiing on Saturday, but she hadn't objected. She hadn't even brought up the conflict. Like me, she was sinking as inexorably as our mother; it was taking more time, but the course for us both was clear. Eventually, it seemed, we both would hit bottom.

☽

"And so we meet again," said Dr. Cindy Yager, smiling. "Want to split another granola bar?"

This time I was not in her office. I was in her examining room instead, a few doors down from her office and across the hall, seated atop the cushioned table with a paper sheet. It resembled the examining room of the pediatrician I had seen as a little girl and the examining room of the family practitioner I saw now as an adult. Narrow, antiseptic, and decorated with a diploma and a health poster—this one about proper sleep hygiene, with a child's crayon drawings of sheep and stars and a four-poster bed. The biggest difference between this room and the ones in which I had been examined before? We were on the fourth floor of an impressive hospital complex and so there was a window. The view of Lake Champlain and the Adirondacks was similar to the one in reception: a tourist postcard that trumped most artwork Yager (or any physician) was likely to use to try and brighten the space. I was still in my jeans and a sweater, but I knew the flimsy gown loomed. There was a folded one beside me on the examining table.

"No, I'm fine," I said, trying to sound agreeable. My father and Paige were in the waiting room. Paige and I had flipped a coin to see who would go first. I'd lost.

"This will be a pretty low-key physical," she said, leaning against the counter opposite me. "I won't be drawing blood, for instance. Mostly I just want to get a medical history."

"Did my mom tell you much about my sleepwalking as a girl?"

"A little bit. With your permission, I'll want to ask your father what he recalls."

"That's fine. I mean, I really didn't do much. I woke up a couple of times and didn't recognize them. Pretty common, right?"

She held her clipboard against her chest like a shield and corrected me: "There was more. Considerably more. You know that."

I realized that my mother must have told her about the time I wound up in their bathroom after the miscarriage. But I was a little taken aback by how dire the physician made it sound. "The bathroom and the Barbie dollhouse," I said.

"Yes. And your father told me about the night you emptied out your bureau when you were in kindergarten. All your clothes were on the floor in the morning."

I had never heard this story. I tried to downplay my surprise with a joke. "Well, I do that now when I'm awake—before dates."

"And then there was the time you wandered downstairs and rearranged the logs beside the woodstove."

I sat up a little straighter and tried to muzzle my wariness. This, too, was news to me. "What did my dad—or maybe my mom— tell you about that?"

She shrugged. "You took the wood that was piled near the stove and made a little corral for your plastic horses on the carpet."

"Sounds pretty harmless," I said defensively, but I wished I could recall anything from this nocturnal adventure.

"So, is it now my turn to ask you some questions, Lianna?"

"May I have one more?"

"Absolutely."

"Am I definitely going to have to spend the night being wired? And, if yes, when?"

"That's two questions," she replied, raising a single eyebrow good-naturedly. Then: "Not definitely, no. Let's see. And it would probably be in a month or so, based on my schedule."

"Paige, too?"

"Correct."

"So, we're talking December for the both of us?"

"That sounds about right."

"Do you still do the sleep studies at the hotel?"

"We do."

"I am so not looking forward to that," I told her. "All the wires. My mom said you even wire the eyes."

"Your mom fell asleep. You'll be fine."

"If it comes to that," I said hopefully.

She nodded. It was clear she was confident that it would.

☽

"I thought she was nice," Paige was saying from the backseat in the car on the way home, referring to Cindy Yager. Our father was driving, and I was in the front seat beside him.

"I'm glad," our father said, his face lost in the evening shadows.

"But I wish Lianna and I could have our sleep test in the same room. It would be kind of like we were on vacation." For years when our family went away, our parents would have one hotel room and Paige and I would share another.

"Kind of," I agreed, though I understood why we needed separate rooms and how the experience would be nothing at all like a typical night at a Sheraton. I knew that Paige understood this, too.

"And a hotel breakfast the next morning? That's cool," she went on.

"Waffles," our father murmured, knowing my kid sister's affection for them. "I have always liked waffles in winter. They are definitely a winter food group for me."

"Dad?" she asked after a moment.

I saw him glance into the rearview mirror. "Yes, sweetie?"

"Where were you the night Mom had her sleep study?"

"I was home with you girls."

"And then you picked up Mom after you got us off to school? You went and got her?"

"Oh, no. Your mom drove herself home from the hotel that morning. Twice."

"Twice?"

"Well, not really. But your mother was so disoriented when she woke up in the morning that she forgot her eyeglasses in the hotel room. She had actually driven about five miles before she realized why the world was so foggy."

"Kind of dangerous," I said. "Will we be that disoriented?"

"I doubt it. Your mother was a rarity in a lot of ways."

"Don't worry," Paige said to me. "You won't come home and build a pen for your toy horses by the wood stove."

"I should never have told you that," I said.

"Nope," she agreed. Then to our father she asked, "But you'll be spending the night at the hotel while we're being tested, right?"

"Yes. Absolutely. But you really have no reason to worry—no reason at all."

"I guess."

"And let's face it," I added. "Most of the time you're a world-class sleeper."

She folded her arms across her chest. "This was my big idea in the first place, remember? I think you are way more worried than I am."

That probably wasn't true: Paige was anxious, too. That was clear. But she was right: as I had confessed to Cindy Yager, I was dreading that night.

☽

The day after Paige and I were examined at the sleep center, Gavin showed up at our house. It was late Friday morning and I was—as I was most of the time—alone. I considered not answering the bell when I saw who it was, but I did. I was unable not to: I could feel my color rising. On some level, I had to know that by opening the door I was letting him back into my life. I told myself that I would find out what he wanted and send him away, but I must have known in my heart that in the end I would be incapable. I didn't believe he was coming with new information about my mother's death. If the investigation had had some sort of unexpected breakthrough, he would have contacted my father. Besides, he had brought flowers. It was clear he had come only for me.

"I see you're expecting company," he said, pulling off his aviators and smiling. I had brushed my hair that morning, but otherwise I had dressed primarily for Joe the Barn Cat. I was wearing my pajama bottoms and an especially ratty college hoodie.

"What do you want?"

He extended the bouquet in my direction. He raised his eyebrows boyishly. I took the flowers without saying a word and motioned him into the house. He knelt and started to untie his shoes, and I told him not to bother.

"Because I'm not staying long?" he asked.

"Because I haven't vacuumed today, and your shoes don't look all that messy."

"The house looks nice. It was so crowded the last time I was here, it was hard to see how well designed all the spaces are—how light and open it is, especially for an old Victorian in Vermont."

"My mom was an architect, remember?" I got a vase from the dining room sideboard and a pair of scissors from a kitchen drawer. I remembered how my mother always snipped the stems of cut flowers before placing them in water. He'd put his sunglasses down on the kitchen island exactly where I wanted to arrange the lilies and irises and daisies. I pushed them against the wooden knife block. "What would you have done if my father was home? You know I didn't want him to know about us. I wasn't even sure you wanted him to know about us." I hadn't snarled, but neither had I hid my disgust.

"His car was gone. And—oh, by the way—he teaches Friday morning."

"Is there nothing you haven't researched about my family? Do you have any idea how creepy you just sounded?" I asked, irked by his knowledge of the Ahlbergs and our routines.

"A: there is plenty I don't know about you. And B: at different times in different conversations, both you and your father have told me that he has a class on Friday mornings. Contemporary American Poetry. It didn't take a stalker to figure that one out."

"And that ethical line?"

He shrugged. "A gray area. I know cops who've done much worse."

I shook my head. "You know, I used to be afraid that you and my mom were lovers. Now I wonder if you killed her. I really do, you know." I had said it facetiously, but a part of me still doubted him.

"And yet you let me into the house."

I motioned at the knife block and arched my eyebrows. I squeezed the scissors twice so they made a loud snipping sound.

"Why do you keep wanting to view this story as a late-night crime drama?" he asked me. "Why can't this be a romance?"

"I used to think it might be. I told myself that very thing in the car when we were driving to Montreal."

"And wasn't that a great day? A great evening?" He spread out his arms and grinned almost impishly. "Why can't I be your Mr. Darcy? Or, given my age, your Colonel Brandon?"

"Have you actually read Jane Austen?"

"Not a single word. But I have a sister."

"Well, this isn't a Jane Austen novel."

"Fair enough. But we're not talking Hitchcock, either, Lianna," he said softly. "Your mother's story is a tragedy; it's horrible. It's devastating. But it's not your story. It's not our story—at least it doesn't have to be."

"Someone killed her."

"Stop thinking like that."

"Stop thinking like that? How can you say that?"

"Because I can."

"Because you and the rest of the police can't solve the crime. Because none of you really know anything," I snapped at him, frustrated. "It's not your mother who was murdered."

"We don't know your mother was murdered!"

"Of course she was."

"No. We don't know that. You don't know that. We know she had a head injury. We know she wound up in the river. That's all we know."

"Then what? Name one thing that could have happened to her. She sure as heck didn't just walk into the river where we found that piece of her nightgown."

"Must we do this?"

"Yes!"

He folded his arms across his chest and leaned against a pantry door. I waited. "Fine. She didn't walk into the river. She jumped off the bridge and hit her head on a rock."

"She would have drowned, you know that."

"She jumped off the bridge and hit her head on a rock but made it back to the surface. She hung on to the rock. Or maybe she dog-paddled to the shore but couldn't climb out. She was too weak and injured. She died there and slipped back into the current."

For a long moment I stood there, picturing this. I had thought about this possibility, but only in the abstract. I had never envisioned the specifics: my mother awakened by the cool river water and the blow to the back of her head, clinging to a rock as she bled out before, finally, losing consciousness. Or making it to the riverbank and trying to climb from the Gale, but too injured or frail, and so there she hangs on until, finally, she slides back in. In both scenarios, I heard her crying out for help. But maybe she didn't. Maybe she was disoriented. Or she was incapable. Either way, she dies alone on the surface or the side of the river.

I sat down—collapsed, really—onto one of the barstools around the kitchen island. I felt a little dizzy, as if I had bent over and stood up too quickly. I rested my head on the palm of my hand. Gavin remained where he was, staring straight at me. Gone was any hint of levity from his expression. "God . . ." I murmured.

"Remember, your mother was my friend, too. If there was a killer out there, don't you think I would be pretty damn invested in finding out who that person was? Don't you?"

"So you think she went back to the bridge."

"I don't know what else to think."

"Why was a part of her nightgown on that branch?"

He shrugged. "It was between your house and the bridge. It was near enough to the road."

"What else?" I asked.

"What do you mean, what else?"

"What other possibilities have you considered?"

"Stop torturing yourself. Please. For your sake and mine. Would you do that?"

"Does my father know this theory?"

"I guess."

"You guess?"

"We have never discussed these . . . specifics."

"Oh."

"You're a tad more passionate, Lianna."

"I know. He's given up."

"You sound so dismissive. He lost his wife. He's mourning."

"Well, I lost my mom."

"People are built differently."

I sighed, gathering myself. "I guess."

"Are you going to be okay?"

"Yes."

"Honestly?"

"Honestly."

"Good. Can I tell you one more thing?"

"Sure." I waited. I watched as he started to smile and his eyes grew playful.

"You look cute in pajamas."

"Really: Why did I let you into the house?" I asked.

"Because it's almost noon and you haven't gotten dressed. Clearly I'm the bright spot in your day." He went around the island to stand behind me. Over my shoulder I heard him say, "Since we both know you aren't going to tell your father and Paige that these are from me, I suggest you say you got them to cheer yourself up."

"See what a good liar you are?" I murmured. But then I felt him kissing the back of my neck, and I had neither the strength nor the inclination to stop him.

☽

Much of the world grows quiescent in autumn, but Vermont can feel especially depressing and (yes) dead those first weeks of November. The days are short and growing shorter still. But I watched the endless election news from Florida—the world's ultimate game of musical chairs had actually ended in a tie—and so I saw sunshine and blue sky there. On television. Often I saw all that warmth after starting a fire in the wood stove.

And yet a notable exception to the meteorological grayness that envelops northern New England that time of year are the mountains where we make snow. I was never the skier that my sister was, but even I appreciated that a whole other world existed when you slid off the top of the lift and paused for a moment amid the evergreens iced with vanilla.

On the Saturday morning after Gavin had come by my house, I watched Paige and the rest of the ski team practice on one of the black diamond trails, a little awed by their speed and athleticism, the way they bounced over the moguls, but then I set off on my own and skied the intermediate slopes where I was most comfortable. The sky was cloudless and blue—a respite from the usual gray—and in my breath I saw the promise of the holiday season.

Summer—and my mother's death—began to seem very far away. I told myself I was getting better, not growing callous, and it did not diminish my mother's memory when something would take my mind off her.

$$\smallint$$

"I thought you looked pretty good out there," I told Paige as we were driving home that afternoon.

"Your goggles must have been fogged up. Or you couldn't see in the glare. I sucked."

I was a little startled. "You didn't suck."

"I'll be better on Tuesday," she said. That was the day when the team would have its next practice. Then she asked me, "So who really gave you the posies?" She had brought up the flowers out of the blue to try and catch me off guard; I knew her well enough to know how her mind worked.

"I told you," I answered blandly. "I treated myself. I treated us."

"I don't think so. I think whoever brought them is the same

person who left his sunglasses at our house. The Ray-Bans sitting right now by Mom's knives."

A little flutter of panic rolled over me, and instantly I started rummaging in my mind for names I could claim had been in our kitchen. But I drew a blank and said nothing. I kept my eyes on the tortuous two-lane road down from the mountain so I wouldn't have to look at my sister.

"Not even going to lie, eh?" she said, and then she laughed. "Feeling a little busted?"

"Only a little."

"Are you going to tell me?"

"I don't know."

"Please?"

She must have sensed I was weakening. She turned off the radio.

"Fine," I said. "But don't tell Dad."

"I won't."

"One of the detectives investigating Mom's death gave me the flowers. A guy with BCI—"

"BCI?"

"Bureau of Criminal Investigation. A part of the state police."

"A state trooper?"

"Sort of."

"And he was at our house yesterday?"

"That's right," I said. I couldn't tell whether she was a little floored because I was seeing a cop or because the cop had been at our home. But when she spoke next, I understood it was the latter that had caused her voice to rise ever so slightly in astonishment.

"Why? What happened? Did they learn something new?" she asked.

"No. He came by to bring me the flowers."

"That's it?"

"Isn't that enough dish for one car ride?"

"How long have you been seeing him?"

"Actually, I hadn't seen him in a while. I thought we were over. But then he showed up with the flowers and I guess we're not."

"What's his name?"

"Gavin."

"Gavin what?"

"Rikert."

"Is he old?"

"No!" I didn't take my eyes off the road, but I knew she was smirking. "You talked to him the day Mom disappeared."

"I talked to so many people."

"I know. We both did," I agreed.

"He was at the funeral, wasn't he?" I could hear in her voice the way she was putting his name to a face.

"Yup."

"Any special reason why you don't want Dad to know?"

"I'm not sure. It's a little weird that we're dating. I guess it happens sometimes. But, also, he and Mom were friends . . . sort of."

"Friends," she murmured, as if she were trying the word out. Then: "What kind of friends?"

"It's complicated. They were—"

"Okay, that's just gross," she said, interrupting me. "Are you really about to tell me that our mom had an affair, and now you're dating the guy? The same guy? Seriously? If so, then you are responsible for the most puke-worthy thing in the history of the world."

"It wasn't like that at all."

"Then what was it like? Explain it to me."

"First of all, Mom was not having an affair with him," I told her. "Okay? She loved Dad."

"Go on."

"Second, they were friends from the sleep center."

"Is he a sleepwalker, too?"

"Yes."

"And what do you mean by 'friends'?"

"Just that. They had coffee a couple of times to compare notes about their sleepwalking."

"Okay, so you're involved with something that's puke-worthy—but not historically so."

"Why would you say that?" I asked.

"God, haven't you had enough of sleepwalking?"

"Sleepwalking doesn't define him any more than it defined Mom."

She put the heels of her feet on the seat and wrapped her arms around her ski pants. "Did he say anything more to you about the investigation? I'm sure he did."

We reached the bottom of the hill and the traffic that invariably formed at the stop sign this time of the day in November: a long line of salt-splattered cars with skis and snowboards in roof racks. "Yeah, he did," I confessed. "But don't get your hopes up. It was nothing really helpful."

"Tell me."

"He thinks maybe she jumped off the bridge. She jumped off the bridge and hit her head on a rock, but she wasn't killed right away. That's why she didn't drown."

I expected her to say something right away, but she didn't. I turned to her. She was staring straight ahead and she looked grim. "You're right. That's not very helpful," she said finally, her voice soft and throaty. "But it is awful. Just . . . awful."

I nudged our mother's car forward and waited once more. "You, okay?" I asked.

"Yeah, I'm fine." Then: "I mean, that's something we both guessed might have happened. It's just a horrible way to die."

"Yup."

"So, Mom wasn't murdered. Is that what they're saying now?"

"Well, they're not saying anything. That's just the guess of one detective."

She sighed and stared out her window. At the corner was a log cabin diner and sandwich shop that catered to skiers.

"You want anything?" I asked. "A hot chocolate?"

She shook her head.

"Maybe some popcorn to munch on?"

"No," she said, a yawn interrupting and elongating that one small syllable. "I just want to go home." Then she leaned back against the headrest and closed her eyes.

☽

Would it have made any difference if Paige had told our father about Gavin? Would it have made any difference if I had?

I used to wonder about this, playing out the cause and effect that either of us might have unleashed, the alternate ways our family's tensile core might have been fractured. When I would be awake in the small hours of the night, I'd speculate that something might have changed had either of us, for different reasons, told our father then that I was seeing the detective. A grown-up—someone more grown up than I was at twenty-one—would have done something.

But as I stared out the window at the night sky or at the dark ceiling above me, I could never see what that something might have been. What is the opposite of postponing the inevitable? Prepone? Expedite? Hasten? Eventually, I came to the vaguely Calvinist certainty that telling our father would only have accelerated our fate. It would, in fact, have changed nothing. After all, by then the die had been cast.

IT WAS DARK and macabre, but I made deals. Think Kübler-Ross. I would say, it's okay if I have sleep sex, just so long as I don't get out of bed. Please, I would pray, whatever I do, let it be only in this room.

Because most of the damage that I did and most of the pain that I caused happened when I left the room. When I got out of bed. Despite all the nocturnal hypersexuality they filmed, they never captured what I was really capable of—because that would have meant following me out into the night.

CHAPTER SEVENTEEN

OVER THANKSGIVING, WHILE visiting our grandparents in Concord, Paige and I watched a stack of VHS cassettes of my family.
Our mother had brought them to Massachusetts the last time we
had had Thanksgiving here so she could share them with her parents. The two of us watched them on Thursday night, long after
we had finished dinner and everyone else—including my aunt and
uncle and our cousins—had retreated to their bedrooms to read or
sleep. My father was in almost none of the short videos, because he
was usually the one behind the camcorder. So, it was mostly my
mother and Paige and me on the TV screen. There was my mother
dipping me in a blue kiddie pool I vaguely recalled in our backyard, and there were all three Ahlberg females at Disney World in
front of Peter Pan's Flight: above and behind us was the crocodile
with his Victorian lantern and rows of dagger-like teeth. (Our
father zoomed in on him and made the iconic tick-tock sounds
with his tongue.) There we were hiking Camel's Hump one year
and Snake Mountain another. There we were skiing. There I was
doing a magic trick at a middle school variety show, making the
bright-red bowling pins I had given a father and mother from the
audience disappear from the tubes they were holding and then
reappear in a box at their feet.

In the end, the experience was far more wrenching than looking at the images in the photo albums had been: the sound of
Annalee Ahlberg's voice wrecked my sister and me. When we had

started to watch, mostly we had been laughing at the memories and making jokes about our parents or how we were dressed. But the experience grew sad fast. Soon we were watching in almost absolute silence; without saying a word, one of us would eject the cassette when it was over and put another one in. We no longer looked at each other, both of us lost in our private yearnings for our mother—a need for her that was almost like food after days and days without eating. I know I cried myself to sleep that night, and I think it is likely that my sister did, too.

☽

My father and I were cleaning up the kitchen and loading my grandparents' dishwasher after breakfast on Black Friday. "Are you still nervous about having to spend a night wired in a couple of weeks?" he asked me, referring to the sleep center.

We were alone in the kitchen. I had been leaning over, lining up plates in the bottom rack. I stood up. "Yes. I think I'm going to hate it," I told him. "I think it's going to be awful."

"No. I told you, even your mother fell asleep." He was drying the skillet in which our aunt had made scrambled eggs. After a long moment he said, "The night your mother died . . ."

I waited.

"Did I ever tell you about our last phone call?" he asked.

"No."

"Did she?"

"You mean before she went to sleep?"

He nodded.

"She didn't," I answered. "I guess I figured you two talked that night. But Mom never said anything."

"Good."

"Good?"

"I was busy at the conference. I was presenting an important paper the next day—at least I was supposed to. And I was seeing people that night. When I think about our very last conversation, I've always been afraid that I was a little short."

I was moved that he wanted to get this off his chest and had selected me as his confessor: I hated to think of him living with that regret. But I also felt a small pang of anger that he had been—as he put it—short with my mother. And that might have been that, those two reactions jostling for my attention. But then he asked two more questions in rapid succession that left me as unsettled as ever.

"So she never said a word to you about our conversation that night?" he asked once more.

"No."

"And you never said a word to the police?"

"No," I repeated. "There was nothing to say. Why?"

He sighed. "No reason, really. I just don't want them to think any worse of me than they already must." Then he added, "I hate platitudes. I really do. But sometimes I believe we would all be better off if we always treated people like this was the last time we were ever going to see them."

☽

"God, what would your mother have done if she'd had boys?" my grandfather said to me that afternoon. We were standing outside a gallery near the corner of Newbury and Fairfield in Boston. He was smiling as he peered into the gallery window and pointing at an oil painting of a woman in her early thirties from the 1920s surrounded by her three children—all boys, which was what had triggered his observation in the first place.

"She would have figured it out," I said lightly, but recalling my mother with pride. "You know your daughter. She would have figured boys out just fine."

It was brisk, and the air was charged with anticipation for most of the people we passed on the street. I hadn't expected my grandfather to come with us into the city, but my aunt and uncle had offered to stay behind in Concord with my grandmother, and I was pleased. It made the excursion seem a little more festive. It meant that my father and Paige and I weren't once more left alone to our own devices and private pain.

"You're right," my grandfather said. "After all, look how well she did with Paige!" He was joking, of course, a reference to the simple reality that my sister was something of an athletic outlier among us. But boyish? Not Paige. It was an offhand remark about one of his granddaughters that was nonsensical, and maybe another day I would have let it go. Looking back, my father certainly planned to. But I didn't.

"Since when is it boyish to be a great athlete? Kind of a sexist thing to say, don't you think, Grandpa?" I asked, and I put my arm around Paige's shoulder, squeezing it through the down of her parka. I was hoping to convey solidarity, nothing more.

"You're right! I am showing my age. I'm sorry, Paige," he said.

But Paige surprised me; she probably surprised us all. She ducked out from under my arm, pulling away swiftly, and stood with her back to the gallery glass. "I don't need you to defend me," she snapped, setting her jaw stubbornly. "And I don't need you to say you're sorry, Grandpa. I just don't. Mom . . ."

"Mom what?" I asked. All of us—my grandfather, my father, and I—waited.

"Mom knew me better than anyone," she said, and she shook her head, a little disgusted with the three of us. "And I knew her better than anyone." Then she used her fingers to brush her windblown black hair back behind her ears and glared at us, her head lowered ever so slightly. I almost told her she was beautiful when she was mad—because she was—but I didn't dare say another word.

☽

The rest of my family returned to Concord late that Friday afternoon, but I stayed in Boston and met my college friend Erica, whose family lived in Brookline; she'd taken the Green Line into town but said she would drive me back to my grandparents' after we had a drink. She was twenty-one now, too, and it felt very grown-up to be able to meet at a bar in Boston and each of us have a glass of wine. Erica had never been the stoner I was, though she drank considerably more keg beer at college than I ever did. I had seen her once since we had left Amherst in May, and that had been at my mother's funeral. We hadn't gotten to speak very much that day; she had driven up from the college that morning and driven back that afternoon.

We met at five thirty outside the bar, arriving there at almost the same moment, and when we peered inside from the doorway we saw beneath a galaxy of Christmas lights that it was packed shoulder to shoulder with raucous people in their twenties and thirties, and it was so loud it would be impossible to have a meaningful conversation. There was no place to sit. We would get hit on by young stockbrokers and young advertising executives, and it was absolutely no place for a real reunion. We left and started walking aimlessly down Boylston toward the library and Copley Square, and it was dusk and the streetlamps were beautiful. It felt like it might snow.

I noticed that Erica didn't want to talk about college, changing the subject gracefully whenever I mentioned what had once been our shared world. I could tell she felt bad that I wasn't coming back in the spring: it was as if she were leaving me behind. But when she brought up my mother's death, trying to deflect my inquiries about her thesis or our mutual friends, I brushed her aside. I needed a respite after last night's videocassettes and the fact that I had just spent all day with my family. So she actually asked me about my magic, feigning interest in the children's parties that—other than Gavin and the local elementary school and the ski slopes—were the only part of my life that existed outside of the red Victorian. I looked at her and raised an eyebrow. My magic, it seemed to me that moment, was ridiculous. Lianna the Enchantress was ridiculous.

"I miss watching you practice!" she insisted, and I thought about all the times I had made her watch me make scarves disappear in ornate little boxes or paper flowers appear in what had been empty glass vases. I stood up straighter as we strolled; suddenly I was afraid I was collapsing in upon myself, shrinking with sadness and loss. I wanted Gavin, I realized, I wanted that feeling of anticipation I had when I knew I was going to see him; I wanted that rush I felt when I was back in his arms.

"I think my sister will have a stroke if she hears me one more time," I said, and I could sense how remote I sounded.

Erica said nothing in response—really, what was there to say?—and it's possible that our friendship might have begun to evaporate forever right there on Boylston Street. We had lost all commonality, and now we would just grow apart. But then an empty cab stopped at the traffic light, and Erica abruptly pulled me inside it.

"Where are we going?" I asked.

"One of my friends from high school is having a party. She has her own apartment now in Cambridge."

"Really? I won't know anyone."

"Doesn't matter. It will be good for you. It will be good for us."

The taxi smelled of beer even worse than the bar, and when I looked down I saw why: an empty Heineken bottle was on its side, the last of its contents on the floor mat. When the cabbie accelerated through the light, the bottle rolled against the bottom of the seat and tinkled with a weirdly appropriate holiday-season cheer. The driver heard it, swore in a language I didn't recognize, and stopped at the next red light. There he climbed out, opened the back door, and grabbed the bottle with the urgency of a mother plucking a child from harm's way on a busy city street. He was furious. He slammed our door and dropped the bottle into a metal garbage can on the corner—or, to be precise, smashed it into the garbage can. We could hear it break even inside the vehicle. When he got back in, he turned to us and said, his dark eyes piercing us with rage, "My cab is not a speakeasy. No drinking, do you two understand?"

"It wasn't my Heineken," I said. Erica was glaring daggers at him from her side of the seat.

"I know that! It belonged to the idiots I kicked out before I saw you two."

And then we set off, and it might have been the smell of the beer and it might have been the way the cabbie drove with undisguised rage, starting and stopping, but suddenly I was clammy and nauseous. Before I could stop myself, I added to the reek of the cab by vomiting between my legs and onto the floor.

"No, no! How dare you!" he yelled. "How dare you!"

"I'm sorry," I groaned. "Can you stop? Please? Can you pull over?"

Erica found a small packet of tissues in her purse, but they were mere sandbags against a tsunami. The driver pulled over against the curb, still blocks from Storrow Drive, and I mopped the floor mat and the back of the front seat. (I wouldn't allow Erica to help; I was ashamed and this was penance.) I had a little bottle of perfume in my purse, and without telling the cabbie I sprayed some into the rear of the vehicle. Erica paid the angry man, tipping him well after my meltdown.

"I am so sorry," I said, taking a deep breath. "Now what?"

She looked at me as deeply as she ever had: "Are you seeing someone? Are you pregnant?"

"No. I'm still on the Pill," I told her, and then added quickly, "Not that it would matter, because I'm not seeing anyone. I'm just . . ."

"Tell me."

"I just think I'm really close to falling apart some days."

She put her arm around my shoulders and started walking me past the long block of stately brownstones, some of which already were festive with Christmas lights. I saw one family trimming their tree through the bay window, and I felt as if I had traveled back in time to my parents' or even my grandparents' childhood. The father was actually wearing a sweater vest. "We're just going to get you some crisp, fresh night air. We'll promenade," she said. She waved cheerfully at a woman walking a pair of tiny dogs in black dog booties and an older couple in elegant Burberry trench coats and scarves; she knew none of them. We had walked four blocks and I was feeling better, and my dreamlike fear that our friendship was failing began to evaporate. We'd be fine. Still, I apologized once more.

"Stop that. You've been through a lot."

"I guess."

"I still remember meeting your mom. Parents Weekend our first year."

I nodded. She hadn't met my mother the day I moved into the dormitory because my family had already come and gone. They had dropped me off and settled me in by the time Erica and her parents arrived.

"I thought she was so glamorous," Erica went on. "Not what I expected from a rube like you from Vermont."

I knew what Erica meant. I wasn't insulted at all. "She was, wasn't she?"

"And she used to walk so fast," said Erica, nodding. "Those great big strides. She was wearing such hip boots that weekend we met. I loved them."

I recalled how my father sometimes teased her for walking so quickly. When Paige had been little, she'd practically had to skip to keep up (which was usually fine with Paige; like her mother, she was rarely a body at rest). "I remember those boots," I said.

"I mean, even when that annoying client called her that afternoon, your mom was so together. That was among my very first impressions of your mom: dialing down a madman. She was so firm. So totally in the captain's chair."

"The Friday of Parents Weekend," I murmured.

"She was so chill. Ice queen cool. And whoever it was, was so . . . desperate. Remember?"

I did. I had forgotten, but it came back to me now. It was the sort of moment that might bewitch a young person meeting my stunning, statuesque mother for the first time. We had been walking across the quad toward Johnson Chapel, Erica's family and mine, and my mother had taken a call on a cell phone that was still a clam shell. She slowed her gait to give herself privacy, and we had gotten a little ahead of her. But soon we were at the entrance to the nineteenth-century brick chapel, where the president was going to address the parents, and my mother was now two dozen yards behind us on the grass. My father seemed at ease, but I wanted us to get inside and choose our seats. Erica's family did, too. And so I had gone to retrieve my mother, and Erica had, for whatever the reason, accompanied me.

"I would tell you to relax and get some sleep—get over it—but obviously that's not the answer," my mother was saying, the autumn sun on her hair. Her back was to us. "And, frankly, this is neither the time nor the place to discuss this. I'm sorry, but that's just how it is. I can't help you. I never could help you. Don't you see? I can't even help myself." When she turned and saw the two of us motioning for her to hurry up, she looked at us and said firmly into the phone, "I'm sorry, but I think you need to find another architect." Then she snapped the phone shut. "Well, I just fired a client," she told us. She sounded neither bitter nor sad. She sounded as if a weight had been lifted from her shoulders.

As Erica and I walked along that Boston street a little more than three years later, I recalled the e-mail I had found on Gavin's computer—the very last one from my mother. The one where she had canceled on him because it was my first Parents Weekend, and she had written that she and my father and Paige were driving to Massachusetts that Friday.

My mother hadn't been speaking to a client as she had stood on the college quadrangle before Johnson Chapel. She had been talking to Gavin. If she had been firing anyone, she had been—and I knew these weren't the right words, but they were the ones I heard in my head that Thanksgiving weekend—firing him.

☽

All young parents watch their children sleep. We stand over the crib, the bed with rails, and then the bed without rails, and we smile at the utter miracle and welcoming innocence that is a child asleep. We watch them dream, wondering what they are seeing as they stretch out their small fingers or pedal their knees once or twice. We savor the aroma of baby shampoo or strawberry shampoo. We adjust a blanket. We kiss a forehead or cheek. Before we leave, we check the thermostat.

I do all that now, decades removed from the summer my mother disappeared.

But you can bet that I also watch my own children for any signs of parasomnia. I watch for arousal disorders and night terrors and sleepwalking. I think more than any parents I am likely to meet at my children's elementary school about—and here is a technical term that many husbands (though not mine) would find baffling—sleep-stage transition impositions.

So far there have been none. There have been no parasomnias at all. Both of my children seem fine. I pray—and I pray with a self-taught and childlike innocence, the way I learned when I was twenty-one and would roam alone through the red Victorian—that they have been spared that part of their family history. The odds still are against them.

They have their grandmother's eyes and their grandmother's lush yellow mane. A boy and a girl. Someday, they will be knockouts.

☽

On Saturday morning, over Thanksgiving weekend, while Paige was asleep in the guest room we shared at our grandparents' and my father was grading papers, I drove to Somerville to have breakfast with Rowland the Rogue. I had suggested any old diner or bakery, but he insisted on having me to his home, and that meant we ate in his pleasantly retro kitchen: the dining room, after all, was cluttered with old magic tricks. But the kitchen was perfect, even though I always felt when we sat there that I was visiting the set of a black-and-white sitcom from the 1950s. The appliances were from the Eisenhower administration, and one time he had shown me the warranties with pride to prove it. The knobs and handles were chrome, and looked like they were from a space-ship in a low-budget science fiction film, and the white siding on the stove and the refrigerator was badly chipped. Though he had traveled for much of his career and lived on second-rate room ser-vice at second-rate hotels, he was a very good cook: rather effort-lessly he made me eggs Benedict that morning and served the two English muffins on rose-colored china that had once belonged to his mother. For a while he regaled me with tales of tricks that had failed or illusions that had bombed, and how he had responded onstage. I had a sense he was exaggerating: he would not have had the career that he did if he were flubbing routines as epically as he was suggesting in his stories. He would not have been on prime-time television shows.

"Tell me more about the Sleepwalker—that illusion you per-formed on *Sonny and Cher,*" I said, dabbing with a napkin at the hollandaise sauce that I feared was on my lips. "Were you a good enough hypnotist that you could have done the trick without using an audience plant?"

He folded his arms across his chest and rocked back on the two hind legs of his chair. "I could have hypnotized a person and convinced her to walk to a platform and wind up doused in a dunk tank. But you know how the levitating woman works. I need an accomplice. I need a mesh form roughly the shape of her body under the sheet. I need a secret escape from the couch, so she can get offstage."

I did know the secret behind the illusion, but somehow hearing it spoken aloud made me a little sad. On some level, I had wanted to believe there was more hypnosis involved than elaborate stage-craft. "But you called it the Sleepwalker," I said.

"I did."

"Why?"

He shrugged, still tipped back on the legs of his chair. "It conjured dreams. It conjured a lack of control. It conjured the undead: zombies and vampires and ghosts. And, of course, a lot of magicians have levitated their assistants. But what's really the fun in that? It screams 'trick.' It seemed to me that it was far more dramatic to levitate a person from the audience. Yes, I am sure some people knew she was a plant or suspected she was a plant. But, still, the idea that she was being moved by me like a marionette? Far more interesting."

"You had her dunk Sonny Bono on TV that night. How did it normally end? Most of the time you didn't have a foil like that."

"No. Most of the time? I would whisk off the sheet and she would be gone. Vanished. The audience would gasp. A moment later, with a great splash, she would break the surface of the water tank, and I would help her out rather gallantly."

Years earlier I had told Lindsay about my mother's sleepwalking and about the night I had walked her in from the bridge. "Of course, if you really wake up underwater, I imagine you're likely to drown. You'll take in a great gulp of water and the rest won't be pretty," I said.

"No. But many of our illusions are like that. It's also not pretty if you actually saw a woman in half—I imagine."

He was right, of course. "Thank you for coming to my mother's funeral," I said.

"You've already thanked me. You don't need to keep thanking me."

"Well, it's good to see you."

"I'm glad you're here."

"Sometimes these days I feel guilty when something makes me happy."

"That's just what your mom wants," he said. "She wants to be sure you never go on living. She wants to be sure you are miserable and in mourning forever."

If he had been younger—if he had been my age—I would have taken a dollop of hollandaise on my finger and flung it at him. Instead I just shook my head and smiled. I liked the fact that he had referred to my mother in the present tense.

⟩

My father and Paige and I drove home from Concord on Saturday afternoon, and we stopped for gas at the midway point, which was roughly Warner, New Hampshire. We had taken my mother's Pathfinder because it was roomier and more comfortable than my father's Accord. He was behind the wheel and pulled into the gas station and convenience store just east of the interstate exit. I hopped from the passenger side to open the gas tank and fill up while my father and Paige wandered into the store to use the restrooms and get snacks. It had snowed here the night before, but little more than enough to glaze the trees and dust the brown grass. None had stuck to the roads, and now the sun was out once again. I thought of Paige's team on the ski slopes without her. It was, I knew from experience, a glorious day to be on the mountain.

As I was walking around the front of the vehicle after replacing the nozzle in the pump, I noticed it: A modest dent. A pucker. It was on the bumper, near the right headlight. About six inches higher, between the grill and the light—just below the hood—was a second concave ding. A strip of blue paint not quite the width of a pinky had peeled away inside it. I wondered if another car had backed into the SUV in a parking lot at some point that autumn and I hadn't noticed, or whether the dings had occurred when my mother had been behind the wheel and thus had been there for months. The damage was in a spot I was unlikely to notice, and obviously I had other distractions that fall. I wasn't annoyed by the nicks because they were minor, and I might not have thought much more about them if my father hadn't emerged from the store that very moment. He was pulling his black leather gloves back on and at first was oblivious to me. He was squinting up into the sky and enjoying the sun on his face. But then he saw me hunched over by the right headlight, and he came rushing over.

"Look at this little dent," I said, and I pointed. "And here's another."

"I did that," he said.

I stood up straight. "You? When?"

"Oh, months ago. Spring semester. I pulled in too close to a streetlight at the college. One of the ones in the lot near the library."

"I never noticed."

He smiled in a way that I am sure he thought was conspiratorial and funny. "Fortunately, your mother never did, either."

"You never told her?"

He brought his gloved index finger to his mouth and pretended to shush me. I think he thought he was being funny.

I THINK MOSTLY of her eyes. They were open.

CHAPTER EIGHTEEN

I WENT TO see Gavin when we got home from Boston late that Saturday afternoon. "What do you know that you're not telling me?" I asked him that night.

Two days earlier, on Thanksgiving, a young drug dealer had been shot in his squalid little apartment in Burlington's old North End, and Gavin had been working around the clock ever since. We were sitting on his couch eating takeout kebobs from a Middle Eastern restaurant around the corner from his building. We were both having juice instead of wine or beer. In his case, it was because of his sleep sex; in mine, it was because the simple thought of alcohol after the Boston cab ride the night before made me queasy. He had bags under his eyes, but he was happy because they had arrested someone late that afternoon. The TV was on because there was news from Florida as well: that day Broward County had completed its hand recount of the presidential ballots. The sound was almost but not quite off, and I felt oddly grown-up. Paige knew I was with my detective—my "super trooper," she was calling him, often with a roll of her eyes—but our father presumed I was spending the night once again with Heather Prescott.

"I don't know anything I haven't told you," Gavin said, wiping his fingers with a paper napkin.

"You're lying."

"Of course."

"Are you ever going to tell me?" I wanted to be angry with

him, but I was so content to be around him that I couldn't. It had been a revelation in Boston, but the truth was that ever since my mother had died, I really was happiest when I was with Gavin.

He knitted his eyebrows at me, but he was smiling. "I don't know what you think I know that I'm not telling you."

"It seems like I only learn things from you when I've already started to figure it out and you fess up."

"Like the fact I saw your mother a few days before she died."

"Yeah," I said, not trying to diminish the facetiousness in my tone. "Kinda like that."

With the remote he muted the sound on the television. "And yet you're here," he said, regarding me.

"I am." I thought back to my mother's phone conversation more than three years ago on the Amherst quad over Parents Weekend. "Do you remember a phone call with my mother in October 1997? It would have been on a Friday afternoon, a day when my mom was going to see you, but she canceled. It was my first Parents Weekend at college."

"I do."

"Why were you so desperate and—just maybe—selfish? What did you say that led my mom to cut you off?"

"Whoa! I'm not sure I was either. I mean, maybe I was. Maybe I am. But I'd had an event the night before, and it was the last straw for my girlfriend. That, if you must know, was when we broke up. And I was on my meds—same meds as your mom—but I'd started taking an antihistamine, and I wanted to know if your mother had ever had a drug interaction like that."

"With an antihistamine?"

"That's right."

"Were you on one this fall?"

"I took one a couple of times, but never when I was going to see you. Why risk it? And it wasn't a bad allergy season for me. Maybe it was the drought."

"If it was just about Benadryl or whatever, why was my mom such a . . . such a bitch to you?"

"She wasn't!"

"She said, 'I can't help you. I can't even help myself.' I heard her."

"She was being honest. And maybe my experience the night before just made her sad. Too sad. Maybe even close to despairing. It's really not curable what we have. The clonazepam seems to help keep us in bed. At least it does more often than not when we have an incident. But it doesn't dial down the rest. You know that now as well as anyone. And so maybe being around me just got to be too much for your mom. The support group became, I don't know, too hard. Too painful." He looked at me intensely. "Let me ask you something."

"Go ahead."

"On some level, is it possible that you just see me as a way to learn more about your mother?"

"Like I'm using you, because you know what really happened and I don't?" I said evenly, clarifying.

"Precisely."

I ran my fingers through my hair and found the blue horseshoe headband I was wearing. I thought of the way my father often lectured with a prop for emphasis, and pulled it out. I pointed it at him dramatically. "I am not using you," I told him firmly.

"Have you told your father about me?"

"I didn't think you wanted me to."

"Your friends?"

"No. But it's not like I'm hiding you from them. If they saw us together in Burlington, I'd introduce you."

He took my headband and gently combed it back into my hair. "And later," he murmured, his face close to mine, "you would tell them not to tell your father about me."

"You have kebob breath," I said, instead of refuting what we both knew was the truth.

"You do, too," he whispered. And then he kissed me.

☽

That night I awoke and I felt him before I heard him. He was aroused and on his side, once again trying to find me in his sleep. Perhaps we both should have expected it, given how hard he had been working and how overtired he was.

The T-shirt I was wearing was above my navel, and his hands were underneath it, fondling me—groping me—roughly. I thought of the man I knew when he was awake and how he would never touch me like this. I thought of how I wanted to be with that man tomorrow and the day after tomorrow. And that meant knowing I could corral the animal he could become in the small hours of the night, and (if possible) love that part of him, too. And so I pried his fingers off my breasts and rolled him onto his back. It was a feat of wrestling that demanded strength, but not the superhuman effort I had anticipated. When I climbed on top of him, the city, the apartment, the bedroom—including Gavin—went quiet. I pressed his wrists against the mattress, turned on by my own power, and lowered myself onto him.

☽

I went to the bathroom to freshen up before going back to sleep. I wanted a clean washcloth and looked for one in the cabinet under his sink. I wasn't sure what I'd find, but it was the middle of the night and I wasn't thinking especially clearly. I squinted against the brightness of the ceiling fixture, wishing he had a night-light.

It was amid the extra rolls of bathroom tissue, unopened tubes of toothpaste, and spray bottles of tile cleaner, that I saw it. It was all the way in the back against the far wall. His leather shoulder bag. I didn't believe I had seen it since the day we'd met. It was a handsome bag, the leather well aged and the buckles made of brass, and I hadn't forgotten what it looked like. I recalled how it had been slung over his shoulder the very first time I saw him, that August morning my mother had disappeared, when he had been emerging from the carriage barn where my parents parked their cars.

And instantly I knew. I knew it all.

I grabbed the bag almost frantically, knocking over the toilet paper and the cleansers, some of which fell out and rolled against the sink pedestal. In my hands, I was surprised by its heft, but that only confirmed for me what I was going to find as I worked the buckles. And when I peered inside, there it was: one of Paige's swim towels, folded and rolled into a tube. I pulled it from the bag and for a moment cradled it against me as if it were one of my stuffed animals from my childhood. I was woozy and scared and sad—but mostly sad. Finally I forced myself to unroll it. To see it, to see it all. When I did, I was almost hypnotized by the image of seashells and beach, the sand once so white now stained red, and the great, swirling Rorschach of my mother's dried blood.

☽

In the morning, Gavin found me sitting on the couch, still clad in only his T-shirt. I must have looked waiflike and pathetic to him, and I could see in his eyes that he thought my despair was about the man he had become, once more, in his sleep. But then he noticed the towel in my lap and his shoulder bag on the couch beside me. And he understood. He reached for the attaché and tossed it onto the carpet beside the coffee table. Then he sat down next to me, where it had been.

"I was planning to burn it," he said. "I was planning to burn the bag and the towel."

"Where?"

"My aunt and uncle's hunting camp. They have a little cottage up in the Northeast Kingdom."

"Why didn't you?"

"Life just intervened. Either someone was there or I had too much work here. And it was going to be . . . hard. Emotionally."

Hard. The word echoed for me.

"The thing is, my parents gave me the bag when I graduated from college," he went on. "You know what a fuckup I'd been, I told you. The fact I'd made it? Graduated? It meant a lot to them. And the towel? That was going to be difficult to burn, too, but for different reasons. Cops don't burn evidence. At least good cops. Burning it was, I don't know, crossing a line. So maybe I kept finding excuses not to go to the camp and just do it."

"You found the towel in my mom's car?"

He nodded. "It was in the backseat. I cleaned the grill and the bumper. I cleaned the top of the windshield where it met the roof."

"My father knows, too, doesn't he?"

He spoke with an air of resignation. "A father doesn't say those things aloud to a cop. And a cop—in this case, at least—doesn't say them to a dad. I can't tell him what I know. Excuse me, what I believe. But I encouraged him rather strongly to bring your sister to the sleep clinic."

"He didn't seem all that worried when I told him that Paige was afraid she'd gone sleepwalking."

"He probably didn't want to alarm you. He probably didn't want to alarm her. But he was. He is. Even if you hadn't told him about her sleepwalking, he would have found an excuse to get her to the sleep center. He told me you girls had appointments before you did."

"But why me?"

"Think misdirection. You're a magician."

"So I'm going to be wired at the clinic for nothing?"

"Not for nothing. But not because you're a sleepwalker."

"But what if she got in the car again in her sleep?"

"Your father has been giving her your mother's clonazepam."

"He's drugging her?"

"He's medicating her, Lianna. There's a difference."

"And she doesn't know?"

"No. A half tab ground up in her milk. Or orange juice. Whatever."

I thought of the night when Paige complained that the milk had gone bad. I was sure I would recall other moments, too, as time went on. I pointed at the leather bag on the floor. "My mom's DNA is in there, isn't it? From the towel."

"Yes."

Outside, it was growing light and I heard the annoying, monotonous bleep of a garbage truck in reverse. The sky was streaked with the deep, beautiful violet of a bruise.

"My dad told me the dings on the car were from a streetlight. He said he had done a bad job of parking at the college." My voice was small, incredulous.

"Was he convincing?"

I shook my head. "Not in the slightest."

"Is that when you knew?"

I sighed. "He hadn't been driving that night: I knew that. After all, he was in Iowa. And I wasn't driving. At least I didn't think I was."

"So Paige."

"I remembered how much she used to like to drive in and out of the barn, and back and forth in the driveway. Would she take the car out at night? It hadn't crossed my mind until I saw the dings. But I told myself I was crazy." The conversation felt surreal to me. Even now, the recollection of what we were saying—acknowledging life's spectacular, numbing horrors in such quiet, measured tones—can leave me unsteady.

"If it hadn't been an SUV, I doubt your mother would have been thrown so far. It took that high a center of gravity," he said. "Her body hit the grill. Then her head, I believe, hit the corner where the windshield met the roof."

"Was Paige speeding?"

"Well, she was driving fast. Fast enough to . . . to send your mother over the riverbank. I'm sorry."

"No," I murmured, "I asked." She was an athlete. A ski racer. She was intense. She did almost nothing slowly. "Does anyone suspect it might have been a hit-and-run? Did you have to investigate that?"

"We went to a few auto-body shops in the area to see if any-one had brought in a car or truck claiming they'd smacked into an animal, but obviously that avenue went nowhere. It was make-work."

Finally I put the towel down. I laid it gently atop the shoulder bag on the floor, imagining it was a quilt draped upon a coffin. "When you told me that my mom came to see you a few days before she died, you said she was afraid she was going to sleepwalk with my dad away," I said. "You were lying about that, too, weren't you? She came to see you because she was worried about my sister."

"Yes." He sat forward, his chin in his hands, and gazed out the window. "Does she have any inkling? Any idea at all?" he asked.

"I don't think so," I answered, but when I thought a moment more I couldn't help but wonder at Paige's sudden resolve not to travel to Chile to ski the coming summer. I remembered the dream my sister had shared with me—the one where she and Joe the Barn Cat were following our mom down the road. Had she been reach-ing out to me, trying to tell me something?

And then I recalled the hours and hours she had spent walking along the riverbank looking for something.

"Tell me: Was my mom sleepwalking when it happened?" I asked.

"Her eyeglasses weren't in the bedroom."

"Meaning?"

"She probably put them on. We never found them."

"Of course. She'd never wear them while sleepwalking."

"We don't know that. I said probably. Maybe her eyeglasses will turn up any day now in the kitchen or the bedroom or under the seat in her car."

But we did know that. We did. My mother wasn't sleepwalk-ing, and I didn't correct him. I think I knew that moment that my sister had found our mother's eyeglasses. Paige had found those great turquoise ovals our mother wore when she wasn't wearing her contact lenses. She had unearthed them from whatever brush or leaves they were beneath as she walked day after day along the side of the road that paralleled the river. The odds of my mother and my sister both sleepwalking at the very same moment? Infinitesimal. Annalee Ahlberg had been awake. Wide awake.

Looking back, that might have been the cruelest irony of all.

EPILOGUE

THIS IS WHAT I mean about fate: when, eventually, I told my father I was dating Gavin Rikert, it meant that now there were three of us who were complicitous. Three of us who knew. And while we never spoke of it, whenever we were around Paige together—as we would be more and more often, especially in the first eight months of 2001 and then again the year after I finally finished college, before Gavin and I married, when I was again living at home—it was an increasingly awkward conspiracy of silence.

Should I have stayed home through Paige's last years of high school? Perhaps. My father was not left completely alone trying to rein in his younger daughter's increasingly dangerous late-night excursions. He had the sleep center. Her treatment was similar to my mother's, and worked in the same ways and failed in the same ways. But the more Paige walked, the more she knew she was her mother's daughter. (Was she her father's as well? Absolutely. Whether she was Warren Ahlberg's daughter biologically has long become irrelevant. For one season, blinded by the tears that came at me in brackish waves following my mother's disappearance and death, I questioned his paternity. I am ashamed of that dreamlike madness.)

And, yes, the more she walked, the more she must have known she was her mother's killer, too. Her visions from that August night grew crisp, the memories lucid, and the truth unavoidable. I imagine her squirreling away the eyeglasses in a drawer or jewelry box somewhere, a renunciate totem she is unable to live with or without.

She went to college far from Vermont, already distancing herself from those of us who knew her best and suspected what she had done. After graduating, she went to work for an airline as a flight attendant because it meant that she could travel and stay in nice hotels. Her base was Los Angeles. She was, she told me one time when she was drunk, feeding her beast. She said she was ravenous when she was asleep. She came home once a year at Christmas. She never allowed my father and me to visit her.

And then, at twenty-six, she disappeared, too. She did not disappear the way our mother did. She went, as she put it, off-line. Off radar. She could no longer bear even that lone, annual return trip to Bartlett, where our father continued to live, and the Victorian's proximity to the Gale River. She could no longer subject herself to what she seemed to view as the pitying—perhaps in her eyes, even judgmental—gazes of my father and Gavin and me.

She lets my father and me know she is alive, but she discourages us from trying to find her. Last year, she sent him Red Sox tickets on his birthday. For Christmas, she sent her niece and nephew trinkets and books. She assures us that we need never fear for her safety: she knows the pain that killing herself would cause us. Breathing is her atonement. That's just how she's built. Sometimes I post oblique messages for her on the social networks that no one would understand but her, hoping to convey how much my father and I miss her and how nothing could have prevented what happened, because I am sure that in a sad, melancholic way she stalks the Ahlberg family. How could she not?

Before she went underground and cut us off, she mailed me her journal. I read it and reread it once. Then I buried it in a gift box that had once held a sweater in Gavin's and my attic in Burlington, hiding it behind the larger cartons where I stored the magic tricks I have been unable to say good-bye to. I never showed the journal to my father or to Gavin. There are no clues in it that would help us find her.

And, as Gavin reminds me, she doesn't want to be found. At least not yet. He says she will come home when she is ready: when she is at peace. He says as a magician (albeit retired) I should know better than anyone that what we believe has vanished is really just hidden.

He may be right. The earth is as rich with magic as it is with horror and sadness. One day, I will pull back the curtain and there she will stand, smiling and rolling her dark eyes at me.

And this time it won't be a dream.

YES, LIANNA, YES. Since you wonder but are afraid to ask, I'll tell you. Live with it. I do.

Mom wasn't out sleepwalking. Mom was out looking for me.

Acknowledgments

ONCE AGAIN, THANKS are in order.

First of all, the experts: Dr. Garrick Applebee, a sleep medicine physician, for teaching me about sleepwalking and other parasomnias; Mike Cannon, with the Colchester, Vermont, Technical Rescue Team, and Essex, Vermont, police officer Andrew Graham, for discussing with me the specifics of search and rescue; Emmet Helrich, formerly a lieutenant with the Burlington Police Department and now the coordinator for Vermont's rapid intervention community court, for helping me understand how this sort of investigation would proceed; Michael Mangan, PhD, for his book *Sleepsex: Uncovered;* and Dr. Steven Shapiro, chief medical examiner for the state of Vermont, who shared with me the mysteries of the morgue.

I am deeply grateful to my friends at Doubleday for all they do before (and after) my books are published: Todd Doughty, Emma Dries, Jenny Jackson, and John Pitts.

And then there are my agents: thank you, Jane Gelfman, Cathy Gleason, Victoria Marini, Deborah Schneider, and Brian Lipson.

Finally, I want to thank Victoria Blewer and Grace Experience, two of my earliest and best readers—always.

A NOTE ABOUT THE AUTHOR

Chris Bohjalian is the author of nineteen books, including such *New York Times* bestsellers as *The Guest Room, The Light in the Ruins, The Sandcastle Girls, The Double Bind,* and *Skeletons at the Feast.* His novel *Midwives* was a number one *New York Times* bestseller and a selection of Oprah's Book Club. His work has been translated into more than thirty languages, and three of his books have become movies (*Secrets of Eden, Midwives,* and *Past the Bleachers*). His novels have been chosen as best books of the year by *The Washington Post, St. Louis Post-Dispatch, The Hartford Courant, Milwaukee Journal Sentinel, Publishers Weekly, Library Journal, Kirkus Reviews, BookPage,* and *Salon.* He lives in Vermont. Visit him at www.chrisbohjalian.com or on Facebook or Twitter.